My Disappearance in Providence and Other Stories

ALFRED ANDERSCH

✦✦

My Disappearance in Providence and Other Stories

✦✦

Translated by Ralph Manheim

1978

DOUBLEDAY & COMPANY, INC., GARDEN CITY, NEW YORK

All of the characters in this book are fictitious,
and any resemblance to actual persons, living or dead,
is purely coincidental.

ISBN: 0-385-01391-4
Library of Congress Catalog Card Number 73–9005
Translation Copyright © 1977, 1978 by Doubleday & Company, Inc.
Printed in the United States of America
All Rights Reserved
First Edition

Contents

My Disappearance in Providence and Other Stories

Brothers

The Kien brothers sauntered through Jenisch Park and crossed the deserted street.

"Look at that! No cars!" said Jakob. "Everybody's home listening to the special communiqués."

On the shore path between the road and the Elbe, Franz Kien headed down the river. Jakob followed him. The water was flowing downstream.

"Low tide," said Franz.

"I knew it," said Jakob. "I looked at the tide table at home."

He loved Hamburg and North Germany. So did Franz, but not as much as Jakob.

They passed groups of Sunday hikers.

"Not as many as usual," said Jakob.

"Still too many."

"I bet there isn't anybody in Haseldorf Marsh."

They thought of the flat meadows, the trimmed willows, and the ship canals with boats rotting in them.

"That's where we should have gone," said Franz.

"We'd have had to start earlier," said Jakob.

Now they were sorry they had spent the whole morning by the radio at Franz's place.

"It's nice here too," said Jakob.

"It stinks!" said Franz.

The sun across the river was halfway down the sky. Jakob decided to take a picture and they stopped. He took two, one to southwestward against the light, the other with the sun behind him of the harbor to the east. He looked down at the finder of his Rolleiflex; in the first exposure, the distant Altes Land dike, which formed the horizon, was a dark line high up in the picture, between the shimmering gray surface of the water and the flat rectangle of an almost white sky; in the second, the tanks in the oil port, the launching ways in Waltershof, and the docks deeper in the harbor were well lighted, red, rust color, and black at the lower edge of a monochrome autumn sky.

"It won't show much in black and white," said Jakob. "Too bad they haven't started making good color film."

Franz looked at his brother as he stared resolutely into the finder. Jakob was shorter than he, more solidly built; his hair was reddish, and so was his face, which always looked flushed. He had a strong, square chin, which he thrust forward when he was thinking hard or examining something as now. Nobody else in the whole family has a chin like that, Franz thought.

"You'll just have to start painting," he said. "Why don't you go to your painting class?"

Jakob looked at the image in the finder longer than necessary before pressing the shutter release. Then he snapped the finder back into place.

"Painting isn't so simple," he said as they went on. "You can't imagine."

He was studying lettering, typography, and graphic techniques at the provincial art school.

"You could learn to draw at least," said Franz. "I'm told the life class is excellent."

"Don't pester me about it," said Jakob. "I just don't feel like it."

They stopped again and watched a squadron of planes flying southward across the Elbe. Below them the captive balloons that had been put in place some days before hovered motionless in a circle over the harbor. Only after the planes had passed did they begin to move again; yellow against the blue sky.

"Maybe the war's started already," said Jakob.

"It's possible," said Franz.

"We should have stayed by the radio."

"We'll find out soon enough."

"I wonder if we'll be mobilized right away if it starts."

"Just tell them about your TB," said Franz. "Anyway, you're too young."

Jakob was seventeen. From his tenth to his twelfth year he had lain in bed with bone tuberculosis.

"I'll be eighteen in November," he said. "And my TB is cured."

Franz didn't argue. The way Jakob looked now, solid, almost husky, they'd be sure to put him down as fit for active service.

"They're bound to assign you to a motorized unit. I can guarantee they'll put me in the infantry."

"Maybe they don't even take men who've been in concentration camps," said Jakob.

"Too good to be true," said Franz.

Seven years before, when he was as old as Jakob now, he had been a member of the Young Communist League in Munich, where the Kien brothers had lived at the time. Looking across the surface of the river, he thought of the years he had spent in various suburbs of Munich.

"Hamburg's better than Munich," he said.

"Definitely," said Jakob.

"But we won't be here much longer," said Franz.

They had reached Blankenese and were walking along the shore road. There were few people in the cafés. The little sea captains' houses on the hillside were painted white. Squat and white, they huddled in the midsummer green of their gardens.

"Maybe I'll start painting one of these days," said Franz.

He was always saying such things; they upset Jakob and made him angry. Franz wanted to paint, Franz wanted to write. Instead, he wrote advertisements for a paper factory. For one thing, he was married and had a child. He'd never paint, thought Jakob. Not with his mentality. Franz was a head taller than Jakob, slender, with a pale, flat face and a high forehead; he wore tortoise-shell glasses with thick lenses, a correction of ten diopters. Though the brothers looked very different, there was still a resemblance between them. They had the same brown, rather small eyes, and the same short, wiry hair, except that Jakob's was reddish and Franz's dark brown.

"What have you got tomorrow morning?" Franz asked.

"Hand setting," said Jakob.

"That must be interesting."

"It's pretty boring."

He didn't want to admit to Franz that he had been developing a taste for the graphic arts. It was Franz who had thought of sending him to art school. He supplemented their mother's pension with a small sum for Jakob's tuition.

"Maybe you could set one of my poems," said Franz.

He thought of what it would be like to see something of his own in print.

Jakob had never seen any of his elder brother's poems. He was as pleased as Punch.

"You'll have to wait for a few months," he said. "I haven't got that far."

"Too bad," said Franz. "God knows where we'll be by that time."

"Oh well," said Jakob, "I could give it a try."

"Let's get away from the houses," said Franz.

Jakob would have liked to stop at one of the cafés for coffee and cake, but he said nothing. It was still a long way to the high embankment, at the foot of which the beach was wide, especially at low tide as it was now. They hadn't mentioned their destination, but it had been plain to both of them from the start.

"It's already five o'clock," said Franz.

The sun had sunk and its horizontal rays flooded the sky above the water with light.

"Hubby has to be home on time," said Jakob.

Out beyond the Schweinesand two fishing smacks were riding down with the tide.

"They won't be able to go out very far," said Franz. "I hear the whole North Sea is mined."

So far there hadn't been a single outbound ocean ship such as they ordinarily saw when loafing about Haseldorf Marsh on Sunday afternoons: when you watched them from behind the dike, the ships seemed to be going through the meadows, because you couldn't see the river. Here below Blankenese there was no dike, but an embankment thrown up by the current. Jakob looked up; a few pine trees were perched on the edge of the embankment, some of their roots hanging in mid-air. He thought of taking a picture but dropped the idea, though the trees were interesting from a graphic point of view.

When they came to the sandy beaches, they sat down on a low dune, took out their pipes, and filled them. Jakob had a leather tobacco pouch; Franz took his tobacco directly out of a package. He

used a lighter. Jakob's matches kept going out and it took him
some time to light up. Franz watched him.

"Yesterday," said Jakob when at last his pipe began to draw, "I
got Linde's *Lower Elbe* out of the library. It's marvelous! The photographs are old-fashioned but first-class, done with plates, they
don't make them like that any more. Some of those marshes must
be wonderful, especially on the right bank. Have you ever heard
of the Wilst Marsh?"

"Of course," said Franz. "That's where they still have the old
windmills that pump the water from one canal to another. There
are whole rows of them along the canals."

He knows everything, thought Jakob.

After a while he asked: "But you haven't been there?"

"No."

Franz Kien had moved to Hamburg two years before. During
the first year, before he had sent for his mother and Jakob, he
often went to the factory on Sunday. There he could write better
than at home, especially while his wife was with child. Now and
then he would leave his desk in the advertising department and
look down the deserted factory yard. Or he would go to the machine room where the paper hung down from the rolls in broad,
stiff strips.

"Let's go there together sometime," said Jakob. He still had no
girl friend.

"I don't know," said Franz. "If the war starts, I probably won't
feel like it any more."

"I will," said Jakob. "And when it's over, I'll do a picture book
about the marshes. Or maybe just about the Wilst Marsh. If I
come through alive."

The Kien brothers were from South Germany, but their ancestors had been North German—North German and Slav and
French.

"You've absolutely got to read Joseph Conrad," said Franz.
"*The Mirror of the Sea*. The chapter where he describes the
mouth of the Thames. After the war I want to go see the mouth
of the Thames. And London and a few other things."

The Thames can't have anything the Elbe hasn't got, thought
Jakob. You've got to concentrate on one thing.

In the open air, their pipes burned out quickly. They stood up

and strolled across the sand to the water line. The river was still
flowing downstream.

They looked for shells and picked up a few little whitish ones.
Jakob found a greenish-yellow Donax with fine radial ribs.

"We'll find better ones on Amrum," he said. "Next summer."

"We'll never get there now," said Franz.

The sun hung low over the Altes Land. The sand they were
walking on shimmered red.

When they boarded the train at Blankenese station, they were
tired. In Altona they had to change. There they saw the extras:
the war had broken out. The people read the news, folded their
papers, put them in their pockets, and went to their trains. Franz
got out at Dammtor; he lived in Eppendorf. Jakob rode on to
Berliner Tor, where he took the streetcar. He lived with his
mother on Horner Weg.

++

Daughter

++

Dr. Richard Wenger, director of the X-ray laboratory at a clinic in Davos, and his daughter Thérèse arrived in Calais at about eleven o'clock in the morning. They had taken the express that leaves Basel at 12:50 A.M. and spent the night in couchettes. Dr. Wenger had taken second-class couchettes rather than first-class *wagons-lits* for financial and educational reasons, and also because he thought Thérèse might as well get used to this mode of travel, since she would be coming home for the Christmas holidays in just such a couchette. As it happened, they were lucky; only one other passenger had come into the compartment during the night—in Metz. He had climbed into one of the upper bunks as quietly as possible and without turning on the light, and had got off at Lille.

After the train pulled out, Dr. Wenger had read *The Times* for a while. He had bought it in the Basel station to see what was going on in London. He would have a free evening in London after taking Thérèse to Oxford and thought he might go to the theater.

He and Thérèse lay down on the two lower bunks and drew the woolen blankets over them.

"Isn't it rather like a ski hut?" he had said.

"I can't bear ski huts," Thérèse had replied.

Before turning out the reading lamp, he had looked across at her. She was already asleep. She had turned over to the wall, and all he could see of her was the mass of dark hair that she was always fighting battles with.

Again that morning it had taken her a long time to do her hair. When she came out of the washroom, she asked:

"Do I look all right, Daddy?"

"Pretty as a picture," said Wenger.

"Me pretty?!"

"All right, then you're ugly."

"No," she said. "I'm not ugly. It's just that I'm not especially pretty."

They stood in the corridor, and Thérèse let the passing landscape divert her from the subject of her looks. She was delighted with the pocket-handkerchief-sized houses along the roads between Saint-Omer and Calais.

"That's what I call houses!" she exclaimed. "Not like the dopey châlets in Davos."

"Do you think our house is dopey?" asked Wenger. "After all, it's a châlet."

"Oh, Daddy," she said. "I think our house is wonderful, especially the inside. If only it weren't a châlet! Châlets are so bourgeois." She stopped for no more than a second. "You and Mama aren't bourgeois. And I realize that's the only way you can build a house in Davos. This flat country is marvelous! Later on I want to live in country that's perfectly flat."

"You'll have to marry a Dutchman," said Wenger, "or a Russian."

"Nobody can marry a Russian," said Thérèse. "Besides I'm not going to marry a man just because he lives in a flat country. I'll just marry some man and then I'll say: All right, let's go someplace where it's flat!"

"But suppose he doesn't want to?"

"I'll find out in advance if he's a flat man or a mountain man."

The weather became clearer and clearer as the train approached the coast. On the station platform in Calais they could feel the wind.

Thérèse pointed at the ferry and sang out: "Daddy, is that our boat?"

"Yes," said Wenger, "but please stop shouting 'Daddy!' "

Most of the people with them in the passport line seemed to be English, and it embarrassed Wenger when Thérèse called him "Daddy" loud enough to be heard. The doctor was an Anglophile, he liked her to call him Daddy at home, but here in Calais among these English travelers it upset him. They'd take him for some kind of Americanized German, when actually he was only a Swiss Anglophile. But he couldn't very well run around explaining the difference.

While taking a turn around the ship, they came across a hippie. He had settled down in the smoking room and was spreading out the contents of a large and filthy duffel bag on the floor. His hair hung down over his shoulders, he wore glittering earrings and a long sheepskin coat with the fleece side out.

Wenger saw Thérèse pass the hippie quickly, doing her best not to stare at him, whereas most of the people stopped and examined the young man without compunction. Thérèse had never seen a hippie, except in illustrated magazines and on the covers of Beatles records. There were no hippies in Davos.

The air was so clear that when they went out on deck they could see the English coast.

"I've never had such weather for a crossing," said Wenger. He wondered if he mightn't have preferred a slight haze, from which the Dover cliffs would emerge only gradually. Today the Channel looked to him like a stage on which the curtain had risen too soon.

"One should always go to England by boat," he said. "You have to feel that you're going to an island."

He was annoyed with himself for falling into this pedagogic tone. Maybe this long trip wasn't the right thing for Thérèse after all. It would make Oxford seem so dreadfully far away. After all she was barely sixteen, and this was her first time away from home. They should have flown: by plane it was less than an hour from Zürich to London; it would have seemed like no trip at all to her.

She looked across the harbor to the sea. "It's too bad Mama can't be here to see this," she said.

Wenger's wife was also a doctor, a pediatrician with a good practice. It was only in the early summer, when it was very quiet in Davos, that Richard and Madeleine Wenger were able to go away together. Usually they went to Sardinia for a few weeks, always to the same hotel. They bathed or drove up into the mountains, where they left the car on the road, walked into the *macchia*, and sat awhile, listening to the cicadas. Now, at the beginning of October, Dr. Madeleine Wenger couldn't possibly have left Davos.

"She's already seen it," said Wenger. "I met your mother in England."

They had attended Professor Matthew's course in roentgenology at the Hospital for Sick Children in 1947 when they were both graduate doctors; Wenger had stayed with roentgenology, his wife had gone into pediatrics. She was a French Swiss and came of a medical family in Nyon; they had married in 1948. In 1949 they had had a son, Ulrich, now in his last year of high school, and two years later a daughter, whom Madeleine had insisted on calling Thérèse after her grandmother, who must have been a character. Thérèse never tired of listening to stories about Thérèse Badiou of Nyon; her mother was a good storyteller, especially in French.

The sky was so blue because of the brisk east wind, and Thérèse was seasick, not so badly as to throw up, but enough to send her below. When Wenger went down to see how she was doing, he found her in the smoking room, lying on a sofa with her eyes closed; not far from her, the hippie was strumming his guitar. She was even paler than usual; her pale face rested in the dark nest of her hair. As they were approaching Folkestone, she appeared on deck, freshly washed and combed, just in time to admire the white cliffs—a procession of tall, rigid, transparent ghosts striding northward.

They set their watches back an hour. "That's great," said Thérèse. "We've gained an hour."

In the train to London, they looked around for the hippie, but he was nowhere to be seen. Just before the train pulled out, he appeared on the platform accompanied by a policeman. He didn't board the train but was taken into some office.

"Daddy!" cried Thérèse. "Did you see?"

Wenger nodded.

"They've arrested him! Why? Because he's a hippie?"

"Certainly not for that reason. Besides, they haven't necessarily arrested him. Maybe it's just a baggage check. It seems they examine those people's baggage very carefully."

"For drugs?"

"You're very well informed."

"I'm sure he hasn't got any drugs. He showed me everything in his duffel bag."

"Thérèse!" said Wenger. "I thought you were seasick!"

"Yes, I felt terrible. I only spoke to him for about ten minutes, then I lay down."

"He knows German then?"

"No, he spoke French. Not very well, but we managed. He spent the whole summer in France and North Africa. He gave me something."

She opened her handbag, took out a little necklace of sea shells, and handed it to her father.

"Cowrie shells," said Wenger. "Very pretty."

He handed it back to her. She looked at the necklace for a while, then put it back in her bag.

"It must be awful," she said, "to wander around like that all the time. He says he hasn't got a home any more. He doesn't want one, he says."

Wenger watched her put the necklace away. She had on a brown tailored suit from a fashionable sports shop in Davos. Under her jacket she was wearing a thin, light-blue jersey. Her clothes were very becoming to her, but a shell necklace, even if it was pretty, wouldn't go with them. Thérèse looked well scrubbed and well bred but not stuffy. Though her mother was not a lady of fashion—she was more the Madame Curie type—she had managed to impart some of her family's Geneva chic to her child. Dr. Wenger was well pleased with his daughter's looks.

During the trip through Kent, her spirits revived. She was delighted with the meadows, the autumn trees, and the farmhouses with their little pointed, cone-shaped towers.

"Those are hops storehouses," Wenger explained. "Nowadays it's mostly people from London who live in them, artists and writers, that sort of thing."

"Marvelous!" said Thérèse. "Does the country around Oxford look like this?"

"Oh, I should say that Oxfordshire is even more beautiful. More grandiose. You'll like the Thames Valley. And some time you'll have to visit the park of Blenheim Castle. You've never seen such trees."

"If I like it, I'll paint pictures of everything."

"I hope you do."

Thérèse had always been first in her art class at the Davos high school. The previous winter she had won first prize in a student

competition. The subject assigned had been "Davos in the Year
Two Thousand" and Thérèse had painted a magnificent, though
rather terrifying, vision of ski trails twining their way between sky-
scrapers. Her painting had been displayed in the window of the
Schweizerische Volksbank. People had stopped to look at it, at first
with amusement, then rather dejectedly.

Unfortunately she was a total failure at mathematics, and the
principal had dryly informed the Wengers that she would never
get her diploma. Yes, he said, she was gifted in languages as well
as art, but was utterly inept at subjects requiring rational thought.

Thérèse's parents were surprised at her artistic bent. "I have an
uncle who paints," Frau Dr. Wenger had recalled, "but only as a
hobby." After consulting various people and talking the matter
over with Thérèse's drawing teacher, they had decided to send her
to the Zürich School for Applied Art. But the introductory course
did not begin until after Easter; in the meantime, her parents
thought, it would be a good idea for her to learn English, since in
school she had studied only Latin and French. Wenger held that
in this day and age ignorance of English was a variety of illiteracy.
He had written letters, read prospectuses, examined references,
and finally chosen St. Sidwell's Hall, a school in Oxford. His wife
seemed rather less pleased with the idea.

"We can surely find someone here in Davos to give her private
lessons," she had argued.

"That's not at all the same thing as learning English in England."

"But don't you think she's a little too young?"

"Thousands of girls her age go to England for six months."

She had raised no further objection. Thérèse herself seemed to
look forward to her stay in England.

"At least I won't have to ski this winter." She turned her head;
some horses were standing in a meadow, a cloud the color of a tea
rose hovered over them, and she wanted to look at the passing picture as long as possible.

"Do you really dislike skiing so much?"

"I hate it!"

"But we've never forced you to ski."

"What else is there to do? In winter. In Davos. But it makes
me vomit."

"I wish you wouldn't use such expressions."

"I'm sorry, Daddy. It just slipped out. Will there be a lot of snow over here?"

"It doesn't usually snow in southern England."

"That's great!"

"Just wait until you've had a few weeks of rain and fog. You'll miss Davos."

"Never. There can't be too much rain and fog for me. I like rain and fog much better than sun and snow."

Then came South London, the endless rows of identical houses, the Thames.

They took a cab to the hotel on Curzon Street where Wenger always stayed. Every time he went there it seemed to have aged a little; it was beginning to look almost shabby. He had last been in London three years before. They spent only a short time in their rooms and went out into the bright afternoon.

Thérèse was aghast at the length of the mini-skirts on Piccadilly.

"Daddy!" she said. "Man!"

"I am indeed a man," said Wenger, "but aren't you putting a little too much stress on it?"

He affected an air of indifference, but to himself he had to admit that he too was rather bewildered by the new style in skirts.

This time Thérèse seemed hardly to have heard his reproof. She was feeling more and more miserable.

"I'll just have to throw all my clothes away," she said.

"Are you out of your mind?" Now Wenger was really indignant. "You're better dressed than any of these girls."

Thérèse stopped still. She was almost in tears. "The way I'm dressed is square!" she said. "Square, square, square!"

For the first time Wenger regretted that he had not persuaded his wife to take Thérèse to England. Madeleine would have had a friendly talk with her, suggested ways of altering some of her dresses, and comforted the child. As a father and a male, he simply had no desire to discuss fashions with his daughter. Involuntarily his eyes followed the contours of a pair of legs from the ankles almost to the waist—they were reflected in the window of a leather shop outside which he had stopped—and he concluded that he would have been most distressed to see Thérèse running around in such a skirt.

She soon pulled herself together, took her father's arm, and began to enjoy the famous street. They stepped into Fortnum and Mason, strolled around in its muted splendor, and bought a tin of tea. For Piccadilly Circus it was still too light. They went looking for Carnaby Street. Wenger had promised Thérèse to take her there and was eager to get the chore over with as quickly as possible. They found the narrow street and went into several shops. Coming out of one of them, Thérèse said: "Most of the stuff is just kitsch."

She was sorely disappointed. She had rummaged about among posters, buttons, teapots, and articles of clothing, at first with enthusiasm, then with increasing indifference.

"Fortnum and Mason is kitsch too," she said, "but at least it's genuine kitsch."

There weren't even any Beatles records that she didn't have already. Still, they saw a number of Bob Dylan records that were not to be had in Davos and bought one called *John Wesley Harding*.

"Bob Dylan is better than the Beatles anyway," said Dr. Wenger. "The Beatles only have good words, the music is nothing; Bob Dylan's words and music are both good."

Thérèse made no reply. She was quite satisfied with the Beatles' music. "That's another reason why you've got to learn English," the doctor had said to her on two or three occasions, when he dropped into her attic room at home and found her playing Beatles records. "You don't understand the words at all. The way you join in is pure fraud. You haven't the faintest idea what you're singing."

Sometimes he had sat down on the floor with her and translated a song or two. At first pop music had meant nothing to him, he was a lover of old-fashioned jazz, but after translating some of the songs to himself and Thérèse, he had been carried away, as he admitted to himself.

For dinner they went to a restaurant Wenger knew in Shepherd Market. It hadn't changed. He was tired, and that made him think of the clinic and his work. Over the dessert, he began talking about something that had happened shortly before their departure.

"A horrible business!" He tried to stop himself but couldn't. "A colleague of mine, an elderly doctor, came to see me. He complained of pain in the chest, he told me exactly where. He wanted me to examine him and take a few X rays."

Wenger had the impression that Thérèse wasn't listening very attentively—she too, he realized, must have been rather tired—but he went on with his story because, as he himself was aware, he wanted to tell it to himself.

"So I made the X rays, and when they were developed, I was horrified. They were catastrophic. Usually when you get such pictures, there's no difficulty, the patient is a layman, he can't read the X rays, you can say anything you please. But with him my heart sank. He's not only a doctor but a good one—I knew he'd recognize his condition at a glance."

Wenger saw that Thérèse had lowered her spoon, though she hadn't finished her ice cream. There was no point in his stopping now.

"But the world is full of surprises. He looked at the pictures and said it was all very encouraging, the shadows were quite harmless, and so on. I was flabbergasted. It's incredible how people can delude themselves when they want to." He stopped for a moment. Then he said: "I was enormously relieved, as you can imagine."

"Are you sure he wasn't just pretending?" Thérèse asked. "Maybe he was putting a good face on it for your benefit."

"Impossible. I was watching him closely. A perfect case of self-deception."

"How long has he got to live?"

"Three to six months."

"Father," Thérèse asked, "wouldn't it have been better to tell him the truth?"

That was the question all laymen asked when they heard about such cases. Which was a good reason not to talk about them. You only involved yourself in an interminable discussion about the physician's responsibility, and so on. A doctor's business was to treat patients, not to answer metaphysical questions. Fortunately there was a routine answer.

"That, child, is a very complex problem," he said.

He had put in the "child" because it had struck him while speaking that on this occasion she had called him "Father" instead of "Daddy." He felt that she was displeased with him. However, she finished her ice cream.

It wasn't his way to talk about his practice with his family, though he sometimes exchanged stories with Madeleine. Why had he broken the rule now? On the way back to the hotel he was unable to shake off his bad humor.

In planning the trip, he had allowed for a day in which to show Thérèse around before the term began in Oxford. He started with Lincoln's Inn Fields and the New Square, because he knew Thérèse well enough to realize that she would not be favorably impressed by London if he started with Trafalgar Square or Buckingham Palace. Nevertheless, he arranged matters so that they would see the Changing of the Guard at eleven o'clock, because as a child Thérèse had shown a weakness not only for dolls but also for her brother's tin soldiers. And indeed, she couldn't take her eyes off the damson-blue capes and red plumes of the Royal Horse Guards on their beautiful horses.

But later, as they were walking down Whitehall, she expressed enthusiasm, not about the Horse Guards or the stylistic purity of the Georgian squares, but about the escalators in the tube stations they had been in—"They go so incredibly deep down!" she exclaimed—and about seeing so many colored people on the streets.

"Are there Indians and Negroes in Oxford?" she asked.

"Oh yes," said Wenger. "There are lots of colored students at Oxford."

He knew that she couldn't stop thinking about next day and had to make an effort to seem cheerful. He spared her Westminster Abbey and Parliament and started back to the hotel through St. James's Park, past the ducks and pelicans and the façade of Buckingham Palace. In the afternoon they went to the King's Road. Thérèse wasn't quite so disappointed as she had been with Carnaby Street; here at least there were plenty of eccentrically dressed young men and girls. She looked about for yesterday's hippie but didn't find him. Dr. Wenger wondered how he would feel if in a few weeks he were to receive news that Thérèse had run away from her school in Oxford and begun a new life among the denizens of the King's Road; he had a way of thinking up catastrophes. It was getting dark when they ended their walk in the quiet streets of Chelsea, where there were artists' studios, overgrown front gardens, and houses where Carlyle and Oscar Wilde had lived.

"I keep thinking of my father," said Wenger. After a look at the grayish-yellow Thames, they had sat down on a bench on Cheyne Walk.

"He had a violent temper and he was very sick," he said. "I think he would have been fond of you. He had three sons and no daughters.

"Toward the end we were very poor," he said. "You can't even imagine how terribly poor we were. It was Uncle Hans who sent me to the university after father's death."

"Sometimes I wish we were poor," said Thérèse. "The one thing I don't like about the Beatles is that they've made so much money."

"I wouldn't wish for anything like that if I were you." Again, as on the evening before, he was feeling talkative. "I remember how once on my birthday my father and I went to town. I had been given a few little presents and in the afternoon my father wanted to take me to the zoo. On the way we passed a big movie theater, all Basel was talking about the picture they were showing, *Captain Scott's Last Voyage*. Everybody in my class had seen it except me—we simply couldn't afford it. My father saw me staring at the posters; suddenly he stopped and said: 'All right, you can choose; either we go to the zoo together, or you can go and see this picture by yourself.' "

"Daddy!" Thérèse gasped. "I hope you went to the zoo with your father!"

He shook his head. "No. That's the trouble. I let him buy me a ticket to the movie, it cost as much as two tickets to the zoo, and he went home on the streetcar. We were living in Riehen at the time."

Thérèse sat stiffly erect beside him, staring at the iron work of the Albert Bridge, a disorderly knot of black ribbons that someone had thrown up against the evening sky.

"I didn't enjoy the picture in the least," said Wenger. "All the time I was sitting there I kept thinking that my father had wanted to go to the zoo with me. It still keeps after me."

"Grandfather was a businessman, wasn't he?" He could tell by Thérèse's voice that she had asked the question only to be saying something.

"Yes, but an unsuccessful one. He always thought of himself as a big-business man, but he wasn't even a little one."

Back on the King's Road, they went to one of the cheap chain restaurants. The previous evening Wenger had called up a friend and colleague. Dr. Sullivan had said: "You and your daughter must come to see us tomorrow night; we can't invite you to dinner because we're in the midst of moving." Wenger had wanted to decline, but Sullivan wouldn't hear of it; they had met years before at a medical congress in Amsterdam, and a friendship had developed. The Sullivans had once visited the Wengers in Davos.

At the restaurant, Thérèse's depression erupted. She ate nothing, looked out at the King's Road, which now lay in darkness, and said: "I'd die in London."

Dr. Wenger gave up trying to determine the chemical composition of the cutlet that had been put down before him on a Bakelite plate.

"Nonsense!" he said in an attempt at optimism. "I've just made you look at too many things."

The house in Hampstead was cluttered with crates, baskets, and shrouded furniture, in the midst of which stood Dr. Sullivan, a big man with rather tousled hair, and his wife, who was very small.

"This is the second time you've moved since I've known you," said Wenger.

"Nothing unusual about that," said Sullivan with surprise as he poured the wine. "The house is too big for us now that the two boys have gone off to university. We've sold it and bought a smaller one that's more conveniently located."

Wenger reflected that for him and his wife selling their house would be a world-shaking event.

The Sullivans spoke German. Mrs. Sullivan was a German refugee. She invited Thérèse to spend her first free weekend with them.

Also present was the elder of the Sullivans' sons, who was studying at Oxford. His father had commanded him to "call in for roll-call," as he put it with a twinkle; he had thought John might be able to give Thérèse some useful pointers.

From time to time, while chatting with Mr. and Mrs. Sullivan, Wenger cast a glance at Thérèse and the young man who were talking French to each other. Young Sullivan was small, soft-spoken, calm, and self-assured. Wenger observed how he gradually lost the air of amused condescension he had at first adopted with Thérèse.

In the cab on the way back to the hotel, Thérèse was in high spirits. "He said I speak French very well," she said. "He's at Christ Church College, he's studying economics. His term begins on Monday and he said he'd come to my school to see how I'm getting along and prevent the worst. Daddy, what can he mean by that?"

"Didn't you ask him?"

"I did, but he wouldn't tell me. He wants to show me around his college."

"You're in luck. It's one of the most beautiful in Oxford."

"Do you know what else he said? He said my school is very popular with the students, because of all the girls."

"I hope you'll find a little time for all your studies," said Wenger playing the "heavy father" as he sometimes did, in a tone compounded of irony and menace. This time he omitted the menace, for he was glad the evening had put Thérèse in better spirits.

They were both surprised at the run-down condition of the Oxford station. The concrete walls of the underpass leading to the exit were crumbling, and the smell was distinctly unpleasant. Wenger had been to Oxford twice before, once for a congress, once as a tourist, but both times he had come by car, and he shook his head when he saw the reception this lovely city had to offer those who arrived by rail. Thérèse's trunks, which they had checked in Basel, had arrived. They had a long wait for a cab. Looking across the freight yard, they saw some of the famous towers, blue-gray against the light. The cab took them through a residential area. Before leaving home, Wenger had looked at the map in the *Blue Guide* and found to his regret that the school was not in the center of the city among the medieval colleges, but on a wide thoroughfare leading out of town to the north.

"The bus will get you into the city in a few minutes," he said. Thérèse made no reply, just looked at the little houses and their front gardens.

St. Sidwell's Hall proved to consist of two rather large houses in Neo-Gothic style. The entrance hall was a confusion of girls and suitcases. The secretary at the reception office was friendly but businesslike. She sent Wenger and his daughter to Miss Maverdine in the annex. But Miss Maverdine was nowhere to be found. The sleeping quarters were in the annex, the girls were going about choosing their beds. A few were accompanied by their mothers, but most were alone. Wenger felt definitely out of place; it would certainly have been better, he thought, if his wife had come with Thérèse. Thérèse struck up a conversation with a German girl and they chose beds side by side.

Wenger exchanged a few words with the girl's mother, a lady from Baden-Baden.

"I had a rather different picture of the school," he said.

"That's putting it mildly," the lady replied. There was no haughtiness in her tone, only a shade of worry.

The rooms were clean but hopelessly run-down. The lower half of the walls was painted chocolate-brown, and in the wooden floors there were deep scratches that had been waxed over for many years. The clothes cupboards and curtains seemed to have been made from the same dingy, crumbling substance.

"I suggest that you get settled," Wenger said. "I'll call for you in two hours." He fully expected Thérèse to say: "I refuse to stay here," but she did nothing of the sort. Before he left, they discussed practical matters for a while.

If she refused to stay, he thought in the cab on his way to the Mitre Hotel, I'd be in a fine fix. He had been looking forward to the hotel, but as he stood at his window looking out at the High Street, he suddenly found that it meant nothing to him.

"Do you know," he said, after joining Thérèse, "I think we've come here with Swiss ideas. I suppose you know what a Swiss boarding school of this class would be like."

In saying "of this class," he was thinking, with an inaudible sigh, of the price. St. Sidwell's was far from cheap; Dr. Wenger's Anglophilia was costing him a pretty penny.

"Yes," said Thérèse, "two years ago I took that summer course in Montana, remember? It *was* different."

"I should have known and prepared you for it," said Wenger. "English boarding schools are known to be rather shabby, but there's a pleasant atmosphere."

Even so, he thought, it wouldn't hurt them to get a new carpet. Or throw the carpet out and put in a decent floor. They were sitting in the entrance hall waiting to be told when they might see the headmistress. So far the headmistress had not appeared, she seemed to have gone into hiding.

There was no telling from Thérèse's manner whether she at least found the atmosphere of St. Sidwell's Hall pleasant. But she must have unpacked, for she had changed clothes. Now she was wearing a moss-green woolen dress that made her look pale. She was naturally pale, but now she seemed more so than usual. Her young face, the color of dead nettle blossoms, was caught between her dark, hard, unruly hair and her lustreless green dress. Besides, she had put on too much eye shadow, as Wenger noticed with distaste. In Davos he tended to find fault when she tinted her eyelids blue, but here he held his peace. She was taking it all very well, it seemed to Wenger; maybe too well.

"There are plenty of records," she said. "They've got the Beatles too. And TV of course. And a language lab. Half the girls are English high school students. Only the girls live in, but the classes are co-ed. Incidentally, Miss Maverdine is very nice. She's the housemistress. She invited Pat and me in for a cup of tea."

"Who on earth is Pat?"

"An American girl. I've moved into her room. She's tops. There are three of us, Pat and me and an Italian girl from Florence. Is she gorgeous! Daddy, you've never seen such a beautiful girl!"

Wenger did not like his daughter to call his attention to the beauty of other girls. He showed no sign of enthusiasm.

"Oh well," he said, "you're not so bad yourself."

"I'm not in the same class with *her*," said Thérèse.

Her father decided to take advantage of the opening. "Of course you're a good deal prettier when you don't paint your eyes like that."

She seemed vexed. "You ought to see how the other girls make up," she said. "I can't go around looking conventional."

"It strikes me as conventional for them all to make up the same way."

This was no conversation for a man. Luckily the secretary interrupted them to say that the headmistress would be there in ten minutes; she lived right around the corner.

They went up to the room Thérèse had moved to; this was his only chance to see it because he would be leaving the next morning and wouldn't be coming back to St. Sidwell's Hall.

"Be sure to tell Mama about my room," she said.

At that hour the school was almost deserted. The Italian girl was alone in the room. She had been lying on her bed reading and now she jumped up. She was indeed beautiful, very young and dark, with a soft olive skin, but in these surroundings Dr. Wenger could summon up only fatherly feelings.

Thérèse had settled in a corner by the window. She had piled her suitcases on top of a clothes cupboard. Each of the girls had a small table; the other two girls' tables were in wild disorder, but Thérèse had arranged hers neatly. On it lay a cup with pencils and crayons and the tin box where she kept her paint tubes. A good part of the wooden table top, worn down by many generations of students, was concealed by a new drawing pad. Thérèse had fastened a photograph of her parents and her brother to the wall with Scotch tape. Wenger looked at the picture; he, his wife, and Ueli had stopped to rest while climbing Mount Parsenn; they were sitting under a fir tree chatting. Thérèse had snapped the picture.

"I'll see to it that Ueli writes you as often as possible," he said.

He saw that she had hung the cowrie-shell necklace on one of the bed posts.

Again he looked with distaste at the brown paint on the wall. He made a rough guess at the school's income and came to the conclusion that it could afford more prepossessing colors, even if they had to be renewed more frequently.

They were shown into a room full of books, pictures, and porcelain. While waiting for the headmistress, they looked out at a narrow strip of garden, where carefully staked dahlias were in bloom. Then the headmistress was rolled in in a wheelchair and Wenger saw to his horror that she had no legs. Where her legs should have been there was a plaid blanket. An accident, no doubt, he thought. As a doctor, he could imagine what torments—circulatory disorders, for example—the lady must have suffered. Mrs. Eldon had a proud pale face under her pinned-up hair. Of course she knew and loved Switzerland; she would keep a special eye on Thérèse. With cold affability she conversed for a while with Thérèse in French. She asked Wenger if he had connections at the university.

"I have friends in the Medical Department," he said. He was going to add that he was not planning to visit them on this occasion but stopped himself when it struck him that it would do Thérèse no harm if Mrs. Eldon thought he had close ties with his Oxford colleagues.

"The school is always in contact with the university," said Mrs. Eldon.

She offered them tea, but Wenger thought it proper to decline. She rang and was rolled out. Wenger and Thérèse sat there for a while, alone, gazing in silence at the dahlias in the garden and at the porcelain.

On their way to the bus, Wenger decided that Mrs. Eldon was unhappy because for some reason St. Sidwell's had failed to achieve college status and had remained a preparatory school. But instead of sharing his speculations with Thérèse, he merely said: "It's quite an achievement to run a school in that condition."

Thérèse only nodded, and it seemed to him that at the thought of the legless woman she shrugged her shoulders. Strange, he thought, that Mrs. Eldon should inspire other feelings beside sympathy.

They got out at Carfax. At four in the afternoon the streets were full of people. This, Wenger thought, was Thérèse's real introduction to Oxford; he led her down St. Aldate's to the quad of Christ Church College. The low Gothic buildings around the large deserted quad were silver-gray.

"I won't show you around here very much," said Wenger. "Young Sullivan will take care of that if he keeps his promise."

Thérèse's face brightened at the thought of her date. She touched Wenger's arm because three Negro students were sauntering across Tom Quad.

It suddenly occurred to Wenger that she would enjoy the meadows by the rivers more than all these old buildings. He found the gate leading to Christ Church Meadow, and they walked to the Thames under the high autumn sky. There were the college barges in the olive-green water, but they looked as if they were never used.

Here they were all alone. Thérèse stopped and looked across the meadows at the city, a silhouette cut in lead-colored paper.

"It's lovely here," she said. "I'll come here often and sketch. Or maybe just read."

She was wearing a light-colored raincoat over her green dress, and she had done up her hair in a brown silk ribbon to keep it in order. Her face with its high cheekbones was as pale as usual, but so heightened and hollowed by the colored shadows of the autumn trees that Wenger thought he could see how this child would look in a few years as a grown woman.

To think, he reflected, that there would be no Thérèse if we had really decided not to have her. Thérèse had come along at a difficult time for both him and his wife; Madeleine had been seriously ill the year before, and as externs at the hospital they were none too prosperous; another pregnancy was about the last thing they needed. He had implored his wife to submit to an operation, and in the end she had given in; but then the surgeon who had agreed to do them the favor had suddenly been called away, and during his absence Madeleine had changed her mind.

And so Thérèse was born, and now sixteen years later here they were together under the low-hanging willows on the banks of the Cherwell.

Following the river, they passed Magdalen College on their way into the city. Thérèse admired the belfry. She read the name of the college on a sign at the entrance.

"It's pronounced 'maudlin,' " said Wenger.

"In that case I'll send Mama a picture postcard of it," said Thérèse.

She seemed distraught as they walked along the High Street. Nevertheless she stopped in front of a shop window and admired the scarves in the colors of the various colleges. Outside another shop, she went into ecstasies over a dress.

"Daddy!" she cried.

She gazed at it for a long time. Then she said: "It only costs seven pounds. Can I buy it?"

"You're out of your mind!" Wenger restrained himself from criticizing the dress, from calling it a mini-rag in pop colors, and only observed: "Your allowance is ten pounds. If you buy this dress, you'll only have three pounds left till the end of the month."

"I'll manage all right."

He knew that she wouldn't manage. Thérèse wasn't the thrifty type any more than her mother. That was all right with Wenger, he didn't care for thrifty women. A woman had to know how to spend money, not enough to ruin you, but at least enough to discourage any suspicion that you were living with a low-priced woman.

But of course it was monstrous that Thérèse should want to buy a dress on her first day in Oxford. After all there were certain principles, certain rules of conduct which, for instance, had made him take couchettes rather than a wagon-lit compartment for the trip from Basel to Calais. For a moment, to his own surprise, Wenger nevertheless considered making her a present of the dress. In a moment which he later described as luminous, he realized that on that particular day she needed a dress, and possibly that particular dress. The moment passed. Thérèse was reasonable about it, she didn't complain or even make a show of resignation, but only gazed with boredom at the lighted windows of the department stores and Woolworth's that they passed after turning into Cornmarket Street.

It was time for a cup of tea. The place they went to was jammed with women who had been shopping and—though the term had not yet begun—of students. Wenger would have preferred to walk right out, but they found two places. They were so wedged in between tables and people that they could hardly move. When Wenger ordered tea, the waitress, without asking, poured tea and milk into big, thick-walled cups.

They looked at the brew.

"The English drink tea with milk," said Wenger.

"The lunch today was great," Thérèse informed him. "Roast veal with mashed potatoes and salad. And pudding."

"My goodness," said Wenger, "you could have told me that a little sooner."

"It's so unimportant," said Thérèse.

Wenger thought the remark and the tone in which it was made unpleasantly precocious.

"The school isn't what we imagined," he said. "But I think you'll find it comfortable. In an English sort of way."

He looked around the tearoom. It was all tables and chairs. The walls were bare and the neon light was gray. I should have taken her to the Mitre, he thought. We could have got tea there just as well. When he looked at her again, he saw she had tears in her eyes.

"But darling," he said, "you'll be back home again for Christmas!"

He felt utterly helpless. This tearoom was really too awful. Thérèse put her thumb and forefinger into the corners of her eyes, as she always did when she was trying to fight back her tears. That gesture transformed her into a grown woman. By the time she withdrew her hand she had pulled herself together.

"Yes," she said. "I'll always come to see you in my vacations. From Oxford. From Zürich."

He could hardly object to that. Wenger wanted to say that when she was in Zürich after Easter she would come home on weekends too; after all it was only three hours by train from Zürich to Davos. But he said nothing of the sort. Instead, he blurted out what was on his mind.

"We can't always be together," he said.

After that he felt to his horror that the tears were rising to *his* eyes. He was stricken with panic; good Lord, he thought, short of a miracle I'm going to cry, it's insane, I haven't cried since I was a child, I only hope she doesn't notice.

His arms and legs stiffened, his whole body tensed, he mustn't let this happen: a hysterical scene in a public place and in England to boot. He managed to avert his face.

"Father," he heard Thérèse say, "I didn't mean it that way."

He looked out into the dusk that had settled over Cornmarket Street; after a while he managed to recognize that it was bluish-gray.

When at last he was able to turn back to his daughter, he had made up his mind.

"All right," he said, "I'll take you back home with me tomorrow if you like."

Thérèse said nothing; she only shook her head, almost imperceptibly. She stood up and left the room; when she came back the shadows under her eyes were not quite as dark or her eyelids as blue as early in the afternoon.

Dinner at the Mitre went off as harmoniously as if the Wenger family had been on a holiday trip together. Farewell dinners were in progress at all the tables in the small dining room; students were sitting with their parents who had brought them to Oxford.

"Too bad I can't stay another day," said Wenger. "I'd have liked to show you more of Oxford."

"It's not possible," said Thérèse understandingly, "our classes start tomorrow."

I could perfectly well stay another day, thought Wenger. He had booked a flight to Kloten for the day after tomorrow morning and had already told Thérèse in the train to Calais that he had business to attend to in London. Now he realized that there was no need of such pretenses; she had understood as well as he that their excursion had already gone on too long.

After dinner they strolled for half an hour through the shadowy city. Thérèse took his arm. Under the high walls of St. Peter's Church and Queen's College there were blocks of darkness between the street lamps, but suddenly the full moon, a heavy ghost, hovered over the quads of All Souls. History lay all about them. Innumerable voices told innumerable stories, toneless, forever disembodied, only the lips still moved. Wenger didn't really know what to make of it. What had he said to Thérèse? *We can't always be together.* True, but was it necessary to leave her behind in such a strange place, so far from home, in a room with chocolate-brown paint, in the care of a legless woman? It was absurd. He sensed that Thérèse was cold and found his way out of the black and silvery labyrinth. On Broad Street he found a cab.

Before getting out, she sent her love to her mother and brother and gave him a kiss. While the cab was turning around, he saw her walking up to the door of the school.

Next day in London he walked through streets, stared at shop windows, and looked at people. He spent two hours in a bookshop and bought a few things. At five o'clock he phoned the school and asked for Thérèse.

"Hello!" he heard her say.

"Miss Wenger," he said.

"Daddy!" She seemed delighted.

"How is it?" he asked.

"Great!" she said and reeled off a list of unrelated news items. Obviously she was being kept busy. Perhaps he had been worrying needlessly.

"What were you doing when the phone rang?"

"I was playing the Bob Dylan record we bought in London for Pat. *John Wesley Harding*. Man, is that a record! Pat has been explaining the words to me. She's great!"

Everything was fine. They chatted awhile before exchanging another round of good-bys. Wenger waited a moment before hanging up. And indeed she was still on the phone. He heard her breathing and quickly put his hand over the mouthpiece to prevent Thérèse from hearing his. When she finally hung up, he lay down on the bed and looked at the ceiling. There was nothing to be seen on its white surface. Nothing at all.

After dinner, which he took at the hotel, he decided to go to the movies: *Ulysses*, after James Joyce's novel, was playing on Oxford Street. Two days before, on the train, he had underscored the ad in *The Times*. At present he hadn't the slightest desire to go anywhere, but he gave himself a jolt; you couldn't waste an evening in London sitting around a hotel lobby. In the cab he remembered how he had read Joyce's book twenty years ago. At first it had disgusted him, but then in retrospect it had come to seem more and more beautiful. When he occasionally picked it up, trying to account for this paradoxical phenomenon, his perplexity had only increased; there seemed to be no connection between these cool sentences with their constant outbursts of cynicism and the atmosphere they left behind, an atmosphere of darkness, night, wind, and melancholy. Strangely enough, the director seemed to have had similar feelings, for the picture he had made was dark through and through. Of course it had been an insane idea to film this book; nothing more had emerged than a sequence of dark, sharply cut scenes, culminating in Molly Bloom's great monologue. The portrayal of Molly Bloom corresponded almost exactly to Dr. Wenger's conception of her. The longer she spoke, the more the image on the screen ceased to be anything more than a body, a bed, a night, from which gross, obscene words poured into the movie house on Oxford Street, where two thousand people sat, scarcely breathing under the density of the words. Suddenly Dr. Wenger was afraid. He no longer heard the voice, he saw only the dark, moving components of the picture, which reminded him of the night before in Oxford, the chasm of the Queen's Lane, the silvery shadowy quads of All Souls in the moonlight. It seemed to him that he had abandoned Thérèse in a world of ghosts, of Commendatores and Golems, White Ladies, vampires and Frankensteins. Yes, Oxford was Frankenstein, and Thérèse was in the power of a ghost language. He jumped up and pushed his way past a row of knees. He would take Thérèse away immediately.

Neither on broad, glittering Oxford Street with its crowds nor on the quiet side streets that took him back to the hotel did he recover his calm. Once he stopped and looked at his reflection in a darkened shop window: a man of medium height in hat and raincoat, with a tendency to obesity, though in fairly good trim. The reflection showed nothing. X rays showed something, and so did movies made after books by James Joyce. Mirrors or mere photographs showed nothing, neither fathers nor ghosts, only empty shells.

Yet as he shaved the following morning he had only the mirror before him. His plane from Heathrow to Switzerland was due to take off at nine, duty called, and Dr. Wenger had to hurry with his packing.

++

In Memory of Captain Fleischer

++

The light in the depot was very bright, but yellow, not cold.
Behind the open door the dark-blue night reached out into glassy
depths. Framed in the indigo rectangle stood a marine officer in a
gleaming white cap.

They were issued the comfortable olive-green fatigue uniforms
of the U. S. Army, with a large white PW stamped on the backs
of the jackets. Franz Kien watched Frerks carefully folding the
jacket of his German uniform and packing it at the bottom of his
barracks bag. A few of the men threw their heavy woolen jackets
away. For a while Franz Kien wondered whether to keep his. It
smelled of sweat. The night sent waves of warmth and fragrance
into the depot. In the end, he carried his things to the pile of cast-
off clothing and boots. An American soldier stood beside it, shouting from time to time: "*Schmeissalles weg*—Chuck it all away.
You're getting all new stuff." The light rubber-soled shoes were
wonderfully comfortable. And in the deep breast pockets of his
new jacket he found room for everything: a pad of writing paper,
pencils, two pipes, a package of tobacco, an envelope full of letters
and photographs.

A train was shunted into the depot, and they started off that
same night. Richmond was not blacked out. The next day they
saw Fredericksburg, Alexandria, Washington, and Baltimore. Before Harrisburg they crossed the broad gray Susquehanna; they
saw islands, herons, a hanging bridge made of plaited branches,
and on the wooded banks tree trunks entwined in creepers. On
the station platform in Washington there had been an old man
whom Franz Kien called the Senator. The Senator was tall and
slender with a square-cut gray beard, a broad-brimmed hat, and a
gold watch chain; he was holding two Irish setters on short
leashes. Negroes were passing by.

One morning after Franz Kien had managed to escape from the war, he had seen the Rock of Gibraltar, sand-colored under a yellowish-gray cloud. There were white forts on the African mountains across the Straits.

At night they slept on the black leather seats of the coaches. The train became shorter and shorter; in the end, only their car remained. In St. Louis it was attached to a regularly scheduled express. It was certainly a mistake that Frerks should be in their car. The men who had packed their German uniform jackets had been in the other cars. In Franz Kien's car the barracks bags were lighter.

In St. Louis there was fog over the Mississippi. The Americans lived in wooden houses and sat in rocking chairs on verandas. Near a place called Cairo the dark-gray Ohio looped through dark, leafy woods and flowed into the lighter-colored Mississippi. In a place called Carbondale, their car was uncoupled and they had to wait two hours for another train. A laundry basket full of oranges was brought in. "From the Carbondale ladies," said the sergeant who was escorting the prisoners. "They heard that a shipment of PWs was waiting here."

He gave them a German-language American paper he had bought in St. Louis. They all waited impatiently for their turns; only Frerks passed it on unread.

"He's hopeless," said Maxim Lederer to Franz Kien under his breath.

Maxim Lederer had a rasping voice, he was always clearing his throat, and he always concluded his fanatical tales about life as a refugee with a sharp laugh. He claimed to have been a refugee in Prague; but he had had to go back, he'd have starved if he hadn't. From him Franz heard what had happened to the Communist Party in the last few years. He was only half interested. As he looked out at the countryside and the cities, his mind was busy with the fantastic fact that he had escaped from the war and was now crossing the American continent. Maxim Lederer seldom looked out the window.

During the following night they arrived in Memphis. In the morning they crossed the Mississippi on a high bridge near Jackson. The banks of the Mississippi consisted of sand flats and scrub marshes. Behind the dikes there were flooded woods interspersed with shallow streams, beside which herons and pelicans stood, fluttered into the air, and settled down again. The train moved slowly. The wooden houses of the Negro villages were as weather-beaten as the faces of the heavy old men who stood in the door-ways looking up at the train. Later, they came to the flat-topped drying sheds of Louisiana, empty country, country for the long, monotonous wanderings Franz Kien loved, through dry prairie grass that crackled, through brittle pine woods. In Ruston where they were unloaded there were white horsemen, bent low between cowboy hats and silver spurs. Their small, velvety brown horses seldom raised their heads, for the September day was hot and still.

2

The eagle circling below streaks of misty cloud aroused no desire for freedom in Franz Kien. According to all the rules of metaphor, he thought, that animal is up there to drive me crazy; but as sitting on the back steps of the hospital shack he looked up from his book in the soft afternoon light of the southern Novem-ber, the eagle was nothing more to him than a bird flying sound-lessly over the camp, over the flat country. And the barbed-wire fence in the distance was only a meaningless band of filigree.

He was still reading when he heard steps and voices from inside the hospital. He closed his book, stood up, climbed the steps, and opened the screen door. The hinges squeaked twice before the door closed behind him. Two MPs were standing in the passage between the two rows of beds, holding Frerks between them. His hands were tied together. Franz Kien had never seen a man tied before. One of the Americans asked where they could put Frerks. Franz Kien indicated a bed. The two patients in the ward had sat up in their beds. Then Maxim Lederer came in. The soldiers pushed Frerks over to the bed and gave him a shove when he failed to understand that he was supposed to lie down. Because of his tied hands, he fell on his face and lay motionless. The Ameri-can who had spoken before said he would send the doctor; then he followed the other, who was already on his way out.

Franz Kien and Maxim Lederer turned Frerks over but were unable to undress him.

"Should we untie him?" Franz Kien asked. "What's wrong with him anyway?"

Maxim Lederer shook his head. They covered Frerks up. He stared into space, obviously dead to the world. He had a sweater over his shirt, and though it was Sunday, he wasn't wearing his famous and detested jacket.

"He's cracked up," said Maxim Lederer in his hoarse, impersonal voice. "He'd been lying on his bed all day and didn't go to meals. Then all of a sudden he went berserk. First he tore pictures off the walls, then he attacked the barracks orderly. They held him until the MPs came."

He ended every sentence with his short, throaty, joyless laugh. He showed no *Schadenfreude*, he had nothing against Frerks except what everybody had against him.

"But why have they brought him here instead of to the guardhouse?" Franz Kien asked.

"Because I said he was sick," said Maxim Lederer. "I was one of the men holding him, and I could tell."

Franz Kien took Frerk's temperature. It was 106.

"You see," said Maxim Lederer.

"He must have been sick all day," said Franz Kien.

Maxim Lederer stayed at the hospital, though his night duty didn't begin until eight. All through September he and Franz Kien had picked cotton like all the prisoners; then they had signed up for jobs at the camp hospital. The work in the cotton fields had not been hard; they went down endless rows of plants, plucking the white flakes from the open capsules and tossing them into sacks that hung from their shoulders. At noon they lay dozing in the shade of the trees behind the farmhouse. The house lay silent in the noonday heat. The Negro who had brought them ice water sat leaning against a tree, asleep. He was the only Negro they came in contact with; even in the distance they saw no Negroes working in the fields; it wasn't thought fitting that Negroes should see white men picking cotton. In the afternoon they went back to work; when Franz Kien looked up, the prisoners were blue spots moving about in a shimmering sea of cotton. After a while he and Maxim Lederer found the monotony unbearable. In the meantime the cotton fields had been harvested; now the prisoners were cutting sugar cane with machetes, broad knives curved at the end. Back in camp, they talked about the Negro girls they had seen from the trucks in which they were driven to the plantations.

It was more than two hours before the doctor came. On Sunday it was always hard to reach the doctors. From time to time Franz Kien felt Frerks's pulse, which was pounding furiously. Twenty years later he remembered the feeling Frerks's wrist had given him, though he couldn't remember Frerks himself. Strange: twenty years later, he had forgotten what Frerks looked like. Yet his brain had stored up every detail of Captain Fleischer's image. Whenever he chose to, he could summon up the scene of Captain Fleischer getting out of his jeep at the camp gate in the twilight of that Sunday, passing the sentries, approaching the hospital with his short, precise steps, and run it off like a film. Maybe because he had stood so long at the window and waited for Fleischer so impatiently. Fleischer had his left hand in the pocket of his jacket; his right arm was held rather negligently, and Franz Kien could tell by the cramped bend of Fleischer's wrist that he was rummaging for a cigarette. As usual, he pulled out the cigarette and thrust it between his lips but didn't light it. It shone white in his brown face, below his black, carefully clipped mustache. Between the mustache and upper lip a strip an eighth of an inch was shaved. Everything about Captain Fleischer was thin and precise, including his nose and the gold frames of his glasses. Along with this precision, he was negligent and easygoing, with occasional cramped movements such as that bend of the wrist while walking.

Beyond the hospital grounds, the rows of long, low barracks were shrouded in a greenish chiaroscuro that always made its appearance when the sultry south wind was blowing. In a few of them the light had already been turned on. The gravel paths between the barracks were almost deserted. At that hour the prisoners were washing up for supper.

Franz Kien was glad it was Captain Fleischer, and not his superior, Major Moulton. Fleischer was an internist, not a surgeon like Moulton. Moulton was a Regular Army man, while Fleischer had a private practice in New York. But he wore his uniform with ease. Franz Kien imagined that his uniforms were tailor-made. He stopped Fleischer in the entrance and made his report.

"Oh, it's him," said Fleischer when he caught sight of Frerks.

Franz Kien was surprised that Fleischer should know Frerks, for he seldom entered the living quarters of the camp and never accompanied Colonel Taylor, the camp commander, on Sunday morning, when he passed the prisoners in review. He must have heard about this prisoner, Franz Kien thought, and gone to take a look at him. Frerks was the only prisoner who wore his German uniform jacket at the Sunday morning review. Immediately after their arrival in camp, he had washed it, ironed it, and affixed his corporal's stripes, the parachutist's insignia, the black-and-white ribbon of the Iron Cross Second Class, and the eagle with swastika. They had put him in the second rank, but Colonel Taylor had immediately moved him to the first, called the interpreter, and questioned him about his military career. Hardly a Sunday passed without the commander exchanging a few words with Frerks. He made him leader of a work squad. Frerks was cut off by all the other prisoners. No one spoke to him.

Fleischer was surprised to see Frerks lying in bed with his clothes on. He threw back the blanket and saw that his hands were tied.

"Gee!" he said.

He took the cigarette out of his mouth. Sometimes there was a quiet, dangerous sharpness in Fleischer's way of giving his medical orders. This time it looked as if he were going to lose his temper. But he kept himself under control and merely ordered Franz Kien to untie Frerks's hands and undress him. Franz Kien was furious with himself for not having dared to do it on his own before Fleischer arrived. He knew that Fleischer despised him for it.

Frerks showed little signs of consciousness and was hot to the touch. When he was back in bed, Fleischer examined him and said he had pneumonia. He himself prepared the first penicillin injection. His face was calm again, almost indifferent, as he held the needle up to the light to examine it; again his cigarette was dangling from the left corner of his mouth. Before leaving, he said Frerks should be given plenty of liquid.

Franz Kien stayed on for two hours, listening to Maxim Lederer's fanatical tales of his days as a refugee. He claimed the Communist Party had handed whole units over to the Gestapo for failing to comply with the party line. If his stories were true, the Communist Party was rotten to the core. If they were not true, the man who told them would bear watching. Maxim Lederer had little to say about his return from Prague to Germany; he answered evasively when Franz Kien asked what the authorities had done to him. Franz Kien knew that anything could happen when men caught between two fronts were subjected to questioning. One night at Gestapo headquarters could decide the whole course of a man's life. A dubious character, Franz Kien sometimes thought, I'd do better to steer clear of him; but he liked Maxim Lederer's hopeless, impersonal voice that liquidated the revolution at every sentence. Maxim Lederer never spoke of his private life and never, like all other prisoners, talked about his plans for the future. And another strange thing about him: you could break off a conversation with him in the middle; he wouldn't seem offended, he'd just stop talking and turn back to his newspaper.

On the way back to his barracks under the cloudy night sky, Franz Kien felt the sudden gusts of wind blowing in from the Gulf of Mexico. To him, when he thought about it, the revolution was unimportant. Of course there would be wars, violence, and revolutions, but all that mattered so little. What mattered was the night, the wind, clouds, eagles, the sea, and men asleep in the barracks. . . .

In the morning Frerks's temperature was still over 104, but he was sleeping peacefully. Maxim Lederer said Fleischer had come again during the night and given Frerks another shot of penicillin.

"I had to tell him about Frerks," said Maxim Lederer.

"He's probably wondering whether to recommend psychiatric treatment," said Franz Kien.

"He seemed furious when I told him that none of us would have anything to do with Frerks. I tried to explain that Frerks had isolated himself. He just doesn't belong in this camp, I told him."

Maxim Lederer put away the books and newspapers he had been reading during the night. Through the glass door of the office you could see into the ward where Frerks and the two other patients lay sleeping.

"These Jews with their illusions," said Maxim Lederer. "Do you know what Fleischer said before he left?" And without waiting for an answer: "He stood by Frerks's bedside and said: 'It's easier to hate than to love.'"

Even after that quotation Maxim Lederer's laugh didn't sound angry or scornful, but as usual, clipped, hoarse, and matter-of-fact.

Franz Kien would have liked very much to know whether Fleischer had addressed those words to Maxim Lederer or to Frerks, who was certainly asleep or at best half conscious. Had he looked at one of them or at neither—perhaps at the wall behind the bed? There was no point in asking Maxim Lederer, who certainly hadn't noticed. In view of what had been said before, he couldn't help relating Fleischer's remark to himself. But what if Fleischer had spoken neither to Frerks nor Lederer, but for his own benefit?

The day in the hospital passed quietly, with the usual occupations: making beds, taking temperatures, serving meals. One of the patients had had his appendix out; he wasn't allowed to get up and had to use a bedpan, which Franz Kien didn't mind. The other was syphilitic; every two hours he was given a small intramuscular injection of penicillin. He was afraid of pain, he tensed his buttocks instead of relaxing, and Franz Kien had to wait till he forgot himself for a moment before he could insert the needle. After lunch two out-cases reported, men from the forestry team with poison oak; Franz Kien smeared their swollen hands and legs with ointment.

In the course of the morning, Frerks recovered consciousness enough to provide the most essential information for the hospital records. Born in 1923 in a village near Eutin, no profession, sixteen when the war broke out, drafted in 1940. He said he had been an officer candidate. His father had been a clerk in the district administration. Having said that much, he was exhausted.

In the afternoon Franz Kien had time to read. He also went for a short walk between the hospital and the barbed wire; on the southeast side there was a row of pine trees that sheltered the camp. He picked a bouquet: a branch with wine-red and green leaves, two grass stalks with blades like lance heads, a plant with grapelike red blossoms, and a green stalk ending in a single violet flower. In Louisiana, under the cloudy sky, in the moist, warm air, occasionally stirred by a gust of wind, there were still flowers in November.

At five o'clock when he woke Frerks to feed him orange juice, give him an injection and take his temperature, he remembered how he had sat next to him in the camp movie theater, when a picture called *The Great Flammarion* was being shown. The great Flammarion was an old-time French officer, and it had been uncanny to see a figure out of Europe's warlike history resurrected in Eric von Stroheim and making his appearance in an alien American world. When the lights went on, Franz Kien had seen the ecstatic expression on Frerks's face. That memory almost enabled him to visualize Frerks's features later on, but then they slipped away, dissolving into the vague impression that lean, bony young men usually leave behind them.

Before Maxim Lederer relieved him, he looked at some of Marsden Hartley's pictures in a magazine. The reproductions were poor, but Franz Kien could see nevertheless that "Mount Katahdin in the Fall" was a fine picture. Marsden Hartley had written: "There are no more than two people in this country who know mountains." He had not written: ". . . who know anything about mountains."

Fleischer arrived for his evening call. He had come in the morning and shown Kien how to give an intravenous injection. Franz Kien found it very difficult, and two of his injections had caused Frerks considerable pain. Fleischer was satisfied with Frerks's condition. His temperature had dropped to 103. He asked whether Frerks spoke English; Franz Kien didn't know, but he had observed that when Colonel Taylor spoke to him he answered before the interpreter had time to translate.

When Fleischer arrived in the camp at the beginning of October, he had seemed strangely gentle and sensitive beside the sturdy military figure of Major Moulton. The camp commander and Major Moulton had undoubtedly been displeased when Captain Fleischer brought his wife to camp and showed her around the barracks and installations including the hospital. Captain Fleischer's wife was a marvelously pretty and chic young woman. The prisoners were bowled over. A rumor went around that she had been a model in New York. She wore her soft, bleached-blond hair at shoulder length. She seemed more aware than her husband of the awkward situation; Franz Kien noticed that her graceful, faintly provocative gait stiffened as she approached the hospital side by side with the Captain, who was taking his usual short steps and negligently swinging one arm, while with the other cramped hand he was rummaging for a cigarette.

After one of the couple's visits to the ward, Franz Kien had heard two patients discussing Captain Fleischer and his wife.

"Looks like we got her all hot and bothered," one of them had said.

"You've got it wrong," said the other. "It's him. He gets a kick out of showing us his wife."

The grain of truth in their comments was that Fleischer probably thought he was giving the prisoners pleasure by bringing his much too attractive wife into camp. A big mistake for a man of his intelligence, thought Franz Kien. The only possible explanation was that love made him blind. Franz Kien saw that Fleischer was disappointed that his wife didn't talk to the patients or even shake hands with them, but stood behind them, turning half aside as though prepared to run for it at the slightest sign of danger. After her second visit she didn't come again.

It wasn't until Tuesday that Fleischer was able to talk to Frerks. Even then Frerks was apathetic, though fully conscious. His temperature was down; Fleischer stopped the penicillin and prescribed sulfa pills. He drew up a chair and sat down beside Frerks's bed. He told him why he had come so late on Sunday: he had gone to the Mississippi to see a breach in the dikes. There had been heavy rain in Tennessee and the masses of water had burst the dikes near Vicksburg. He described the watery waste. Frerks looked him straight in the eye, but Franz Kien couldn't tell whether the captain's story interested him or not. He himself would have liked to ask Fleischer questions; he had a feeling that Fleischer understood the Mississippi, but he knew that Fleischer was talking entirely for Frerks's benefit, even though he had picked his subject at random and might just as well have talked about something else, about New York for instance, or the war that was coming to an end. Fleischer spoke softly and fluently; when he broke off now and then, it wasn't because he didn't know what to say next, but because he was taking time out to think about what he had said or was going to say.

"Can we go some of the way together?" he asked after one of these pauses.

Immediately after Fleischer's departure, Franz Kien asked

Maxim Lederer, who had come in during Fleischer's bedside monologue and listened to it, whether he thought that question could
be asked in German.

"No, thank God," said Maxim Lederer. "We're not as sentimental as the Americans."

"It didn't sound sentimental the way he said it," Franz Kien
argued.

But he had to admit that spoken in German, the same words
did sound insufferably sentimental, given the relations between
Fleischer and Frerks. In a pinch he could conceive of saying "It is
better to love than to hate" in German; true, there was pathos in
it, but you could put up with a bit of pathos if you had to. What
was absolutely intolerable was to transform an offhand, friendly
remark into something sticky by translation.

Maxim Lederer went over to Frerks's bed.

"Did you understand what Fleischer was telling you?" he asked.

Frerks didn't answer. He lay with his eyes wide open, staring
into space.

"Captain Fleischer's a Jew," said Maxim Lederer. "Ugh, ugh, a
plain, ordinary Jew. In case you didn't know."

"Cut it out!" said Franz Kien.

Fleischer hadn't waited for Frerks to answer his question. He
had stood up, attended to the other patients, given a few instructions, and left. Franz Kien couldn't tell whether Frerks was disappointed when Major Moulton appeared next day instead of
Fleischer, who had gone off for a few days' leave.

Franz Kien was again sitting on the back steps when he heard
the screen door squeak on its hinges. He stood up as a matter of
course, though Fleischer told him not to. Standing on the upper-
most step in his negligent yet precise attitude, as usual rummaging for a cigarette with his cramped right hand, the captain
looked out at the line of barbed wire in the distance. This kind of
camp should be set up without barbed wire, he said. Then he
came back to the subject of Frerks and spoke angrily of the unfair
way he was being treated. That evening Franz Kien jotted down a
few sentences in his diary, such as "Nobody talks to him" and
"He should be taken into the crowd, not segregated."

He himself did not, like Fleischer, see the barbed-wire fence,
but only the hollow behind it, bathed in brown and yellow, and

in among the trees on the horizon the Negro farm, the bright-colored washing that was always hanging in the yard, and the black cows grazing in the tall meadow grass.

3

When Frerks was well again, he went back to wearing his German uniform jacket on Sundays; it wasn't until the prisoners were shown movies of the concentration camps that he stopped. He made friends with a middle-aged peasant from the Eifel, a primitive anarchist and eccentric who had once been court-martialed. The two could be seen talking together on long walks along the barbed-wire fence. That was after the armistice.

Franz Kien lost sight of him, Maxim Lederer, and most of his fellow prisoners when along with twenty others he was transferred to a camp in the North. Again they traveled in a car attached to regularly scheduled trains. They crossed the Red River at Monroe, rode along the Mississippi for a while after Memphis, then turned into the Tennessee plain.

Sometimes Franz Kien wondered where he and Maxim Lederer and Fleischer and Frerks would be twenty years later. Or the Negro who had brought them ice water at noon when they were picking cotton. Where would they be living, each for himself, twenty years later?

He never thought of the revolution, only of countries. America, Tennessee, Gibraltar, Europe. Of the loneliness of the countries.

He had spent a peaceful fall and winter in Louisiana, the old slave country.

An elderly, heavy-set Negro, a railroad worker, was standing by the tracks when early in the morning they stopped at a station in Tennessee. He was wearing a faded brick-red shirt. When Franz Kien looked at him, the Negro looked back with a long steady gaze, without moving, without smiling.

On the wall of a wooden house beyond the station the words MOSES PLAYHOUSE NICE CLEAN ROOMS MEALS COLD DRINKS were inscribed in peeling paint. Franz Kien would have been glad to get out and take a room there.

+++

The First Hour

+++

What the gate keeper slammed behind him wasn't a gate; it was only a big iron door fitted into a brick wall.

"Well, Ehlers, good luck!" the gate keeper had said.

"Herr Ehlers, if you please," he had said.

And then the door had slammed. The noise didn't bother him, he was used to it. Inside, there was either dead silence or a deafening din: banging doors, thundering steps, the clatter of tin plates, men bellowing. Interspersed by hours when there was nothing to be heard. Nothing. It was only in the shop that the work called for the measured sounds of plane and saw, spoken communications, signs and glances.

When the door had finished slamming, he listened for what sounds there might be outside. He heard the singing of a band saw in the distance, rising to an intolerably high note, then dying away.

On his side of the street the wall went on and on. On the other there were old four-story tenements. The street was deserted except for three cars, parked a long way from each other. They looked as if they had been standing there for years.

Fifty yards farther on, the row of houses was broken by a side street. He read the weatherbeaten Gothic letters of the name of the corner bar, which was known to him from the reports of returnees: THE COOL SPRING. That was the first place all or nearly all of them went when they got out.

A woman turned the corner. She was carrying a shopping bag. Her winter coat made her shapeless. Since he was still standing outside the iron door, she gave him a curious look out of her careworn face. When he stared back, she looked away and disappeared into a doorway. The houses here had no doors, but big open entrances, dark passages leading to inner courtyards.

He thought: Monday, January 2, 1970, 10 A.M.

The weather was gray, not very cold. At least it wasn't raining. His greatest fear in the last few years had been that it might rain on this day, that the weather would make him hurry, perhaps even run to take shelter somewhere, and content himself with the first café he came to. Rainy weather would have spoiled it all.

At last he began to move, as slowly as possible.

They had given him a new suit and a new overcoat; the clothes he had taken off twenty years ago didn't fit him any more. Then, at the age of thirty-seven, he had been slim, the tall, gaunt type; now he was a heavy-set man without contours.

He had objected to the narrow trouser legs.

"They look like stovepipes," he had said.

"That's how they're wearing them now," the clothing-room trusty had said. "They'd all stop and stare at you if you came along in those old bell bottoms of yours."

Besides, they were too small in the waist. He could barely squeeze into his old jacket.

They had also given him a new shirt, new underwear and socks, a blue-and-white striped tie that he didn't like, and new shoes. They were more pointed than his old ones, which for a moment had stood scuffed and ungainly beside the new ones, before the trusty had tossed them into a crate. He had declined the hat they offered him and asked for an umbrella instead. Later on in his cell he had rolled it tight and fastened it with a strip of adhesive tape he had painted black. Of his old things he kept nothing but a black woolen muffler.

He crossed the street and walked along the house fronts. Outside a ground floor window he stopped to look at a vase and a pot of cyclamen on the other side of the pane. The vase was potbellied, painted in a lavender flower pattern; it was dusty and had a crack in it. The cyclamen was like cyclamen. He gazed at these two objects until he saw a shadowy man standing behind the window, in the glossy gray of the voile curtains; apparently he too had been looking at the vase and the cyclamen and was now staring at him. He had on a dark-gray coat and a black woolen muffler; his hands were in his overcoat pocket and the handle of a tightly rolled umbrella was crooked over his arm. He couldn't recognize much in the face; it seemed dull, maybe a bit flabby, only the thin

straight nose had withstood change and stood out clearly. His hair
was still thick; he wore it parted on the right side. In the last few
weeks, he had been allowed to let it grow. It had once been black.
His new hair was steel-gray.

He turned away. From here, no longer directly under the wall,
he had a view of the prison buildings. It didn't hold him for long.
Since the cells were all on the inner court of the rectangular main
building, he knew he would not be able to see the window of his
cell. That was why he had never been able to look out at the
streets around the prison; it wouldn't have helped to pull himself
up by the bars in the hope of seeing something else besides cell
windows. When he occasionally did so, it was to look at the sky,
especially when he thought there might be interesting cloud for-
mations or when the rain was pouring down on the roofs. In the
last few years he had given up this bit of gymnastics; the effort
had become too much for him.

When he reached the corner, he read the names on the street
signs. The street leading along the wall was called Angerstrasse,
the other, that opened out into it, Poelnitzstrasse. He repeated
the names a few times, not only silently, mentally, but also in an
undertone: "Angerstrasse, Poelnitzstrasse." These names were the
first words he spoke. The light in the streets, under the gray,
wintry sky, between the old tenements, was a splotchy brown,
with chalk lines and charcoal lines in it.

It gave him deep satisfaction to think how he had had his way
in the matter of the escort the prison authorities had wanted to
foist on him.

"It goes without saying that we'll get you a room and a job before you leave us," the warden had said, after informing him that
his life term had been reduced to twenty years. "And someone
will escort you to your room."

"I don't want anybody to go with me when I get out of here,"
he had replied.

"I'm sorry. Regulations!" The warden's voice was harsh again.
Possibly he was annoyed that this man, whom he had even offered
a chair, showed no sign of joy or gratitude at having been reprieved.

"I'll leave here alone or not at all!"

He knew that this obstinacy, which, to make matters worse, was not what anyone expected of him—he was known in prison as a silent, acquiescent type—had delayed his release by several weeks. The twenty years were over at the end of November, not in January. They had finally given in. He was well aware they couldn't keep him any longer. He hadn't been reprieved at all. A lifer simply couldn't be held for more than twenty years. Ridiculous to say his sentence had been reduced.

Imagine having to walk through these streets with some escort! Maybe even being obliged to talk to him!

This escort would probably have asked him if he'd care to have a beer at the corner bar outside which he had stopped. Such people, social workers or whatever, thought they knew psychology, thought they understood. Of course his answer—that he wasn't a barfly—would have met with approval, but how much patience would that kind of man have had with his standing there a while and carefully, whisperingly, reading the words on the brewery signs? He wouldn't have given him as much time as he needed.

Finally he tore himself away and walked, still slowly and hesitantly, down Poelnitzstrasse, which looked exactly like Angerstrasse. Once he turned around and looked back at the wall and the prison. His last look at it was from the end of Poelnitzstrasse. By then it was smaller; the dark-red wall and the part of the cement-gray block that closed off the street were a cold two-dimensional surface, a red-gray flag against a background of two rows of old tenement houses. It all disappeared when he turned the corner. He went back to the corner to make sure it was still there; only then did he turn for good into the third street, whose name he likewise read but immediately forgot. On the way he had passed a few people. He noticed that they looked him over and he noticed that they lowered their eyes when he looked back at them.

This slum section, this prison neighborhood, was exactly as he had imagined. It hadn't disappointed him. But then looking toward the cutout at the end of the third street he perceived a rapid horizontal movement, a gray whishing, at once image and sound, and sensed that he was coming to something new, something unknown to him. Before leaving the prison, he had looked at a map of the city; he knew that he was approaching a broad artery leading out of town, and that when he reached it the streetcar terminus would be a few hundred yards to the left. But on the map, which the young clerk who had handled the arrangements for his discharge had explained to him—the warden hadn't shown his face again—this formerly tree-lined avenue was marked by a broad white stripe, which had somehow given him a feeling of peace and quiet.

What a mistake! So he had missed all this! In 1948, when they had locked him up the traffic had been entirely different, a disjointed noise that came and went, not this steady hum. Now the cars were more beautiful, smoother, sleeker, and the trucks were basses, singing monsters, dark and snub-nosed. For a moment he forced himself to admire this street flooded with movement. The stereotype flashing of blinkers, the slower rhythms of stoplights wove a kind of luminous music into the gray of the moving columns. After all, he had never seen anything like this; he should have been overwhelmed. This was morning traffic in a not very big city! Instead, he looked on coldly. He wondered if it was only because he had missed the development of this motorized world that he felt nothing but loathing. Was he envious? He didn't know. He remembered the young clerk saying to him: "Be careful when you get out, Herr Ehlers! Watch your step! You'll be going into an entirely different world." The young man had always addressed him as "Herr Ehlers" as if nothing else would have been conceivable. In speaking of a new world, had he been referring to these monotonously passing tin caverns containing the outlines of people's torsos?

As he went on, it was still the old world for a while when he wasn't looking at the roadway: the same houses as before, and up ahead an open square, bordered by tall, leafless poplars. And on the square an old-fashioned, pale-yellow streetcar with a trailer of the same color, was waiting. It was exactly what he had expected: pale yellow and finely delineated, standing at the end of the line, among kitchen gardens and poplar trees.

He pondered whether to get into the trailer or the main car, then decided in favor of the main car, but stayed on the rear platform.

Two women were sitting inside. When the lady conductor came out to him, he said: "City, please!"

He had settled on this formula in advance. He thought it would sound experienced and offhand. But it didn't work.

"Where in the city?" the conductor asked.

"I meant the center," he said. A bad beginning. He bowed his head, reached into his overcoat pocket for change, and brought out a two-mark piece.

"I'll let you off at Nicolaiplatz," said the conductor after a pause, during which she must have looked him over. "There you'll be right in the center. I'll let you know when we get there."

No doubt she often had passengers like him. Out here there was nothing but the slums and the prison. The people in the street had identified him at a glance. As long as people could see, or at least suspect, where he came from, he wasn't really discharged.

"Thank you very much," he said.

She handed him his change. It wasn't until she had gone inside the car that he dared to look at her. About thirty, he figured. She struck him as pretty.

If she knew, he thought, that she's the first woman I've spoken to in twenty years!

The last one he spoke to, twenty years before, was his landlady's daughter. He had killed her. One day when he couldn't stand it any more he had grabbed hold of her. She had screamed. He put his hand over her mouth but she had kept on screaming until he squeezed her throat.

Wintry gardens; then, before the houses began, a glance at the bay on which the city was situated. He saw ships drawn up at docks, and across the water villas and the crowns of trees.

For a minute or two, as she slumped in his arms, he hadn't realized she was dead. He had shaken her, thinking she had fainted.

In the course of the twenty years he had practiced facing up to her image when it came back to him. He didn't drive it away. He had fully expected it to appear in this first hour. As it happened, it had picked a bad moment; he could literally see it pale in the windless January air over the bay, then vanish completely.

The people who got on at the stops paid no attention to him. After a while he stood squeezed between them, as silent as they were. The conductor called out: "Railroad station." Actually, that was where he should have got out. They had found him a job in

Kiel and given him a railroad ticket. They were expecting him to go to Kiel immediately.

Since he had been living in the apartment for over a year, the court had convicted him of murder rather than manslaughter. Not premeditated, but still murder, a crime of passion as they put it. At the time he wouldn't have minded if they had sentenced him to be hanged, but only a short time later he was grateful that the death penalty had been abolished. He was clearly aware of what he had done. Once he had got into a conversation with a legal-minded fellow prisoner, who had explained: "Life for that! Man, your lawyer must have been an idiot!"

"She would have been alive," he said.

After fifteen years he had gone to see the warden and asked if his sentence could be reduced.

"Hm, murder," the warden had said. "An emotional crime. Well, I can inquire."

Then he had blundered.

"Since I've been here," he had said, "I've known three men who were sentenced respectively for complicity in two thousand, three thousand, and seventeen thousand murders."

"What are you driving at?" The warden was known as an irritable man, who would flare up over nothing at all.

He had tried to explain as gently as possible: "Those men arrived long after me, and they left ages ago."

"Well, if you're going to take that attitude . . ." That was the end of the interview. He had had no news of his petition until five years later, when his time was up.

The conductor came out on the platform and motioned to him. He nodded. When the car stopped, she helped him through the crush to the door. She treated him almost like an invalid.

He waited on the sidewalk until the car had left. Before taking his first steps, he wanted to be perfectly sure the lady conductor had disappeared.

Nicolaiplatz was merely a narrow, elongated rectangle, a break in a long street which was obviously the main street of this medium-sized town. Again he put his hands in his pockets, letting his umbrella dangle from his left forearm, and appraised the street. Lots of people, but hardly a human torrent. Cars passed, not as many as on the suburban street but still a good many, more than he was used to. He actually thought the words *used to*, though he wasn't used to anything now, he'd have to start getting used to things.

Here at last no one would know him or recognize him.

He started off to the left because in that direction the street seemed to be longer and livelier, but stopped almost immediately at a newsstand. This was one of the scenes he had imagined in detail: stepping up to a newsstand and buying a paper. There were papers in the prison, but it wasn't easy to get hold of them; you had to plead with the guards or track them down, and that could be a very complicated chase; altogether, the prison was a labyrinth. As it turned out, buying a paper wasn't as simple as he had imagined; what he hadn't taken into account was that before he could make up his mind to ask for one he would stop and stare in consternation at the nude or almost nude women on the covers of the illustrated magazines. For this he had not been prepared. How long had this been going on? In his day he had seen such pictures in shady little magazines that the dealer hung up in an obscure corner of his stand. Now they were plastered all over the outside, and on the busiest square in town! It was mad. Was this the new world the young clerk had warned him about? He looked cautiously around: the passersby weren't paying the slightest attention to the pictures. They must have gone crazy. Or they were utter hypocrites. Probably both: crazy hypocrites.

When he saw that the man in the wooden booth was watching him, he hurriedly bought a paper. He read the headline: END OF BIAFRA. The word Biafra meant nothing to him.

He put the paper in his pocket. At this time of day he would have been working in the prison carpentry shop. Then at noon he'd be sitting in his cell again. After the first few years they had given him permission to have pictures in his cell. He had pasted up only one, a seascape he had cut out of a magazine. In the end they had also given him a radio, an old contraption with a tinny sound, that he hardly ever switched on. He read a good deal, at night before lights out and on Sundays. The prisoners were awakened at six. In all those years he had only twice screamed, wept, and banged on the door. They had come and given him an injection.

Now he was walking down a main street, past people, under an even gray sky, on a not very cold day.

At ten o'clock he had still possessed four hundred and twenty marks and seventy pfennigs. That's what they had given him after twenty years of work. The streetcar had cost eighty pfennigs and the newspaper forty.

He had prepared himself for the sight of girls in miniskirts. He had learned of their existence from the crude jokes of recent arrivals among the prisoners. The first he saw were reflected in the plate-glass window of a furniture store, outside which he had stopped. He was about to turn around, but they stopped behind him and began to chatter, a group of grown-up schoolgirls. He decided not to move; that way he could go on watching them unnoticed. One of the girls had long slender legs, she appealed to him; the others, he thought, would have done better to cover their thighs. The cars behind him drove across the glass pane. He saw the cars, the girls, some other people, himself, and the furniture. He liked most of the furniture. They were doing a lot with veneers and white vinyl these days. The plastic was pasted on cheap wooden boards; nowadays, he had heard, you paid for the design, not for the material. He himself had fed sheets of this thin, soft material into a punch press. When you pasted it on table tops, cupboard doors, or shelves, you got a smooth surface. In the mirror of a dressing table inside the shop, the pretty girl's long, slender legs appeared for a moment very clearly, then vanished. He had started out as a white-collar worker, a bookkeeper in a factory, and in prison they had also put him to work in an office. After two years he had asked to be trained as a cabinetmaker. At first they had laughed at him; you couldn't learn so difficult a trade at the age of thirty-nine. He had stood firm and finally got his way. A few years later he was one of the best cabinetmakers in the prison. He often said that he would have died if he had had to go on doing office work. Above all, he couldn't conceive of spending his days in an office when he got out. When he finally turned around, the girls were dispersing. Some went down the same sidewalk, close to the curb, close to the cars; others crossed the street. It struck him how everything went together: the tin caverns with the sitting torsos, the bare walking thighs, the shop windows in which cars and thighs were reflected, the objects behind these mirrors which, if you looked straight at them, wiped out the mirror images in front of them.

Looking at the pipes on display in the window of a tobacco shop, he wondered if he should take up smoking again. In prison he had broken himself of the habit. He put off his decision until later.

He saw quite a few women who appealed to him. But it was too late to think of taking up with a woman. At thirty-seven he had still been a bachelor; why then should he marry or even enter into a permanent relationship at fifty-seven? Besides, he had no luck with women. They had nothing against him, they neither liked nor disliked him. There must be something about him that prevented them from taking an interest. True, he had had only two years, from 1947 to 1949, in which to form this opinion. Before that he had been a soldier, then a prisoner of war in Russia. Maybe certain women would take an interest in him now. He was a murderer. They would be deluding themselves. He really wasn't a sex criminal. In prison he had hardly ever masturbated. His murder had been nothing but a stupid accident with a screeching doll.

Enough of that! He had let his thoughts run away from him. Exactly what he had wanted to avoid. He took a side street down to the bay and cautiously crossed the shore road; here there were more cars again and they were going faster. A car stopped right beside him, the man inside cranked down the window and shouted: "Hey, haven't you ever heard of zebra stripes?"

He saw the angry face. Before he could say anything, it was gone. Arrived at the other side, he looked around and found out what the man had been talking about: the corridor of yellow stripes next to the traffic lights.

He wandered around the harbor. Here it was quiet. He watched stevedores piling up crates that a crane was unloading from a big freighter. Between the ships lay the water of the bay. The water and the sky looked as if it were going to snow. How would I know? he thought. I've lost touch with the weather.

It was here that he first began to see the prison as a doll's house. Suddenly it appeared before him, very small, a toy; he could bend over and watch the dwarfs trotting down miniature corridors, past tiny cells, where other dwarfs sat motionless, wizened and beyond salvation.

On the way back to the main street, he stopped outside a travel bureau, impressed by the posters. Could people really travel wherever they pleased now? The place was so full of people that he wasn't afraid to step in. He took his place in line and listened as a man arranged for a trip to Morocco, and a girl for a winter sports holiday in Switzerland. Then he discreetly stepped aside, took some booklets from a table, folded them down the middle, and left. It would be a long time, years perhaps, before he would be allowed to leave the country.

He took his newspaper out of his pocket, tucked the folders into it, and kept the bundle in his hand. With his paper and travel folders, his tightly rolled umbrella, his stovepipe trousers and black muffler, he looked like one of them, he felt. His hair was steel gray but thick and parted on the right side, and his nose was still thin and straight. He would be presentable in spite of his age, he thought, if his face, like the flesh of his whole body, hadn't lost all meaning. It had grown flabby.

At last he found what he had been looking for the whole time: a big café. When he went in, he saw that it consisted of two adjoining rooms; the inner room was raised; to enter it you had to go up two steps. There were not many people in the café. He decided in favor of the outer room, he didn't want to go in any farther. He took off his coat and sat down by a window. He savored the sweet, warm, bright smell of the café. The round table top was of brownish-reddish marble. On it lay an ash tray and a china sugar bowl with silver fittings. So now they left the sugar out just like that!

The waitress came up to him. She had on a blue dress and a white apron. He ordered a cup of coffee.

While waiting, he reached into his coat pocket and took out the slip of paper on which the two addresses in Kiel had been typed: his job and his room. He wasn't going to Kiel—that was definite, as much a part of his program as the sentences: "Either I leave here alone or not at all," and "Herr Ehlers, if you please." Because they had said Kiel, he had immediately thought of Hamburg. If he found a job there, they couldn't object too much; the worst they could do was to threaten him with stricter police supervision. Suddenly he changed his mind. In either case he'd be working as a cabinetmaker and living in a furnished room, so what difference did it make whether the shop and room were in Kiel or Hamburg? He could move later on, with their permission. And the less trouble he gave them, the sooner they'd be likely to let him have a passport. Yes, he'd go right to the station and take the first train to Kiel.

Since he had declined to take anything with him from the prison, he would have to buy a few things first: soap, a razor, a change of socks and underwear, and a small, cheap suitcase.

The waitress brought his coffee. She took the cup off a tray and set it down before him on the table. She put a little silver pitcher of cream beside it.

The cup was light yellow with a blue pattern—some sort of vines. On the saucer, beside the cup, lay a silver-plated spoon. The coffee was deep black, brownish around the edges. Steam rose from it; it smelled good.

He took the spoon from the saucer and set it down on the chestnut-colored marble.

His coat was on the chair to the left of him. His newspaper and travel folders lay on top of it. His umbrella hung on the back of his chair.

First he turned his cup—once, twice—and watched it turning, blue vines around a black circle on chestnut brown.

Then he pushed it away to the far edge of the table. Now it looked shadowy against the light. Cars passed behind it.

He became aware of the blue dress, the white apron beside him.

"Don't you like the coffee?" he heard the waitress say.

"Oh yes, yes," he said, feeling annoyed. "Bring me a piece of chocolate cake."

When she had gone, he drew the cup toward him but still didn't touch the coffee.

The chocolate cake arrived.

"Bring me another cup of coffee," he said. "This one has got cold."

"But you'll have to pay for this one."

"Yes, of course."

"Why did you let it get cold?" she asked.

He looked up at her. She was a woman of forty or more with a tower of hair on her head. In any case, she wasn't just a waitress. She offered resistance.

"Just like that," he said. "I don't know myself."

She shook her head but in a friendly way. Somehow his answer seemed to satisfy her, perhaps because it had been spoken so softly.

He ate his chocolate cake. He had wanted to be alone for a while with his cup, but that wasn't his only reason for ordering it. He had been planning to eat a piece of chocolate cake ever since he started for the café. It tasted pretty much as he had imagined chocolate cake would taste.

The second cup of coffee looked exactly like the first.

He poured a bit of cream into it and watched the little cream clouds rising in the coffee and breaking up. Then he pulled up the sugar bowl, took the paper off two lumps of sugar, and carefully put the lumps in the cup. He picked up the spoon and stirred the coffee. He knew the waitress was standing nearby, watching him out of the corner of her eye, but that wasn't his only reason for doing all this.

After drinking his coffee, he unfolded his newspaper and tried to read. He wasn't able to.

Instead, he looked out the window.

Now he would have liked to smoke. He could have bought a pack of cigarettes in the café. He was never able to figure out why he hadn't hit on this simple idea.

+++

Jesuskingdutschke

+++

For Walter Heist

"It's nothing," said Carla. "A surface wound."

She pushed his black hair aside and examined his skull as well as she could by the light of the street lamp. Marcel stood leaning against the lamppost. Blood ran down over his face in two streams; he wiped it away gingerly when it got in his eyes.

"It's got to be bandaged," said Carla to Leo. "The best place would be my clinic. Think we can scare up a cab around here?"

Carla was a medical student interning at the Moabit Hospital.

"You'd better go home and change first," said Leo. "You must be wet to the skin."

She shook her head. "It's not necessary," she said. "My coat stopped most of it, and I've got a change of clothing in the clinic."

Her hair, which was as black as Marcel's, was plastered to her head. She had on a light-colored belted raincoat.

Leo forced himself to look at the blood that was trickling down into Marcel's beard. Behind him he heard the steps of the demonstrators who were retreating into Kochstrasse. They had stopped running, because the police were attacking only as far as the corner of Charlottenstrasse. The water cannon was still in operation, although the street was already deserted. Turning away from Marcel and Carla, Leo looked at the stream of water, which was lit by the searchlights on the other side of the Wall. Suddenly it was turned off. For a few seconds there was only silence and the black glow of the wet street. Then he saw the police in the background, swarms of helmets and overcoats around the lighted Press Building. About a hundred yards from the water cannon, almost at the corner across from Checkpoint Charlie, a man was lying face down on the sidewalk. A civilian, apparently a doctor, had been let through the cordon of police around the zone crossing, and was going toward the injured man.

Trouble or no trouble, there ought to be cabs at the Underground station, Leo thought, but in that direction we'd be sure to run into trouble with the police.

"Come on," he said. "We'll find a cab at Askanischer Platz."

They were among the last to leave the scene. On Anhalter Strasse the night could have been any April night in Berlin, cool and quiet. Whenever they crossed through the light of a street lamp, Leo saw that Carla was watching Marcel closely, apparently afraid the blood would start spurting again.

A lone taxi was waiting outside the little round park on Askanischer Platz. The driver had his elbow on the steering wheel and his head propped on his hand; he seemed to be asleep, but the moment Leo touched the door handle, he spoke up without shifting his position: "Get your paws off there. I don't take students."

As usual when such things happened to him, Leo thought of the bearlike strength that made his friends refer to him as "the bruiser." He could pull this man out of his cab with one hand. But just as he was going to take hold of the door on the driver's side, he remembered how half an hour before he had neglected to stop the blow that had caught Marcel on the head.

"This man is hurt," said Carla. "We've got to get him to the hospital as quickly as possible."

Instead of answering, the driver only cranked up his window. They saw him picking up the microphone of his two-way radio.

"Let's go to Hallesches Tor," Leo suggested. "We'll take the Underground and change at Wedding."

"We'll get there quicker by walking through the Tiergarten," said Carla.

Leo had to admit she was right, though now, at night, he would have liked to take the Underground from Hallesches Tor to Wedding. On that line, the trains passed under Friedrichstrasse through East Berlin without stopping. The light in the cars that were usually empty grew dimmer, you sat in a colorless twilight, and the stations passed by like yellow-tiled clouds. Stadtmitte, Französische Strasse, Oranienburgertor. On the platforms there were always two Vopos side by side, with their rifles slung over their shoulders.

At the Landwehr Canal they turned right. Reichspietsufer, Leo read. This night, he thought, ought to smell of murder, of köbis and Reichspietsch, of Liebknecht and Luxemburg; it ought to ring with cries for help. But it was only a dimly lighted April night; the canal water lay dense and meaningless between the bright stone banks; now and then a car drove through the vaguely moving circles of light on the roadway.

There was the Wall again to the right of them, sometimes only a short connecting link between the walls of two warehouses, sometimes a longer stretch. They followed it, turning north into the deserted Linkstrasse. A diffuse glow beyond the Wall intensified the darkness on their side of it.

On Linkstrasse Marcel spoke for the first time.

"Lukács's critique of Burkharin is wrong," he said. "Bukharin in his day understood certain things that Lukács still doesn't understand."

"You mean you've found a copy of Bukharin?" Leo asked.

"Right," said Marcel. "In a second-hand bookshop on Flensburger Strasse. I couldn't believe my eyes. The German edition of 1922."

"Man!" said Leo. "When can I have it?"

"Not for a while. We're doing a seminar on it."

Marcel was studying sociology. Since the Institute had folded, the students were temporarily free to choose the topics of their seminars.

"Bukharin was the only one who understood the role of technology," said Marcel. "Here's what he says: 'Every given system of work relations is determined by the prevailing technology.' That's why Lukács attacks him. He claims that Bukharin identified technology with the means of production . . ."

"Which wouldn't be so wrong," Leo broke in. "In architecture at least, I'd say the two were identical."

"Sure," said Marcel. "But Bukharin doesn't even go so far. He only says that the development of society depends on the development of technology. Lukács calls that 'false naturalism.' "

Suddenly they stopped talking. A police jeep had stopped beside them. The police next to the driver jumped out and came toward them.

"Papers, please!" he said.

"Why?" Leo asked. "Aren't we allowed to walk here?"

"If you want to make trouble, you can come along right now," said the policeman.

Leo took out his Berlin identity card and handed it to the officer. As students, they were used to being checked for no reason at all and never went out without their papers.

The policeman looked at Marcel. "What's wrong with you?"

"He fell and hit his head," said Carla.

"I see," said the policeman. "He fell? Just like that?"

"No," said Carla. "He didn't fall just like that. He fell. It happens. I work at the Moabit Hospital, we're taking him there now."

She handed him her West German passport. He took out a notebook and entered their names.

"You have no right to take our names," Leo said.

"I have no right to do all sorts of things," said the policeman calmly. "You'd be amazed."

Leo felt Carla's hand on his shoulder.

"Don't worry," he said. "I won't hurt him."

The policeman looked at him. "I hear you threatened a cab driver a little while ago."

"That's not true," said Carla. "He refused to pick us up. We didn't say a word, we just walked off. Not a word! Even though he said he didn't take students." This in a near scream.

Even this policeman couldn't help seeing that she was only demanding her rights. He turned away from Leo.

"And now let's see your papers," he said to Marcel, while returning Carla's and Leo's.

At the sight of Marcel's Swiss passport, he changed his tone.

"We'll take you to the nearest first-aid station if you like," he said.

"I'd like you to take down my name too," said Marcel.

"Not necessary," said the policeman.

Marcel grabbed his passport out of the policeman's fingers turned around, and started off.

Walking off like that without a word had given them a good exit, Leo thought, as he followed Carla and Marcel, and it was good tactics besides. God knows what would have happened if I'd stood there a minute longer with that pig. But then he changed his mind. Don't boast, he said to himself. You're a phony. Nothing at all would have happened. Marcel probably knows it. He certainly knows it if he saw what was going on before he was hit. Maybe he walked off so fast just now because it made him sick to hear me shooting off my mouth. Just shooting off my mouth.

But Marcel seemed to be thinking about something entirely different. He resumed their conversation while the jeep was turning around and driving off; the sound, like a curse dying away in the night, was still in their ears.

"Bukharin denied that the rhythm of social processes could be foreseen," he said. "He wanted to turn sociology into a natural science. We'll have to discuss all that in depth one of these days. Actually most of the people in the seminar are against him. Too cautious, they think. Some even call him a pessimist. They agree with Lukács, who naturally saw the threat of Bukharin's ideas and clubbed him down with Lenin. 'Some people who call themselves revolutionaries are trying to prove that there is no way out of the situation. That is an error. There is no such thing as an absolutely hopeless situation.' "

"Was Lenin referring to Bukharin when he said that?"

"Hell, no. Lukács just took it out of some speech that has nothing to do with Bukharin. But it's brilliantly quoted. Lukács always quotes brilliantly."

Suddenly he stopped still.

"Leo," he asked. "Are we in an absolutely hopeless situation?"

"Not at all," said Leo. "Look how far we've come already. With a little noise at the universities and a few demonstrations. Why, we've only just started."

Though his answer had been spontaneous, it seemed to him a moment later that it had not been quite sincere, that he had only been trying to reassure Marcel. However, what he had said was his honest opinion, he hadn't said it just to please Marcel. Now he saw the dried blood on Marcel's face and, to take his mind off other things, said as they started off again: "Don't be so hard on Lukács. He's written some very good things. Have you read *Narrative or Description?*"

When Marcel replied in the negative, Leo set out to explain the virtues of *Narrative or Description*, but Carla interrupted him.

"Do you happen to know," she asked, "how Bukharin died?"

"Of course we know," said Leo. "Stalin, the show trials, and all that."

"Words," said Carla. "Stalin, show trials. Empty words."

"What do you mean by that?"

"In court Bukharin called himself a criminal. He denounced Trotsky. The day he was shot, they had to drag a whimpering chunk of flesh out of his cell. He even begged the firing squad for his life."

"Nonsense," said Marcel. "Read Merleau-Ponty if you want to know what happened at Bukharin's trial."

"I have read him," Carla shouted.

While they were arguing, Leo saw a stone in the street and began to kick it. He simply had to do something. This night was turning into a disaster. He ran ahead, still kicking his stone. Then he stopped and waited.

"Why exactly did you come to us?" he had asked her soon after their first meeting, about a year before. She had given him a clear answer. Her father, a surgeon—Carla too was planning to become a surgeon—and director of a clinic in Duisburg, had spent a short time in a concentration camp as a young man. He had taught Carla a rather primitive but effective theory of resistance. "None of us lifted a finger," he had said. "Not one of us. We let them round us up like sheep. It didn't occur to anyone to resist violence with violence, to take up arms and put up a serious fight. We all said it was hopeless. You're only a girl, Carla, but your place is with people who fight when they're faced with violence!" The old man—actually he was only in his fifties—still stood by his convictions; in his letters to his daughter he showed sympathy for what she was doing and only raised tactical questions to save her from gross blunders. Carla's situation is clear, Leo thought. She had a perfect superego, her father. Carla is reliable. More reliable than any of the people who join us because they think their parents are petit bourgeois.

They were skirting the Wall, but now the Philharmonie, Scharoun's stone tent, was on their left. Leo admired the building every time he saw it. Bathed in white light, it made the Wall look like a mere wall.

"I'm sorry," said Marcel, "but I think I'll have to sit down for a minute."

He huddled on the sidewalk. Carla knelt beside him.

"Lie down," she said, "and take a few deep breaths."

He lay down and Carla put her arm under his head. Leo saw her wet shoes and stockings.

"Good God, Carla, you'll get pneumonia," he said.

She only shook her head and watched Marcel's breathing, holding up his head for fear his wound would start bleeding again.

Leo strolled around. He was miserable having nothing to do. After a while, he discovered the inscription on the Wall, which at this point was faintly lighted by the Philharmonie.

"Hey," he called. "Take a look at this!"

Marcel already had sat up. Carla helped him to his feet, they joined Leo and together they read the inscription, JESUS-KINGDUTSCHKE, which someone had written in thick red chalk. Since he had left no space between the three names, they had become a single name.

Leo laughed aloud. "Looks like some of us are raving mad."

The two others remained silent. After a while, Carla said: "You know, it doesn't seem mad to me."

Marcel stared glumly at the letters.

"All these apostles of nonviolence!" he said.

"That hardly includes Dutschke," Leo objected.

"Don't bother me with Dutschke!" said Marcel. "Always talking about the long march through the institutions. Can't he think of anything better than that?"

Leo was all ready for a discussion on violence and nonviolence, but when he turned to go on, he saw a taxi standing on Kemperplatz beside the Philharmonie and ran for it.

In the cab Marcel collapsed; he slumped down in his corner and closed his eyes.

Leo sat in front with the driver. He turned half around and held out his arm, but Carla didn't take his hand.

"No," she said softly. "Not now."

There was no light in the Tiergarten. It seemed almost as though they were driving through the country in the night.

Leo pulled back his arm and sat up straight—the second time he had pulled back his arm that day.

Again he saw the policeman coming toward Marcel, who had gone on methodically and obliviously throwing stones when the police were charging and everybody else was running away. They had been quite right to run, and it had been stupid of Marcel to stay there, throwing stones. The policeman had come running with upraised truncheon. Leo, who had been standing next to Marcel, could easily have put him out of commission. He need only have grabbed the upraised arm and twisted it out of its socket; the cop would have rolled on the ground, bellowing with pain. He hadn't done it. He had stretched out his arm, but too slowly, with calculated slowness, knowing that his move would be too late. The blow had fallen, and Leo had grabbed not the policeman's arm but Marcel's. Whereupon he had pushed, dragged, and carried Marcel out of harm's way. The police hadn't interfered, they never attacked him, Leo was used to that. He was six foot six, no lumbering brute, but a trained athlete, specialized in the shot put and hammer throw. The coach implored him to go easy on politics; if only he'd concentrate on shot-putting, he'd be international class within a year. Leo wore his metallic blond hair close-cropped; with his crew cut and the conformation of his cheek muscles he was usually taken for an American at first sight.

"It was marvelous of you," he heard Carla say, "to stay with Marcel and get him out of there."

He was relieved. So she hadn't seen what actually happened. Besides, it was true: he had stayed with Marcel. Except that he had been afraid, paralyzed by plain physical fear; and to make matters worse, he hadn't lost his head, he knew what he was doing. He was well aware that if he disarmed the cop, five or ten of them would jump him and beat him to a pulp. And Marcel too. Letting Marcel get hit on the head was the lesser of two evils —the same sort of calculation as when, aware that he wasn't breathing right or hadn't braced his right leg firmly enough, he would stop in mid-shot put and let the shot roll off the palm of his hand.

The lighted towers of the Hansa quarter. The Stadtbahn underpass. When they reached the hospital, Marcel didn't want to get out. "Let me sit here," he said. "It's nice here." Carla looked worried.

The outpatients' clinic was an almost empty room. Long experience has shown, thought Leo, that nothing more is needed in this sort of room than an examination table, a medicine cabinet, and three chairs. "Sit beside him. He may topple over," Carla had said before leaving them, and Leo had complied. He thought about purely functional rooms. This examination table, this medicine cabinet, suggested nothing beyond an examination table and a medicine cabinet. Such objects, such a room, fell in with his ideas of architecture—houses and rooms that defined themselves. They were not fetishes.

"I feel terrible!" said Marcel, so far gone that he spoke Swiss German.

Carla came back, bringing a doctor. Though she had been gone only a few minutes, she had managed to change her appearance completely. Now she was wearing a white smock and tennis shoes; she had dried and combed her hair. And with all that, she had found a doctor. Leo had never seen her at her place of work. Here she seemed firmer, more integrated and compact than usual. He would have liked to take hold of her.

The doctor was a tall, thin, stooped man in his forties. He went straight to Marcel; asking no questions, he merely looked at the wound, palpated it and observed Marcel's reactions. It seemed to Leo that the doctor had taken a liking to Marcel. Most people liked him. He had been in Berlin for more than a year but he still looked as if he had come directly from the Café Odeon in Zürich. Though he cultivated a rather shaggy beard and went to great pains in neglecting his appearance, he had a winning look. Even now, thought Leo, his face looks as if it had been drawn by Celestino Piatti, the face of a pale, bleeding, passionate young man on a book jacket. Yet Marcel was anything but a model for commercial art; he was a methodical little fighter, stubborn and persistent, a Swiss with an injured sense of justice.

They had met at the engineering school library the previous fall, while Leo was writing his thesis on the history of architecture. He had piled up a small library on the table in front of him. Marcel always appeared between eleven and twelve o'clock, took the seat to the right or left of Leo if one of them was still available, and read newspapers; now and then he wrote something on a slip of paper.

"I beg your pardon," he said one day to Leo. "But what does *insulae* mean?"

He pointed to the title page of Leo's thesis. He had been sitting next to Leo out of sheer curiosity. He admitted as much.

"That word has been running through my head since the first time I saw it," he said. "Are you writing about islands?"

"No," said Leo. "That's what they called tenement houses in ancient Rome."

"Funny name for houses."

"The *insulae* were the first big dwelling houses. They all had wide streets and open spaces around them to help the authorities keep the *plebs* that lived there under control. The biggest *insulae* were built under Nero. Today it's as good as certain that Nero made his famous fire only to get rid of the slums around the forum; they had become a jungle where it was impossible to keep an eye on the *plebs*."

They spoke in whispers, as one does in libraries.

"Have you been in Rome?" Marcel asked.

"Yes, all summer," said Leo. "I had an Italian scholarship for my thesis."

Since, like everyone else, he was immediately attracted to Marcel, he asked: "What do you do?" He pointed, perhaps a bit disparagingly, at Marcel's newspaper.

Marcel showed him his slip of paper.

"Here," he said. "This is what I've found today. In a single issue."

Leo took the paper and read with amazement the words that Marcel had written in a neat, regular hand with strangely abbreviated downstrokes: *Idlers—bums—troublemakers—riffraff—SA-methods—obstreperous radical teen-agers—hoodlums—gangsters—political madmen—political rowdyism—provocateurs—teen-age muddleheads—mob—terror—excesses—criminals*. And then at some distance from this list, the words *decent people* and *law and order*.

"I'm doing a study on the sociology of language," Marcel whispered. "I'm going to call it 'Before the Pogrom.' How language is used to organize ghettoes and incite to murder."

Leo had stared at the slip of paper. "Do you think it's as bad as all that?" he had asked.

"Don't you?" Pointing at his slip of paper, Marcel had said: "One thing I'm sure of; this kind of thing will lead to murder."

The doctor turned away from Marcel and shrugged his shoulders. "We'll need an X ray," he said.

He asked Leo to help Marcel undress. "First we'll have to clean the wound," he said to Carla. "I'll see if an operating room is available."

When he had gone, Carla said to Marcel, "They'll give you a partial anesthetic. You won't feel a thing." Marcel showed no sign of interest; in the warmth, under the harsh gray light, he apathetically let himself be undressed. But then in his undergarments he went unaided to the examination table and lay down on it. They saw that he had a slender, graceful body. Carla covered him with a woolen blanket.

"So it's more than a superficial wound?" Leo asked under his breath.

"In these cases there's always a possibility of fracture," said Carla.

She shook her head almost angrily when Leo said: "You look great in your white smock."

The doctor came back and said the operating room would be available in ten minutes. He felt Marcel's pulse again, then sat down on one of the chairs. He was obviously tired.

Suddenly they heard him say: "You people prefer the candy of revolution to the bread of reform."

Leo had a sharp answer on the tip of his tongue, but thought better of it; he didn't want to make trouble for Carla. Maybe it was important for her to be on good terms with this medico. Leo had sat down on the window sill, because that was the darkest part of the room; in these medical surroundings he felt too big, ungainly.

It was Carla who answered without hesitation:

"We're sick of eating this society's shit."

Leo looked at the doctor. Would he show displeasure or even disgust? But he seemed used to hearing girls whose shoulder-length dark hair and pale faces gave them a romantic look expressing themselves in scatological terms. He seemed to withdraw into his fatigue.

"Society," he said after a while. "It makes no difference what kind of society you live in. Only one thing matters in any social order: whether it's run by decent people or not."

"Good grief!" said Carla.

Leo spoke up. "You mean with a few nice people on top we'll have a decent sort of capitalism? Do you really believe that stuff?"

"Or a decent sort of Communism," the doctor replied. "Yes, that's what I believe."

"An untenable elitist theory," said Leo. "Sounds good, like all liberal phrases, but . . ."

A nurse interrupted him. The operating room was ready. Carla and the nurse rolled out the table with Marcel on it. The doctor smiled politely at Leo as they brought up the rear. Leo was sorry he had thrown the word "phrases" in his face.

His father was still up when he got home. He and his father lived in a one-family house in Lankwitz. His mother had died at his birth. His father had been in a concentration camp from 1933 to 1945, and when he got out the first thing he did was to make a child. Exhausted by the war and waiting, his wife had died in childbirth. "If she only knew what a heavyweight you turned out to be," Leo's father sometimes said. He himself was small and thin. Now he was sixty-five and might have been taken for Leo's grandfather rather than his father. Until pensioned three years before, he had been a foreman mechanic at the Siemens plant. He paid for Leo's studies with the indemnity he received for his years in the concentration camp; added to the hundred and eighty marks contributed by the Berlin student plan, it was barely enough.

"I'll make it up to you for your twelve years in Oranienburg," Leo had once said. At home with his father, he spoke Berlin dialect.

"Forget it, don't think about it," his father had said. "It couldn't be helped."

Actually he didn't believe that it couldn't have been helped. The fact that in 1933 he had been a member of the Communist Party's section bureau for Berlin Wedding had cost him twelve years of his life. He would sum up his opinion of the party in one sentence: "When it came to theory, the Party was always big stuff." And he would add: "Correct predictions aren't enough."

He wanted to know about the demonstration at the Press Building.

"It's great what you fellows do!" he said. "And all spontaneous. Without a party, without organization!"

They were sitting in the kitchen. Leo, who hadn't had anything to eat since the afternoon, was eating a salami sandwich and drinking light beer.

"When I think how carefully we thought everything over before taking any action," his father said.

He blew gray clouds from his curved pipe.

"Yes, you fellows don't think much, and I wonder if that's good. My guess is that you don't know who you're taking on. Rudi Dutschke certainly didn't know."

Leo could see that his father, in the grip of his concentration-camp trauma, was literally shaking.

"Father," he said. "It's no use. We have to find these things out for ourselves."

"I know," said his father, recovering his composure. "Except that you're heading for defeat. That's sure."

Leo had no desire to talk about victory or defeat; his father had put an entirely different idea into his head. If a great revolutionary party had thought too long before taking action, he reflected, then perhaps he too could be forgiven for stopping to think, for weighing the consequences, and choosing the lesser evil instead of striking out blindly, merely because a friend was in danger.

Except that of course such a line of reasoning changed everything.

He'd have to put the question to Marcel. If Marcel hasn't got a fracture, he decided, I'll go see him tomorrow and tell him I could have stopped that blow. He tried to imagine how Marcel would react.

"That's unimportant," he would probably say. "In every struggle there are changing subjective situations."

Leo would try to explain as patiently as possible. "I was afraid of violence," he heard himself say. "Which means that I have no right to tell other people to practice the violence that I myself am afraid of. And I can't join the people you call the apostles of non-violence any more. Decide to be meek because I'm a coward? No, nothing doing!"

What would Marcel say to that? Leo could think of no decisive arguments to put in Marcel's mouth. Of course Marcel would deliver a systematic lecture: on the objective significance of violence, on the undermining of revolutionary thought by psychology. And he would say all this not to comfort Leo, not to help him over his crisis, but because he really believed in the power of objective knowledge, really believed that subjective weaknesses were irrelevant. What was a single momentary lapse in the long history of the revolution? Nothing.

In the end, he would quote his beloved Merleau-Ponty: "The euphoric revolutionary," he would say, "is an Épinal print."

When his father had gone to bed, Leo called up the hospital. It was a long time before he had Carla on the line.

"Marcel is all right," she said. "No fracture. He'll only have to stay here two or three days."

She told him the visiting hours. He sensed that she was waiting for him to suggest a date. Her aloofness was gone.

After he had hung up, it came to him that he still needed certain material for his paper on the *insulae*. There were a few houses in Ostia that he had not investigated. His father would give him money for the trip. He wouldn't need much.

+++

An Even Better House

+++

Base

Who is Albert Lins, who last Friday, September 24, 1965, purchased Gorteen House, a manor on the coast of Connemara in the west of Ireland? In partnership with Theo Maurer, he owns the Maurer & Lins hardware factory in Stuttgart, specializing in the manufacture of cooking pots and buckets. Nominal share capital DM 200,000, divided equally between the two partners. Gross income for 1963: 29.5 millions. Gross income for 1964: 31.2 millions. A further increase is expected in 1965. Published net profit for 1963: 2.3 millions; for 1964: 2.7 millions. Actual profits are obscured in the balance-sheets (write-offs, investments, transfer to reserves).

Lins and Maurer begin operations in 1948, investing 10,000 marks of their own money in a small wrecked factory in Feuerbach. Maurer, an engineer, takes over the technical end, and Lins, son of a Berlin attorney and himself the holder of a law degree, the commercial end. Bank loans, since then repaid. Lins has definite ideas about design and surrounds himself with leading designers. M & L cooking pots become noted for their modern design. Lins and his creative advertising staff build the M & L image. Modern sales and distribution methods: credit advanced to wholesalers and retailers. Investment in supplier firms. Share of overall market for 1964: 32.4 per cent. Portion of total production exported: roughly 30 per cent. Steady expansion of plant, partial conversion to plastics, new administration building under construction (seven stories, reinforced concrete, to be rented in part). Workers on payroll: 36 in 1948, 581 in 1965. Over Mauer's opposition, Lins pays maximum wages and sets up a pension fund. Albert Lins is regarded as one of the most socially progressive employers in the Federal Republic.

The two millionaires' private fortunes are invested in real estate and securities. Lins also invests in paintings. Cash deposits—at low interest—in savings accounts at the Wurttembergische Bank in Stuttgart and the Schweizerische Bankgesellschaft in Zurich. Article 5, Paragraph B of their partnership contract specifies that no change can be made in the conditions of ownership without the consent of both partners.

British Racing Green

The dockers were winding ropes around his beloved TR 4, built in 1964, when they still had spoked wheels. Even to himself he did not describe its color as plain dark green, but resorted to the words used by the Triumph Corporation in its catalogue. Of course he knew that people made fun of him when he showed off this car.

"Did you hear what Lins called his car?" a business friend would ask his wife on their way home. And he would try to imitate his host's English pronunciation.

"Tráiumph! British *räissing grien!*"

"Wouldn't you say he was too old for an open sports car like that?"

"Exactly! He's getting on to sixty. And those things are as hard as ironing boards. My back couldn't take it." In his voice, mockery would give way to lamentation over the inequalities of this world. "The fact is," he would say, "Lins is a snob."

By her bearing and the look on her face, the lady would show that she agreed with her spouse, but in secret she would probably ask herself whether a man going on sixty whose back was still in such good shape, didn't deserve something better than criticism. From a business point of view, the critical envy of some visitor meant nothing to Lins; he usually kept his TR 4 in the garage of his villa on the Killesberg along with the little English sleigh and the two big Mercedeses, which left no room for doubt that he was *in*.

The crane lifted the car. For a while it hovered in midair, infinitely green against the yellow-streaked blue of the evening sky that arched over the—unfortunately smelly—Liffey and the city.

Then it sank into the belly of the ship. If only they didn't scratch it, Lins thought. Beginning next year, he had been assured, there would be modern car ferries between Ireland and England.

"In a coign of the cliff between lowland and highland"

At 5 P.M., the sun was still high in the sky (nine degrees west longitude). He now had the keys of Gorteen House in his pocket. As he had surmised, the innkeeper at Inverbeg had had them. To his right, Inverbeg Bay at low tide: flat rocks covered with seaweed that looked like chocolate-covered mud. The Gorteen House park: a dark hole; he had to take off his sunglasses. The gate with the weatherbeaten For Sale sign (and the still legible address and telephone number of Gregory in Dublin), the gap beside the gatepost, through which he had squeezed on his previous visit. On the driveway, a soft light filtered through reddish pine needles. No wheel tracks.

Wipe your shoes before entering

The price of Gorteen House was eight thousand pounds. On Thursday, September 23, Lins phoned Maurer from his room on the fifth floor of the Shelbourne Hotel in Dublin and asked him to transfer that sum by wire to Gregory's account. Although Lins made no secret of the drawbacks of the house, Maurer said it was dirt cheap. True, it was far from Stuttgart. "An hour and a half by air," was Lins's answer. He would wait till he got back to tell Maurer that to him Gorteen House meant something more than being only an hour and a half from the office. Maurer suggested that he find some dodge by which to make the purchase price tax deductible; maybe he could acquire a nominal share in some business. Lins owned to himself that he too had thought of representing his acquisition of Irish real estate as an investment. Why, for instance, wouldn't he buy into the carpet factory he had visited in Ballyconneely . . . ? The man had ten hand looms and only five were in use. Lins, who had some notions of textile design himself, had seldom seen a carpet that could bear comparison with the output of this little factory. He had only to bring them over to the Continent, and with the help of advertisements carefully placed in art and architecture magazines—the first thing, of course, would be to launch a rumor!—they would sell like hotcakes, even if they were expensive (because Ireland was still outside the Common Market). He dropped the idea because, after hanging up, he looked over the trees of St. Stephen's Green at the Wicklow Mountains. Far behind them, far to the west, lay the house that would be his next morning. He and Gregory had shaken hands on the deal, and the contract would be signed as soon as the money arrived at Gregory's bank. Lins decided that he would simply make himself a present of Gorteen House, without any dodges and gimmicks. Gorteen House must not become an object of bickerings with the Stuttgart finance office.

Psi Gamma Phenomenon

"It wasn't only after I got the keys and was able to visit the house that I decided to buy it at any price, but when I saw it for the first time, when I crept around it like an Indian and peeped through the windows."

On his way home, Lins decided to start the conversation in Stuttgart with this sentence. It would be a nasty business, and that was why he had to make it clear to Maurer that no logical calculations had led him to buy the house, that it had been a spontaneous, pre-logical act: who could object to that?

Code civil

Lins was born in Berlin in 1906. Graduation from Latin School, 1925; 1926–1932, university studies in Berlin, Heidelberg, Bonn, and Vienna. No fraternity memberships. Law, history of art (under Adolph Goldschmidt and Karl Neumann), philosophy (under Nicolai Hartmann and Moritz Schlick). Law degree. Thesis on copyright law; 1933, protected stay in Oxford; 1934–1939, junior partner in his father's law firm. Lins senior joined the National Socialist Party in 1933 and later became a member of the leading committee of the League of German Jurists. Conflicts between father and son; Lins junior sees "no point in National Socialism" and points out to his father that civic life is being shorn of its substance. Through connections, he manages in 1939 to be drafted into Luftwaffe Intelligence (ground personnel) and until 1942 avoids duty in undesirable theaters of war by attendance at officer training schools. Commissioned first lieutenant. The African campaign. Taken prisoner by the British without having fired a shot. Officers' camp in Canada from late 1942 to late 1945 (by the terms of the Geneva Convention, officers cannot be made to work). Further studies in art history and philosophy (the prisoners are supplied with books by the universities of Montreal and Toronto). And a pause in which to think. Borrows Franz Mehring's biography of Marx from a Social-Democratic fellow prisoner and studies Rosa Luxemburg's analysis of the second and third volumes of *Das Kapital*. He comes to understand the laws governing the circulation of capital and the average rate of profit. As a lawyer, he foresees that the juridical principle underlying the bourgeois democracy which was to be expected after the war (respect of private property) would enable a certain category of people to make big money. He has never been quite satisfied with the lawyer's role as an analyst and intermediary and decides to transfer his activities to the free economy and, in line with his innermost inclinations, to invest a part of his surplus value in free culture. On his return to Germany, he succeeds in selling his East Berlin real estate (a few apartment houses on Chodowieckistrasse and Danziger Strasse) shortly before it is nationalized. With the proceeds, he buys the seemingly worthless ruins of the factory in Feuerbach.

Sinn Fein

On leaving the Abbey Theatre, he sensed that the city was in a state of unrest. He had attended a performance of *Borstal Boy*. At first he had taken it to be a historical play about some long-past war of liberation, but then the audience had started shouting anti-British slogans. He shook his head. Lins had never thought much of political emotion; it struck him as absurd to get excited about a state of affairs that had ceased to exist. Outside the Shelbourne, there were a few policemen; the lights were out in the hotel. In response to his question, he was told: "They usually smash our windows."

"At the sea-down's edge between windward and lee"

The gate with the For Sale sign, which he glimpsed for a moment in driving past. Again the wall on the left, but to the right there was still an open view of the bay, the moors, and the mountains, some transparent, others conical, seven or eight miles away. Foreground, the color of fox fur, blue backdrop. Far and wide, not a soul. He stopped. On an island, sea birds were clamoring. Behind the wall there were no longer trees but rhododendron bushes and drooping late roses. The house could not be seen from the road. He turned around and drove back to the gate.

Sound track

Indeed, the big plate-glass windows of the lounge were smashed an hour later. The demonstrators came from Merrion Square, where they had pulled down the Union Jack from the British Embassy and burned it. Lins looked down on the shadowy tumult over which here and there the street lamps cast their circles of light. The shattering of glass: a piercing screech, followed by the sound of water flowing over small, round pebbles. Gregory, the estate agent, explained to him next day that the Shelbourne was regarded as a stronghold of the Anglo-Irish and Protestants. He himself declined all refreshment as they were looking through the contract. "I don't drink this damned Protestant coffee here," he said. Lins couldn't help laughing. The crackling of the metallic legal paper that was making Gorteen House over to him drowned out the shattering glass of the previous night, which had alarmed him. After all, this stuff about the damned Protestant coffee was nothing but a silly Irish anecdote that would be amusing to tell in Stuttgart.

Désinvolture

Lins disliked to close important deals in his office; he preferred to do so at restaurants, on drives, or in his house on the Killesberg. He conducted the official negotiations in the conference room of Maurer & Lins AG, which had been furnished in excellent taste by a lady interior decorator. He even did his best to make these meetings seem like solemn conclaves, so as to give the other fellow the feeling that something of great importance was being done, but he took care to leave the final decisions open.

These he brought up as though in passing at pleasantly private get-togethers that made his interlocutor feel included in an elite.

Addressing the ball

He had asked Gregory to tell him the best place to play golf in Dublin, and to his surprise the agent had invited him to the exclusive Portmarnock Club on Malahide Island. Gregory was the better player, and not only because he knew the course. Only at putting was Lins superior. Without being asked, the caddy gave him advice, selected the right club, etc. That was something he had never seen before; he was going to protest, but then he noticed that Gregory talked things over very seriously with the caddy. And indeed, it was partly thanks to the boy that Lins didn't come off too badly. And partly thanks to Gregory, who at the third hole had said to him: "Don't play against me, play against the course." Gregory was short, bald, and sunburned; he was wearing pepper-and-salt tweed trousers, a sweaty polo shirt, and ancient golf shoes. Once he made the green over a four-hundred-yard fairway in two strokes. Afterward at the bar, Lins struck up the question of price, observing that Gorteen House seemed to be unsalable and that he was paying cash. Gregory was adamant. The unsalability of Gorteen House, he pointed out, was built into the price. Lins mentioned the political risk, and told Gregory about the poster he had seen in Inverbeg: "We want land for the poor farmers, not for the idle rich." Gregory replied that nobody wanted the square mile of water and stones belonging to Gorteen House. Lins gave up. He caught sight of a woman who was very much to his taste: slender, satiny brown, freckled, a mass of dark, not very long hair, cool, light-gray eyes. Skirt and short jacket of thin doeskin that looked as if it had been worn for a generation. Among the members of the Portmarnock Club, Lins looked like a fashion plate.

"Walled round with rocks as an inland island"

There could be someone living in the house even if it was for sale. For a long time he listened for some sound but had heard nothing, not even a bird call or the rustling of leaves. Finally he had risked going in. Now he was walking up the path for the second time, still treading softly in spite of himself, but with greater assurance, with a feeling derived from the keys in his trousers pocket. On his previous visit, he had only been able to look into one room, through a single window, the curtains of which had been left open. He had seen an oval table, surrounded by Sheraton chairs. A dry twilight; light rectangles on the walls, where pictures had been removed. Behind the house he had stirred up the swarm of flies that had been hovering over the pools of sunlight.

"Compost liffe in Dublin"

While waiting to close the deal, he had nothing else to do but take a look at Dublin. He had gone to the National Museum twice. He had looked at the Book of Kells. The city was crawling with filth, and the famous Liffey stank so infernally that it was impossible to walk on its banks. Occasionally, Lins stopped and gazed spellbound at a street littered with papers, tin cans, cigarette butts, and broken bottles. The cellar shafts were used as garbage dumps. The streets to the north of the O'Connell Bridge were full of flophouse spooks. He fled to the Georgian neighborhoods and walked along the brick façades and colorful doors of Fitzwilliam Street. Then he turned into an alley and discovered the back yards, the decay, the tarred cracks and grimy plaster, the forbidding dilapidation of abandoned slum workshops. He saw a man hammering on the mudguard of a car.

Libido

Lin's mother, born in a 1876, née Von Janotte (Prussian Huguenots, petty nobility), was thirty at the birth of her (only) child. Now, at the age of eighty-nine, she is living in an old people's home in West Berlin. Lins was relieved when she declined to come and live in her son's more than comfortable house in Stuttgart. She has never been an affectionate mother; no animal contact with her child, not even as a baby. The old lady, who only sits on hard, straight-backed chairs, is determined to live a good deal longer. In 1936, Lins marries an actress three years younger than himself, who gives up the stage. In 1938, she bears him a son, who, having shown neither inclination nor talent for business, is now studying medicine. In 1941, a daughter, who writes and is at present living with a German painter in London. On his return from Canada, Lins discovers that he has no further desire to touch his wife. In 1947, she divorces him and marries a pastor, with whom she remains in the German Democratic Republic. In 1948, during the euphoria of founding Maurer & Lins AG, Lins has an affair with his secretary. In 1956, at the age of fifty, he marries the twenty-two-year-old daughter of a Swiss business associate, who has been working in his office as a volunteer. The name Salomé is not unusual in Switzerland. Separation in 1959. When Lins counts the women he has slept with, he arrives at the figure eleven. Last sexual intercourse—without orgasm—in 1962 with a strip-tease artist from a Zürich night club. He had met her at a bar. Price: 150 Swiss francs. Her room, in the Seefeld area, was full of enormous dolls with nauseatingly sweet expressions, whom the young lady, so she said, loved more than anything in the world.

Specalum Sueborum

Maurer would jump out of his skin when he heard that Lins was planning to retire. To gain time, he would start by talking about Lins's mania for houses. Though as a Swabian, Maurer ought to have wanted a house of his own, he did not, like Lins, live in a private house on the Killesberg, but in a bachelor apartment, a very expensive one to be sure, on the Schlossgarten. He was all the more attached to the factory and spoke of it on every possible occasion as his and Albert's work, sometimes going so far as to call it their *life work*. He took it very much amiss when his partner disagreed, saying there were other things in life besides buckets and cooking pots. "I know," Theo had once replied angrily. "I know your books and pictures mean more to you. But don't forget that you couldn't afford all this art stuff without our buckets and pots!"

"The ghost of a garden fronts the sea"

He would have to have the gray stucco removed from the walls of the elongated two-story building; under it, there would be old brown bricks that could be coated with a transparent varnish. The windows were framed in thin stone bands that did not protrude from the walls but were evenly sunk into them in accordance with aesthetic laws which, he told himself, had been lost for the past two hundred years. The roof of irregular slates, neither too flat nor too steep, not overhanging, but ending exactly where it met the walls, was damaged; there were holes in it. The park had not fully achieved its aim of burying the house; it would be necessary to do some clearing, leaving only the oldest trees, and to lay out grass plots between them. He would give the house back to the sea and the moors, for which it had been built. There was too much shade. As on his first visit, he went to the stone balustrade of the terrace and looked down at the section of road where he had turned his car around.

Superstructure I

As a boy of sixteen, Lins buys prints of Rembrandt's landscape engravings out of his pocket money. He still has them. Since 1946, he has been building up a collection. Concentrating on the graphic arts, he has purchased only two dozen oil paintings over the years. He does not specialize, acquires both old and modern pieces, but omits whole periods (mannerism, rococo). The most valuable among his roughly four hundred items: an engraving by Hercules Seghers, "The City with the Four Towers"—printed in two colors (green and reddish-brown) on green-tinted paper; blue is also present in the air and in the middle ground of the landscape; and a print of Munch's color woodcut "Moonlight" (first version, 1896). The collection also includes early colored broadsheet woodcuts, copperplate engravings by the "Master of the Playing Cards," and works of Hirschvogel, Piranesi, Goya,

Meryon, Vuillard, Ensor, Picasso, and Morandi. Lins is never guided in his purchases by market value; he buys what he likes. In painting, his taste is not quite as reliable as in the graphic arts; he owns a poor Renoir and an indifferent Van Dongen. His biggest mistake was "In Praise of Melancholy," a huge monstrosity by Paul Delvaux, the Belgian surrealist. He is trying to exchange it for an Oelze. Still, he has a few fine old German paintings, two Sironis, Magritte's "Présence d'Esprit," a De Staël, and one of Valenti's "Islands." Lins is not interested in personal contact with artists; he does not do his buying in studios but, despite the higher prices, exclusively from reputed art dealers.

Superstructure II

Lins's library comprises some seven thousand volumes. The greater part of it is devoted to the cultural sciences, belles-lettres, poetry, English and French authors in the original languages. No interest in first editions, autographs, and such; preference for complete works with critical apparatus. Special interests: Spinoza, French literature of the late nineteenth century, Sartre. Among modern writers his favorites are Sartre and John Cowper-Powys. Large collection of art history. Lins is always in search of books in which things and existence are represented in terms of things and existence, and in which words and sentences "go back to the things themselves" (Merleau-Ponty, *Phénoménologie de la Perception*). Lins instinctively rejects all semantic theories, although (or because) he makes use of semantic devices in business ("the M & L image"). Since he believes himself unable—despite his academic training—to formulate his ideas on these matters, he avoids scholars and writers. He has no religious needs.

Superstructure III

Lins built his house on the Killesberg chiefly for his collection. At the time, he is living a bachelor existence. The children are at boarding school. Most of the wealthy people in Stuttgart live on the Killesberg. Lins instructs his architect to break with the prevailing Killesberg style: houses in not very large gardens, with large windows, out of which one looks over not very large gardens at houses with large windows. Content: living room sets, floor vases, built-in bookcases, built-in bars, period furniture, pianos, record players, television sets. His architect designs a small, almost square main building, windowless up to the second story; under the roof, an unbroken line of windows, no upper story within. The result is a single high room, lighted from above, in which his paintings are hung above the low cabinets containing his engravings and woodcuts. Two years later Salomé refers to this room as the museum, crosses it on tiptoes, lives almost exclusively in the south wing, and has a room built for her over the garage: from her window she can look out at the street, even if there never is anything going on. Since this south wing, in addition to the bedrooms and kitchen, also contains a living room in which Lins can receive guests—situated next to the "museum," it makes for an easy transition from art to social life—the house turns out in the end to be a typical Killesberg house. On the lawn outside the living room, a medium-sized Barbara Hepworth stone; behind it, bushes; behind the bushes, the house of a well-known lawyer, of whose services Lins and Salomé avail themselves in 1959, when they are divorced.

Superstructure IV

In Lins's house there also lives an elderly (sixty-two) lady—slender, prepossessing—who attends to his household. Monthly wages DM 2000. Excellent cook. Two-room apartment of her own on the second floor of the south wing, television set, small car. Between her and Lins, strictly formal relations. Lins shudders at the thought of telling her that he is giving up the house. His chauffeur, who takes care of the garden, lives in an apartment on the factory grounds; his wife comes three times a week to clean the house. How, Lins wonders, will he solve the servant problem in Ireland? He sees a butler as the right thing for Gorteen House.

Society news

He had obtained a berth for his car, but none for himself. Contemplating the ancient tub that thumped from Dublin to Liver-

pool each night, he foresaw an unpleasant night. The ship wasn't
due to sail until eight o'clock. He walked along the river bank,
bought newspapers and a crime novel for the night on O'Connell
Street, and took a cab to the Shelbourne for a last drink at the
bar. The faces there were already familiar, men who looked at
him, potential friends in tweed suits, with gold watch chains over
their vests, any one of whom would have been glad to tell him all
about Ireland. Once the woman from the Portmarnock Club had
come in with two men, all three in riding dress; she had looked at
him with her cool gray eyes; maybe he would make her ac-
quaintance later on. He himself had never ridden; in Gorteen
House he would keep a dog for the first time in his life. He would
question experts in Stuttgart about the characteristics of the various breeds.

It would be a mistake to underestimate Maurer's astuteness; in
trying to dissuade Lins from the project, he would not bring up
business considerations; no, he would proceed on the assumption
that Lins wanted to hide away from the world because he had
never recovered from the shipwreck of his marriage to Salomé.
Maurer had never said a word to him about his divorce, but faced
with the danger of losing his partner he wouldn't hesitate to strike
below the belt. Lins would swear to him that while making his decision to buy Gorteen House he had never for one moment
thought of Salomé. Maurer would shrug. Lins knows that in such
cases it is always assumed that the husband has proved sexually in-
adequate. The idea of a man in his fifties marrying a girl of
twenty! His removal to far-off Celtic shores would elicit just this
comment from all his friends. No one would believe him if he
went about saying that after a year with Salomé he had been just
as bored with her as she with him. Maybe the easiest way would
be not to contradict Maurer's theory. Maurer would grumble
awhile, but would soon accept defeat. By an apparently incurable
psychological quirk, people would always regard an erotic-roman-
tic explanation for his yearnings as the most plausible. Lins didn't
want to get off so easily.

"You know," he said to Theo Maurer, "in bed with Salomé, I
wasn't really so bad."

Long Live Lord Revelstoke!

To escape from this crumbling city, he occasionally took his TR 4 out of the hotel garage and drove to Glendalough, to the Wicklow Mountains, or to the Boyne Valley. There he regained the certainty that Ireland was timelessly beautiful. Behind the hedges, across the meadows, traversed by streams, ringed about by horses, lay the Indian summer, a red god in blue veils. How right he had been after all to buy Gorteen House! Yesterday, the day before leaving, he had walked across the cliffs of Howth. The cries of the birds over the sea had been entirely different from the cries of last night's demonstrators, which were still ringing in his ears. Then, after a turn in the path, the island appeared, a reddish mountain in the sea, not far from the coast. Through his binoculars he had established that it was uninhabited, reddish, and treeless. Its name was Lambay. Consulting the Blue Guide that evening in the bar, he learned that the whole island belonged to a Lord Revelstoke and could be visited only with his written permission. Gladdened, he looked up from the page. That was why Lambay lay so uninhabited and unspoiled, so like a thing of legend, in the sea—it was private property. Someone had saved the mythical vista of this porphyry mountain in the Irish Sea from the world in the simplest way imaginable: by buying it. In a setting of mahogany, brass, and mirrors, Lins drank a swallow of whisky to Lord Revelstoke's health.

A treasury of fetishes or the salvation of art?

In the hall, no furniture; it was quite empty. Very much as in his house on the Killesberg, the light shone in from above: museum light. But here wooden posts supported a semicircular stairway, yellowed white and festive. Between the posts, he would hang the De Staël, the green-blue seascape; in that recess, it would glow and look like a stage set. To the right, on the clear wall, he would put the little Danube School "Three Kings" in its cassetted frame. In contrast to the De Staël, this painting must be made to stand out from the wall, almost in relief, if the fine drawing were to be appreciated. He would put nothing but these two pictures in the hall. He opened the doors to the two large rooms to the right and left, walked back and forth between them, and drew aside the cotton curtains.

Corpus delicti

Lins has never been seriously ill. In 1958, brief stay in the hospital with acute inflammation of the gall bladder, then a short period of dizziness and fainting spells brought on by his stay in bed, sedation, too much reading, and staring out the window. On the other hand, Lins is not the bristling-with-health type. No sports except golf. No interest in sunbathing. Likes to swim, would like to fish, feels attracted by all games played with balls (boccie, bowling), but does not play them. Takes long walks, preferably alone. In his fifties, succumbs for a time to the German vice: overeating; pulls himself together from one day to the next and with the help of a strict diet maintains his weight at 180 (height: five feet eleven). Does not smoke. Drinks only at dinner, either dry Bordeaux or Swiss white wines; in company, one or two whiskies before bedtime.

Art for art's sake or escape from chatter?

They too were unfurnished, except that in the small room on the left he found the oval table and the chairs that he had seen from outside. The chairs, of course, were copies of Sheraton. He touched the gray marble mantelpiece and a damaged vase standing on a window sill. He would lodge his library in one of the two rooms, on shelves reaching up to the ceiling, and here too he would put his desk; in the other room, he would put the cabinets with their shallow drawers containing his drawings, etchings, lithographs, and woodcuts. These cabinets were hardly more than three feet high, so that he would be able to devote the walls above them—which by then would have been painted white—to changing exhibitions. Exhibitions, to be sure, that no one but himself would see. Perhaps some of his Irish neighbors would call on him now and then.

Local observer

Arthur Byrne, innkeeper in Inverbeg, watched the German gentleman who had taken the keys to Gorteen House as he crossed the shore road and went to his car. Byrne was a sports-car fan; he himself was the owner of an old Lotus that he was always tinkering with, and he was interested to see how this foreigner would start his TR 4. Naturally he did it all wrong. With a car like that, you had to race the motor furiously before releasing the clutch, start with a jolt, and shoot off like a cannon ball. That was how it demanded to be treated; otherwise it faltered. And besides, that was the whole fun of having such a car. If you didn't want that, you might just as well buy some old sedan, in which you'd be more comfortable. Arthur Byrne suffered to see how the visitor let his motor idle quietly for a while, before backing cautiously out into the road. And then he drove off northward along the bay in second or perhaps even in third. The man was too old for his car!

Pondering the impression this German had made on him, Byrne came to the conclusion that he had never seen a man so well groomed. Maureen had come into his office and said someone wished to speak to him. "A very distinguished man!" she had added, visibly impressed. Even his English had been flawless, one might have said immaculate; no one in the British Isles spoke such English. He was wearing a blue blazer and gray flannel trousers, such as many Englishmen wore on vacation, but on him they produced a different effect: richer, fuller; they hid rather than revealed the man's body and bony structure. They didn't look new or newly rich, but the material was too expensive, they were too well tailored . . . in short, he was too well groomed. A big man, not stout, with a face not tanned but slightly yellow—a bit of liver trouble, Byrne diagnosed—blue eyes behind tortoise-shell glasses—the upper parts of the frames were black—long strands of gray, carefully combed-back hair. He seemed fit enough, but his fitness was no doubt a product of massage rather than native constitution. A man who was constantly being overhauled and showed hardly a trace of wear and tear. What did he want with Gorteen House? Arthur Byrne thought it his duty to warn him.

"The O'Gradys gave it up twenty years ago," he said. "It's kind of run down."

"Oh, that doesn't matter," Albert Lins replied. "The location is certainly unique."

There was no knowing what people who stank of money like this man might take it into their heads to do. He remembered the English banker who had bought and renovated Ardmore Castle, that old barn by the sea, and had never stayed there for more than two weeks in the year.

Natura morta or still life?

He would sleep upstairs. The bedrooms were on the second floor, along with a number of smaller rooms. The house was really too big for him, but he would restore and furnish all the rooms. The children would come and see him now and then, maybe Theo Maurer would pay him a visit. In each room he would hang a painting; there would be a Magritte Room, a Sironi Room, and so on. The innkeeper in Inverbeg had told him that during the winter months it rained almost without interruption. He would spend his days at his desk in the library, working. For the present he evaded the task of defining the word "work" in relation to Gorteen House. On winter evenings, when the rain poured down on the house and filled the night with swirling veils, he would play solitaire. One object he did not yet own was indispensable to Gorteen House: a grandfather clock that ticked.

Dream censorship

For the most part, Lins's dreams are commonplace: he is either frustrated or put to the test. He has to go on a trip immediately; he starts to pack his bag, but can't get on with it; in the end, he is incapable of lifting a finger. Or he is climbing a stairway that has no end. The dreams in which he is put to the test relate not to school or university examinations, but to business matters: for instance, he is unable to draw up a contract which only a short while before he dictated to his secretary in ten minutes. Frequent and repeated *déjà vu* experiences: landscapes and city scenes that he recognizes without ever having seen them. He rejects Freud's hypothesis that all *déjà vu* dreams express a desire to return to one's mother's womb. He is also unable to accept Freud's contention that negatives are unknown to the language of dreams; he feels sure that he has several times said "no" or "not" in his dreams. No patently sexual dreams, much less orgasms in his sleep. In one exceedingly pleasant dream that recurs now and then, Lins is walking down a Berlin street leading to the Anhalt Station; the street is lined with secondhand bookshops with the most exquisite works displayed in their windows. In the midst of the dream, Lins says to himself that he is not really on this street but must absolutely go there when in Berlin. On waking, he is very much disappointed and it takes him several minutes to realize that the Berlin street he has dreamed of does not exist. Despite this sort of dream, he does not believe that his secret desires are fulfilled in his dreams, but tends, rather, to believe that his dreams have been sent to punish him.

From the Red Book of Hergest

He would never forget that priest. The sea was really smooth, yellowed by the western sky, below which, in the dusk, the Wicklow Mountains and the hills of Meath formed a black, jagged line. Lambay was still a porphyry mountain. Heedless of the other people in the lounge, the priest had taken off his soutane, disclosing a white shirt, a round clerical collar, and suspenders. White amid the black of his fellow clergymen, he began, the moment Albert Lins sat down near him, to drink his health. Though the priest was drunk and had taken off his soutane, the other clergymen were listening to him. He was telling a story, a Welsh legend, as Lins later surmised: the story of Ceridwen and Gwion. From time to time, he paused to raise his glass to Lins, the cultured Irish priest honoring the cultured foreigner. Lins did not respond, and kept his eyes on the *Irish Times*. The tourists had long since gone to their cabins; laughing and shaking their heads, they had abandoned the shabby lounge, because the Irish drunks were molesting their wives. Lins knew that if he were to return even one of the priest's toasts he would spend the rest of the night submerged in a never-ending flood of words; just that had happened to him at taverns in Sligo and Galway, and he knew that he could

not compete with the liquor consumption and rhetorical stamina
of a specialist in Gaelic mythology or Yeats. Those sessions had always begun brilliantly and ended in a nightmare. Once settled in
Gorteen House, he would have to avoid such excesses. After relating how Ceridwen, who had been transformed into a hen,
swallowed Gwion, who had been transformed into a grain of
wheat, in consequence of which she found herself with child on
resuming human form, the drunken priest suddenly stood up,
lurched a few paces, and began shouting obscenities at some nuns
who were sitting in the opposite corner of the lounge. There was
no uproar. The numerous men who were sitting there drinking
and singing in an undertone scarcely turned their heads. The nuns
sat stolidly in a circle, exchanging whispers, until at length the
oldest of them turned her disdainful profile in the direction of the
priests who, catching her meaning, led the scurrilous shepherd of
souls away and put him to bed somewhere. After midnight Lins
went back up on deck. To the right he saw a powerful beacon,
which he judged to be Holyhead Light. Wasn't it rather risky, he
wondered, to settle in a country where a priest could break off in
the middle of a legend to address a group of nuns as whores of
Jesus Christ and advise them to get fucked by you know who?
The air was bitter cold; it drove him back into the stench of beer
and sweat. He had guessed right; his night could not have been
more unpleasant. From time to time he managed to doze off.

"Here now in his triumph where all things falter"

Entering the park, he had to fight his way through thickets of
bamboo and rhododendron, which would certainly kill his pines
and oak trees if he didn't have them cleared away. Still, he would
leave a few clumps of rhododendrons standing, so that in May he
might see the sparkle of their red and violet flowers above the
grass and below the dark green of the pine needles. He would sit
on a bench, looking at the back of his Georgian house, which by
then would have been restored and rid of its swarms of flies.
Wearing a blue apron, the butler's wife would emerge from the
house with a dish and call the dog to come and be fed. At the end
of the park, the wild country began, moss and rocks, treeless,
traversed by crumbling stone walls and fuchsia hedges, dotted

with ponds, now silken yellow because the sun was already low in the sky. (Two days later, Gregory showed him on a cadastral survey map that a square mile of this pond country belonged to Gorteen House.) So he would walk along the edges of the ponds in high rubber boots. In a room specially set aside for the purpose, he would keep a set of fishing rods and landing nets and a cabinet with cubbyholes for hooks and floats, lines and sinkers, flies, wobblers and spinners. Flowers and trout. Moss and bird calls. Rain and thoughts.

Kind regards from the Styx

He was cutting faded dahlias in a garden which was neither the garden of his house on the Killesberg nor that of Gorteen House; all he knew was that it belonged to a house where he was living all alone. While busy with the flowers, he noticed that someone had pinned a gray card to the inside of the open cellar door. Startled, he approached the door and reached out for the card to see what was written on it, but to his horror felt an unknown hand light on his and press it against the card. At the same moment, he realized that the gray card, on which he could make out nothing but a blurred stamp, was a threat: it meant that he would be murdered if he went back to the house. He turned around to seize the unknown hand, but it had vanished. For a while, he strolled around the garden, circling the house, a late-nineteenth-century villa, but not daring to go in. He decided to look for help, but the streets were deserted; the one man he met shrugged his shoulders and said it was obvious, he would be murdered if he went back to the house. Finally he went back and crossed the front garden; he pressed the handle of the door, which opened instantly. When he woke up, he saw that it was no longer black behind the lounge portholes, but gray like the card on the cellar door. Stepping over the sleeping bodies on the floor, he went on deck; the ship had already entered the Mersey estuary. He couldn't see the water; it was hidden by low-lying fog, through which the ship of the dead moved with hardly a sound. Overhead, the lightless morning of an overcast day, at the edge of which the towers of Liverpool hovered like gossamer monuments.

"Stretched out on the spoils that his own hand spread"

He would often stroll down to the shore; there he would observe a crab in one of the tidal pools, or listen to the waves beating against the cliffs, or take out his binoculars and watch the cormorants on the tablelike cliffs, or take off his clothes in a sandy cove, and swim in the cold water under a green-gray sky. When he had his fill of the wideness of the sea and moors, he would drive to Coppinger's Court, a ruined old Jacobean house tucked away in a valley, and look for the fish otter he had once seen in the brook nearby, black and slippery, busying himself in the water weeds. From such outings, he would return home to his books and pictures, to his austerely clutterless desk, on which there would be nothing but the book he was reading at the moment and a copybook in which to take notes. Behind him would be his cabinets; he would take out the Italo Valenti print he had decided to consult a short while ago when these feathery watermarks had caught his attention in a cove on Greatman's Bay. He would take it out, look at it, and put it back again.

Cassandra

In the gray of dawn on the Liverpool docks, the crucial dialogue with Theo Maurer. All on board were still asleep; everyone knew the dockers wouldn't start unloading before seven o'clock. Only Lins had gone ashore. He was cold. He walked about in the warehouse that was open on the pier side, and read the signs DUNDALK, NEWRY, DROGHEDA. The Mersey was deep in fog. A strange brown-gray light, in which Theo predicted that once he had finished restoring and furnishing Gorteen House he would be bored to death there. It was unfair to make such predictions, because there was no answer; all he could do was insist with helpless exasperation that the contrary was true. Then he constructed a Theo winding up for verbal blows that would no longer be softened by Swabian dialect, and made him go the limit.

"You've read books and looked at pictures. Once in a while you've told me about things that Sartre wrote. Or shown me why a line in a drawing has to be the way it is and no different. That was the most you could manage. As a businessman—yes, as a businessman, you're somebody. As a connoisseur of art and literature—it's time somebody told you, Albert—you're kind of boring. And now, just because you've chosen to retire you expect all that to change. You'll be bored, Albert, because you're a bore."

Actually, there would only be a business conference with Theo, culminating in the crucial discussion of Article 5, Paragraph B of their partnership agreement, this in the presence of lawyers. From time to time when the fog over the water lifted, he looked on shivering as crate slats, newspapers, and orange peels drifted down the Mersey with the outgoing tide.

"When attitudes become form"

All in all, Lins estimates the cost of restoring Gorteen House—repairing the roof, replastering the façade, painting, putting in plumbing and central heating, clearing up the park, and laying out gardens—at fifteen thousand pounds, or almost twice the purchase price. He would have to hire a local architect who knew the local craftsmen and building contractors. When it was finished, Gorteen House would be the finest little Georgian house in western Ireland. Lins would make the same use of the words "Georgian house" as he had of "British racing green," except that there would be no one to make fun of him, no one to call him a snob. He would be a snob only if when he was finished he had the whole thing crated by Christo. For Connemara even that would be a sensation. Lins would never do such a thing. He is a member of the cultural section of the League of West German Industrialists.

Vignettes from the life of a country gentleman

He would attempt to compile a catalogue of the works of Hercules Seghers; the last was done in 1907 and is deplorably out of date. This would necessitate brief trips to Amsterdam, Munich, and Vienna. He would translate *Weymouth Sands* and *A Glastonbury Romance* into German—he felt up to it—and have the rather bulky volumes brought out (at his expense) by a German publishing house. It was simply revolting that respectively thirty and forty years after their appearance such books should still be unavailable in German. He would undertake a comparative study of the definitions of concepts employed in all the philosophical dictionaries he could lay hands on; the outcome might be a kind of satirical text consisting entirely of quotations and requiring no literary activity on his part. He would compile anthologies for his own use, for instance, a collection of descriptions of clouds or of encounters with fire; or he might draw up a catalogue of the forms of developing consciousness. In the garden, he would probably concentrate on a collection of irises; for this, he felt sure, Ireland provided ideal conditions (moisture, soil). Of course, there would be ornithological observations, and perhaps he would finance a film if he ran across some young people interested in making the film he had in mind (curves, angles of incidence, flight studies of all kinds). Geological undertakings. Islands. A fast motorboat. Fishing. Golf.

Members only

Among the dockers who were now arriving, Lins found numerous examples of the Sean O'Casey face: the straight nose, the wide, thin lips, the oblique planes of the cheeks, the fixed eyes under steel-rimmed glasses. They wore gray or brown jackets over blue or vaguely white trousers. Their hair, in so far as it could be seen under their peaked caps, was gray or white. They were slim, middle-aged, even-tempered, soft-spoken, and hardy. They were pouring tea into cups from white enamel bottles. By now it was light over the water, a black-white-and-red-painted tanker named Mountstewart passed by, and in the distance the gates of the warehouses glittered green. Frozen to the marrow, groggy from loss of sleep, Lins would have been glad to drink a cup of the hot tea with milk, but he didn't dare approach any of the groups. He owned to himself that he had never looked at the workers of Maurer & Lins AG as he was now looking at these Liverpool dockers. Maybe he had never really seen them at all. Suddenly, at a command that no one gave, the dockers set to work. The first car they removed from the Dublin night ferry was a white Mercedes with Dar es Salaam license plates.

"As a god self-slain on his own altar"

Weary of hearing the sound of his own steps, he sat down on one of the chairs. He looked out at the terrace, became aware that the house faced northeast, a curious orientation for a house on the west coast of Ireland, but as a result it was sheltered from the west wind and looked out over the moors, the brown-blue patches of which could not at present be seen because the overgrown rose bushes cut off the view. They would have to be cleared away. Once that was done, he would sometimes, looking up from a book, be able to see a flock of wild swans lighting on a strip of moor. The view from the living room corresponded to the view from outside the living room. The roses, a bright red variety, mingled with the twilight, just as the other day, before he had the keys to Gorteen House in his pocket, they had been reflected in the window pane. Behind glass roses, he had looked into his future, which at this moment was already becoming his past. Nothing of him would endure; in order to become rich, he had spent the best years of his life building up a bucket and cooking-pot factory, and he did not believe in a spiritual life wrested from one's material life and existing in some sheltered corner. Nevertheless, he would be able to sit in this room as an observer, to look on as the moors mingled with his books, as his pictures took flight with the flocks of birds, to determine whether there were sentences that could stand up under the shadows of clouds. An utterly egoistic existence, to be sure. But what else was there left for him, since he himself was not able to make clouds or flocks of birds? He could only collect them.

"Death lies dead"

After a brief glance at the "For Sale" sign, he had turned his car around and driven to the gate. Finally he had screwed up his courage and gone in. Then he had peered into the living room through a window in which roses were reflected; he had looked at the oval table, the chairs, the walls with the light rectangles, where pictures had been removed. Gorteen House was dead. It

was so dead that there was no longer even any death in it. It was
deserted. If he bought Gorteen House and lived in it for the ten
or fifteen, or perhaps even twenty years he had left, then someone
—twenty or a hundred years later—would peer in through these
windows at the last vestiges of the objects in the midst of which
he had lived, and perhaps experience the same feeling of nonbe-
ing. He doubted, to be sure, that it would be possible to keep the
property intact by a provision of his will; the rights of private
property were sacred, but hardly sacred enough to protect a dead
from a living owner; perhaps it was only Ireland that gave him the
idea that certain titles and inheritances might simply be forgotten. Still, he might choose an heir and leave him everything, his
fortune and his art collection, on condition that he leave Gorteen
House intact. But why? Merely because he knew that he would
leave behind him no other trace of his life? *Kilroy was here.* Ridiculous. These people—what was their name again? the innkeeper
in Inverbeg had told him—had vanished from Gorteen House
without a trace. The O'Gradys. There was no one here. No one.
The house was deserted. Deserted. There was no immortality. He
wanted Gorteen House. He had to have it.

On the metaphysics of coupon clipping

Lins is well aware that if he retires to Gorteen House he will be
transforming himself from an owner of the means of production
into a man living on the income from his capital. Oughtn't he at
least to remain a silent partner in Maurer & Lins, if Maurer
offered no objection? A half measure. If Maurer's flair for business
proved inferior to his own, he would keep having to step in. Such
interruptions would make his life in Gorteen House a farce, and
they would occur, for in his heart of hearts Lins regards himself as
indispensable. He therefore decides to invest his share of the capital in securities, real estate, and long-term savings accounts. No
schizophrenia! It shouldn't be very hard to exchange the status of
a producer for that of a gentleman of means. He tells himself that
in the present state of society only an adequate private income
can provide absolute freedom.

Who is Albert Lins?

The passengers had all gone their ways. Car after car had been unloaded and left the pier. By ten o'clock only Lins, beside himself with impatience, stood in the open warehouse, watching the last dockers landing his TR 4. Again the crane let it hover awhile in mid-air, before cautiously lowering it onto the cement loading platform. The worker who removed the cables said that beginning next year there would be modern car ferries running between England and Ireland. Inwardly, Lins wished him and his car ferries in hell. Why in God's name hadn't he left his car in a Dublin garage and taken a plane to Stuttgart? His first motions were nervous, and the engine didn't start until the third try. Driving soothed him instantly. We watch him for an hour or two, as he crosses Liverpool, breakfasts in Warrington, and takes the road to Wales to avoid the traffic in the Midlands. Somewhere amid the hedgerows of Wales we lose sight of him.

A Morning at the Seashore

They had decided to get up early during their vacation, and go to the beach in the morning when no one was there; instead, they slept late and breakfasted late. The children were up before them, and in a half sleep they could hear them playing in the garden behind the house. The garden was nothing more than a patch of cleared woodland with a few bushes on it and a chicken-wire fence around it.

After breakfast, his wife took the children, two little girls of four and five, to the beach. He watched her pack the big red beach bag. She had on a short blue dress and cloth shoes the color of her hair, a faded blond. Her arms and legs were burned brown.

The house they had rented was on Place Gambetta, which despite its imposing name was merely a large sandy space, surrounded by pine trees through which his wife and children passed on their way to the dune. The trees cast faint shadows on them. Now and then the children turned around toward him and shouted something. His wife also turned around once and waved. She was wearing big dark sunglasses that made her sunburned face even smaller and more compact than usual.

He went into the house for a book. The house was furnished without taste. The new tubular chairs were awkwardly shaped and the cupboards were finished with cheap veneer. The price for three weeks was 1,500 francs. His wife had thought it much too expensive, but he had proved to her that they could afford it. He was an engineer, employed by the Dortmund building office. All in all, this trip to the Atlantic coast for his annual vacation would cost him hardly more than a month's salary.

He settled down in a steamer chair in front of the house, after setting up the beach umbrella so as to put him in the shade. He would have preferred not to spend his vacation at the seashore. He couldn't lie on the beach all day because of his sensitive skin.

Besides, it bored him. Plagued by the sun or by grains of sand, he would keep shifting his position, smoothing out the towel he was lying on, or jumping up and busying himself with useless errands. Only the actual bathing gave him pleasure. But his wife loved the seashore, and it was the best thing for the two little girls.

Before starting to read, he watched the French people crossing the square on their way to the beach. They came in families or close-knit groups. No one was alone, and there were hardly any couples by themselves. They had shriller voices and they were more self-assured in their bearing than Germans. They were a nation. He was glad that the thought of belonging to a nation came to him only rarely. The French children from the summer camps in the woods crossed Place Gambetta in orderly bands, singing songs.

He was reading a book about the Catharists. His interest in Catharism had been aroused by a television documentary about the Catharist cult sites in southern France. The Catharists had an explanation for the existence of evil: they believed, or rather, they had once believed, for they had been exterminated, that Creation was the work not of God, but of the Devil. If I were religious, he thought, I'd be a Catharist. He had brought the book because he had found out that the resort they were going to was in a region where the Catharist faith had once been predominant; but on his excursions through the back country, he had found no reminders of this past. Maybe he should have consulted someone familiar with the local lore, but for that he and his wife spoke too little French.

He read only a few pages; he was unable to concentrate. The sky above the tree was too glaring, too light blue, too flat. And the bathers, the young people on their bicycles, and the motorcars hardly fitted in with the subject matter. He went inside and drank a glass of mineral water, although he was not thirsty. He sat down at the dining room table, drew his typewriter across the cheap veneer of the table top, and wrote a letter to his bank. He had not gotten around to paying certain bills before leaving. There were the following payments to be made: DM 231.50 for electricity for the second quarter of 1970; DM 4,880 for the mortgage on his house in a housing development in the suburbs of Dortmund; DM 115.20 for a check-up on his car (a VW 1500); DM 72.50 for the telephone; and a few installment payments. He gave the most thought to the payment on his house. In order to buy it, he had had to take out a mortgage of DM 80,000 at 8 per cent, which involved him in semi-annual payments of DM 3,200 in interest plus DM 2,000 for amortization. (Consequently, the payments would diminish as time went on, but not very considerably.) Three years before, when he had decided to buy the house, his wife had advised him against it, but he had shown her that—considering the interest as rent—they would be paying only 533 marks a month, and after two years only 480. Yes, she had said, but you'll be paying more in interest than the total amount of the mortgage. The house will cost you at least twice what it cost to build it. His wife had been a private secretary before marrying.

He completed his list, addressed the envelope, and sealed it. He was proud of the fact that he was able to pay his bills punctually on what he saved out of his salary. In general, he was proud of himself, of his clear, orderly mode of life. Though a graduate not of engineering school but only of a technical school, he had managed to obtain a responsible position at the municipal building office. One of these days, they would give him civil service status. On completing school, he had worked for a few years for private construction firms, but their passion for profit had disgusted him, and instinctively he was drawn to the security of a government position. It was his opinion that the whole construction industry, in which he included the mortgage banks, should be taken over by the government, like the railroads and the post office. For this reason, he had joined the Social Democratic Party; though the party program provided for nothing of the sort, he felt that this was the safe place for himself and his ideas.

He took off his trousers, slipped into his swimming shorts, and put his trousers back on over them. Then he locked up the house and went to the beach. From the top of the dune he saw, as he had seen every day, that the beach was too enormous to be covered by bathers, even at the height of the season. Here and there, the bathers formed colonies, loose, constantly changing aggregates of bodies and beach umbrellas, but between them and around them there was always an empty yellow and white space, which lost itself to the north and south in horizons of light-gray mist. Today, the ocean was fringed with wide waves, approaching at long intervals; from where he was, he could not judge the height of their foaming crests, but apparently they were not dangerous, for the beach guards had raised the green flag on the pole beside their cabin, which meant that swimming was permitted. He pushed up his sunglasses for a moment to judge the actual color of the ocean: it was a compact steely mass, to all intents and purposes colorless, under a frosted glass sky, as empty and meaningless as the children's cries that rose up to him from the beach.

He found his wife and children at the usual spot, under the blue umbrella they had rented. The two little girls jumped up with delight, and for half an hour he strolled about the beach with them, helping them to find shells. When they came back, his wife was lying in the sun. He undressed and sat down in the shade of the umbrella. They talked in an undertone about the children and the people sitting or lying nearby. He was thirty-five years of age, born in 1935. He had known his wife for seven years, since 1963; they had been married for five years. She was now thirty. She was still slender, and the color of her hair had not changed; her faded blond pony tail lay on her brown back. He had once read somewhere that in French a woman with hair like that was called a *fille aux cheveux de lin,* and later on he had heard a piano piece by Debussy with that title on the radio. He had bought a record of it, and for a time they had listened to it together almost every night. He decided to dig out the record when they got home and play it for her again.

She had already bathed, so he went in without her; only the two little girls ran after him. He passed the two beach guards, policemen from Toulouse, who had taken a course in lifesaving. As usual, they were standing motionless with folded arms, looking out at the sea, brainless statues of gods. One of them said to him: "*Attention, monsieur!*" He turned around and saw that the yellow flag, warning the bathers to be careful, had been hoisted in the meantime. He nodded. The two little girls stopped at the first garland of foam.

He saw that the first—or was it the last?—enormous wave was breaking far away. Resolutely he went toward it; today he was determined to swim, though he knew it was forbidden when the yellow flag was flying. He had already had experience with these waves and knew that the only way to get past them was to dive under. For a moment he watched the wave as it towered over him. Then, when the inner mass rose again, he dove horizontally into its green base. He felt the tug of the backwash for a moment, but then it released him. Quickly he prepared himself for the second wave and dove under it. Then he was in the open sea, which presented no further difficulty. Swimming cautiously, he let himself be carried from the deep valleys to the high crests. He knew he would be in danger when he turned back toward the beach. To postpone that moment, he swam farther and farther westward. He tried to figure out how to deal with the undertow as he approached the beach, but came to no conclusion.

The waves smoothed into a compact swell, from the height of which he saw the beach as a thin strip, a narrow, trembling line of umbrellas and shadows, far in the distance. He decided to turn back. He was very much surprised when still in the open sea, long before the surf line, an enormous wave struck him in the back and in breaking engulfed him in a waterfall. He swallowed water. He extricated himself but only in time to see another great wall coming down on him. It pressed him to the bottom and to his horror he felt his body spinning. He lost his sense of direction. Once he felt the sandy bottom, then there was only water around him, a liquid weight, and his eyes filled with the color green.

++

The Windward Islands

++

It was much too early. As they left the Deutsches Museum the day before, Sir Thomas Wilkins had asked Franz Kien to come to the Hotel Vier Jahreszeiten at two o'clock but it was only one when he got out of the streetcar at Odeonsplatz. He had one mark seventy in his pocket and decided to have a cup of coffee at the Café Rottenhöfer. Late that afternoon, the Englishman would pay him for his services as a guide: two tours; he was hoping for twenty or thirty marks.

Instead of turning directly into Residenzstrasse where the café was situated, he detoured by way of Theatinerstrasse and Viscardistrasse, so as to avoid passing the National Socialist Memorial and having to raise his arm in the Hitler salute.

At that time of day the café was almost empty. A few women. At one table two SA men were sitting. Franz Kien had not expected to meet anyone he knew. As recently as the previous fall the Café Rottenhöfer had been the meeting place of "his" group in the Young Communist League. Franz Lehner, Ludwig Kessel, Gebhard Homolka and a few others, plus the girls: Adelheid Sennhauser, Sophia Weber, and Else Laub. Franz, Ludwig, Gebhard, and the others were still in Dachau; Adelheid was in some women's prison. Franz Kien had once tried to look up Else Laub, but her mother had opened the door by a crack and said in an angry whisper: "What do you want? Go away! We're under police surveillance!"—in a tone suggesting that Franz Kien was to blame for the attitude of the Gestapo. Suddenly he caught sight of Wolfgang Fischer. He was sitting at a table in the rear of the café, talking with young men unknown to Franz Kien.

Franz Kien was delighted. He went directly to Fischer's table and held out his hand.

"Wolfgang!" he said. "It's great to see you!"

Wolfgang Fischer had not been a Communist but a member of

the International Socialist Combat League. Quite as a matter of course, Franz Kien thought in the past tense, though he knew that small remnants of certain Communist and Socialist groups still existed illegally. The Young Communists had regarded the ISCL as an eccentric sect; its members were vegetarians, teetotallers, and believers in moral purity. They were not Marxists but supporters of a Heidelberg philosopher by the name of Leonard Nelson. Though they obviously felt themselves to be an elite, they were modest and reserved, and for that they were well liked. They had been in close contact with the Young Communists, gone on excursions with them, and attended their meetings with a view to discussion.

Wolfgang Fischer raised his head and looked at Franz Kien, but did not take his hand.

"Yes," he said. "Isn't it great to see a Jew?"

Wolfgang Fischer was a few years older than Franz Kien. He was studying chemistry at Munich University. He was stockily built, with short-cropped red hair and the reddish, freckly skin that goes with it. Everything about him was hard: the small blue eyes with their red brows, the tight skin over his muscles and bones. As a long-distance runner he had been prominent in workers' sports activities; Franz Kien had once watched him running the ten thousand meters; he ran like a machine, quickening his pace only in the last five hundred meters, so as to add another lap to his lead over all the others, who were already one or more laps behind. At the finish he had shown no signs of fatigue. He was a Socialist from ethical conviction. In conversations with Franz Kien he had taken the view that socialism would win out, not as a consequence of necessary dialectical processes, but because it was grounded in justice. Modestly, calmly, and matter-of-factly, he expounded the doctrines of Kant and Leonard Nelson. The eighteen-year-old Franz Kien, a beginner in Marxism, could not stand up to him in discussion; he had merely felt that if Wolfgang Fischer was right the decision in favor of socialism was a matter of pure will, and instinctively he doubted the efficacy of pure will. But he felt drawn to Wolfgang Fischer, to this resolute man who spoke gently to him and treated him with patient friendliness.

Such a sentence from Fischer's mouth came as a complete surprise. Franz Kien was so taken aback that he could think of no reply. Slowly he withdrew his hand, conscious that he was blushing with embarrassment.

"What do you mean by that?" he asked finally.

He had been meaning, quite as a matter of course, to take the empty chair at the table.

"What I mean?" Franz Kien had never heard Fischer speak in such a tone. "Don't play innocent! You know perfectly well. I mean that today all you Germans feel the same way about us Jews."

He averted his eyes from Kien and spoke into the air. For some reason that he himself did not understand until later, Franz Kien was unable to tell Wolfgang Fischer that he had spent the spring in a concentration camp and that he still had to report to the Gestapo once a week.

Maybe I could tell him if I were sitting at the table with him, he thought. But as it was, standing, aware of his flushed face, he only managed to say:

"You must be off your rocker!"

"It's easy to say that to a Jew today," Wolfgang Fischer replied instantly. He motioned with his shoulders to the young man sitting beside him, who was looking uncomfortable, obviously embarrassed by the scene. "Please go away. We're leaving for Palestine in a few days and we have a lot of things to discuss."

Franz Kien turned abruptly and left the café. In his confusion he failed to notice which way he was going, but just in time he saw the SS men standing motionless beside the memorial tablet and changed his direction. On his way down Residenzstrasse toward Franz-Josef-Platz, he remembered that he had wanted a cup of coffee. But then Fischer had expelled him from the Café Rottenhöfer. Little by little, it occurred to him how he might have answered Fischer. For instance, he could have said: "The ISCL people have not been arrested. There are no ISCL members in Dachau. Not even Jewish members. In Dachau there were only Communists, Communists, Communists." Then he remembered the middle-class Jews from Nuremberg, whom he had seen in Dachau.

He went to another café where he had never been. It was across the way from the Hoftheater and consisted of one tiny room. He would have liked a piece of almond cake with his coffee, but he hadn't enough money. In those days he didn't smoke. After a while he succeeded in shrugging off the incident with Wolfgang Fischer. It was mad, simply mad! After his coffee, because the cake had been denied him, he felt a faint but gnawing pang of hunger, for which there was no real justification because he had eaten an adequate lunch at home. He knew he would carry his hunger pang around with him all afternoon, while showing Sir Thomas Wilkins the town. He would keep hoping that Wilkins would interrupt the tour and treat him to tea and cake. At the bakery next to the Franziskaner he bought two rolls and ate them, standing in a doorway. That stilled his hunger.

"An Englishman with the title 'Sir,' " his brother had lectured him, "is always addressed by the title and his first name." Consequently Franz Kien had avoided the direct form of address while guiding Sir Thomas Wilkins through the Deutsches Museum. The day before yesterday, Sir Thomas Wilkins had bought a Wagner score from Franz Kien's elder brother and asked him on the occasion whether he knew a student or other cultivated young man who might show him around Munich. Franz Kien's brother worked in a music store on Maximilianstrasse. Franz Kien himself was unemployed. He had been unemployed for three years.

"I haven't the faintest idea how to show anyone around Munich," he had objected. "Besides, I don't speak English."

"The gentleman speaks German," his brother had replied. "And you know Munich very well. Pull yourself together. Sir Thomas is a high English colonial official. It's not every day that you meet such a man. Besides, it's a job." The lesson about the form of address had followed. Franz Kien could see that his brother would have liked to guide the Englishman himself.

"I just don't feel like it," he said.

"I've already accepted for you," said his brother. "Eleven tomorrow morning at the Vier Jahreszeiten." He inspected his brother. "Your hair has grown in again. Nobody will see a thing."

Franz Kien's hair had been shaved off in Dachau, and had taken an amazing length of time, nearly all summer, to grow in.

All evening he had racked his brains about how to show someone around Munich, but no ideas had come to him; he had felt paralyzed.

After meeting Wilkins in the hotel lobby, he had awkwardly

suggested a number of possible itineraries. Suddenly Wilkins had raised his head, looked out through the plate-glass window into the rain, and announced that he would like to visit the Deutsches Museum. It turned out that he had already been in Munich several times, though not in the last twenty years. He spoke so knowledgeably of Munich that Franz Kien couldn't help wondering why he needed a guide. Of course there wasn't much else one could do in the rain, but Franz Kien nevertheless had the impression that the Englishman had wanted to help him out of his perplexity. With a sense of relief, Franz Kien stood up to go, for surely no guide was required for a visit to a museum, but without a moment's hesitation the old gentleman said amiably that of course they would go together. He ordered a cab. It was a long time since Franz Kien had ridden in a taxi. He was glad that Wilkins expressed no desire to see the mines. The mines in the Deutsches Museum were a bore. Wilkins explained an 1813 model of a Watt beam engine with water pump, the Bessemer process of converting iron into steel, and other inventions of which Franz Kien hadn't the faintest glimmer. Despite his English accent he spoke excellent German. He said he had studied in Dresden in 1888. In the fall of 1933, the year 1888 had a legendary ring in Franz Kien's ears.

At two o'clock Wilkins suggested lunch. He wanted, he said, to "eat something typical of Munich in a typical Munich restaurant, perhaps *Leberkäs* or *Schweinswürstl*"—two of the dishes he remembered. Franz Kien pondered. It was hard to find anything in the vicinity of the museum. Then he remembered a restaurant on Paulanerplatz, where he and his Party friends had often met. Under the Englishman's large black umbrella they crossed the bridge over the green-foaming Isar and made their way through the streets of the Au district. The proprietor recognized Franz and said: "Hm, so here you are again!"—but no more. Possibly he was as displeased as Else Laub's mother to see Franz Kien again, but he didn't show it, he merely dropped the subject, and naturally Franz Kien was just as glad that he should ask no questions in the Englishman's presence.

There was neither *Leberkäse* nor *Schweinswürstl*, but there was fresh *Milzwurst*, so they sat at the freshly scrubbed table eating fried *Milzwurst* with potato salad and drinking beer. Over the meal Sir Thomas Wilkins told Franz Kien that his last post had been that of civil governor of Malta; before that he had been military governor of the Windward Islands, and before that a judge in East Africa. It seemed to be of the utmost importance to him that Franz Kien should understand the difference between a civil governor and a military governor. He had the most to say of the Windward Islands. "My home was in St. George's, Grenada," he said. "I went from island to island on my yacht. But there was very little to do. Those people don't quarrel much." He fell silent and seemed to be dreaming. "But it's very hot down there," he said then. "My sister was always knitting. When her ball of wool fell to the floor and I stooped to pick it up, I was bathed in sweat."

Franz Kien found this mention of Wilkins' sister so unusual that he ventured to ask if he were married.

"Why, of course," Wilkins replied with alacrity. "I have two children. They're grown up now. My wife lives in London. We see each other now and then. My sister has been keeping house for me in the last few years."

And quite naturally, without irony, he went on: "A man should definitely have been married once. But it needn't be for his lifetime."

They went back to the museum. Wilkins was enthusiastic about the planetariums. He kept going back and forth between the Ptolemaic and the Copernican planetarium, explaining the differences to Franz Kien. Together they climbed into the car under the mobile model, from which one could follow the earth in its orbit. Up until then these planetariums had never meant much to Franz Kien. Despite the light effects in the darkness, he had found them dull and boring. And besides, he had never taken much interest in the stars and constellations. He had been unemployed since the age of sixteen and politics had been his sole preoccupation. (In Dachau the prisoners had been forbidden to leave the barracks after dark.)

That night he had taken out his atlas and located the Windward Islands. They formed the southernmost archipelago of the Lesser Antilles.

Today he had resolved to greet Wilkins with a "Good day, Sir Thomas," but when the Englishman entered the lobby, the words refused to come out and he had only bowed. Wilkins had simply addressed him as Franz; it hadn't sounded condescending.

"What will you show me today, Franz?" he now asked.

"As if I showed you anything yesterday!" said Franz Kien. "You showed me the Deutsches Museum."

Wilkins smiled. "Today the weather is perfect," he said. "Now it's your turn."

The weather was indeed perfect, a fine September afternoon. Franz Kien led Wilkins through narrow, almost deserted streets which began directly behind the hotel, to the church of Sankt Anna in Lehel. He did not know whether Wilkins was interested in churches or art, but he had decided to show the foreigner a few of the things that he, Franz Kien, loved in his home town. In the church he spoke like a real guide about Johann Michael Fischer and the Asam brothers. He couldn't tell what impression this piece of Bavarian baroque was making on the Englishman. On a man who bought Wagner scores! In the oval interior Sir Thomas Wilkins sat down in one of the pews, but instead of studying the Asam frescoes merely looked into space. Franz Kien stood beside him and waited. The pew was so narrow that the Englishman had to raise his knees. He had a gray mustache. Even now, in his somewhat absent state, his eyes had a friendly look. Up ahead of them a woman was kneeling.

On Galeriestrasse a blue streetcar was ringing its bell. They went to the Hofgarten. At that time the lime trees had not yet been cut down and the concert pavilion was a weatherbeaten yellow under the early-autumn foliage. They walked under the arcade and Franz Kien stopped in front of the Rottmann frescoes. The Greek landscapes faded into surfaces of twilight blue, brown and red. It was easy to see that these frescoes would not last much longer. Wilkins said that Greece was just like that. He spoke of the trips to the Greek islands that he had taken from Malta.

They emerged from the park at Odeonsplatz, which Wilkins remembered well. Again they saw SA men in their brown uniforms. There had been a few in the Deutsches Museum. Franz Kien had expected Wilkins to remark on them, perhaps even to ask questions about the political situation in Germany, but he had said nothing. Instead, he asked Franz Kien how long he had been unemployed.

"We've been having a bad economic crisis in England too," he said after Franz Kien had replied. "But things are looking up now. They will here too. You're sure to find work soon."

He seemed to be looking at the brown and black uniforms as he looked at everything, calmly and matter-of-factly. Franz Kien kept wondering whether to tell him about his stay in Dachau, but he couldn't make up his mind to do so.

He managed to steer Sir Thomas past the Feldherrenhalle into Theatinerstrasse without his catching sight of the National Socialist memorial. When they came to Perusastrasse, he stopped and said: "If we go straight ahead, we'll come to the Rathaus. It's hideous. If we turn right, we'll come to the Frauenkirche." After a moment's hesitation he added: "To tell the truth, it's hideous too. Would you like to see it?"

Wilkins laughed. "No, of course not, if it's hideous. Show me something nice."

Franz Kien led him into Perusastrasse past the Main Post Office to the Alter Hof. He hadn't been there for a long time and remembered it as being more interesting, more mysterious than it actually was. In reality, the Alter Hof was merely a rectangular group of old, relatively well-built houses occupied by government offices. Still, there was the oriel with the "Golden Roof." Standing there with Wilkins, Franz Kien felt ill at ease. Maybe he had made a mistake in coming here, though Wilkins admired the Alter Hof and said it reminded him of certain medieval buildings in Edinburgh.

Possibly because of this feeling of uncertainty, he now, instead of leading Wilkins past the Food Market to the old Rathaus, headed for Franz-Josef-Platz, which was nearer. There, to Franz Kien's dismay, the Englishman took an interest in the Residenz, first examining the south façade, then despite Franz Kien's attempts to guide him in a different direction, walking around the western wing.

Across from the Café Rottenhöfer, Franz Kien stopped, he pointed out the building across the street and said: "That's the Preysing Palace. It's the finest rococo palace in Munich. Down there, on the wall of the Feldherrenhalle, the National Socialists have put up a memorial tablet. Where the two SS men are standing."

Looking down Residenzstrasse, Wilkins saw the two motionless figures. Even their steel helmets were black.

"Memorial tablet?" he said. "What is it in memory of?"

"The Hitler putsch of 1923," said Franz Kien. "The first attempt of the National Socialists to take power. They staged a demonstration and the police fired. A few people were killed."

"I remember," said Wilkins. "Didn't General Ludendorff take part?"

"Yes." Franz Kien didn't know whether there was irony in his voice when he said: "He was the only one who didn't lie down when the police fired."

"The police must have had instructions not to hit him," said Wilkins. He added: "But I don't mean to imply that General Ludendorff wasn't a brave man."

Franz Kien looked across at the Café Rottenhöfer. Wolfgang Fischer must have left long ago. Franz Kien could have told Sir Thomas about the night of the Hitler putsch. In the middle of the night his father, who worshiped General Ludendorff, had put on his infantry captain's uniform and gone out to take part in the putsch. How gray and lifeless the apartment—situated in a middle-class suburb—had seemed when he was gone! Franz Kien had been nine at the time. That night he had hoped his father would return victorious and fill the night-blind wardrobe mirror in the hallway with life. But when he came back three days later, he had taken off the uniform without a word. He had died a few years later, but not too soon to see Franz join the Young Communists. Franz thought of his dead father. What would he have said about Dachau? Franz Kien sometimes basked in the illusion that his father would have disapproved of Dachau, especially if he, his son, had told him what went on there. But his father had been a Jew hater, an Anti-Semite like Ludendorff. And now Wolfgang Fischer was emigrating to Palestine.

"Everybody seems to be saluting the tablet," said Wilkins.

"It's compulsory," said Franz Kien. "But we don't have to pass it," he added, taking it for granted that the Englishman would have no desire to pass the memorial. And pointing to Viscardigasse, "We can take that street over there to Odeonsplatz. Everybody who doesn't want to salute goes that way. It's not much longer."

He tried to smile when he explained: "Everybody in Munich calls it Goldbrick Street."

"Goldbrick Street?" Wilkins repeated. "Ah, I see."

After a moment's thought he said: "No, I'd rather go straight ahead."

That, Franz Kien realized later on, after giving a good deal of thought to his stroll with Sir Thomas Wilkins, was when he should have spoken up. He need only have said: "Excuse me if I leave you for just a few moments. I'll meet you on Odeonsplatz." Perhaps, no certainly, Wilkins would have understood and either said nothing or asked him to explain. True, Franz Kien had no idea how Sir Thomas would have reacted to his explanation. Quite possibly he had no objection to the National Socialist regime. He might even have sympathized with the Nazis. It was certain that he felt no affection for the Communists.

But Franz Kien had lacked presence of mind. Once he had failed to speak up, there was nothing he could do but go on at Wilkins' side. Instead of escaping while there was still time, he had engaged in futile speculation: what would happen when Sir Thomas passed the memorial without saluting? Franz Kien knew that two Gestapo plainclothesmen standing across the street from the memorial, in the doorway of the Residenz, would come up to Wilkins and demand an explanation, but would withdraw with apologies when he—as haughtily as possible, Franz Kien hoped—produced his English passport. The speculation was futile because, while Franz Kien was still visualizing this easy little victory, he saw the Englishman raise his right arm in the Hitler salute. Quite mechanically, he followed suit, not looking at the memorial across the street, but observing Wilkins' face, which was in between. He saw that it took on the same expressionless look as when, picking up his knees in the narrow church pew, Wilkins had sat staring into space.

They lowered their arms at the same time. Wilkins suggested tea at the Annast. They found a table by the window with a view of the Theatinerkirche and the end of Briennerstrasse.

While Franz Kien was still wondering whether the Englishman might not have given the Hitler salute because he thought it unworthy of a gentleman to take Goldbrick Street, he heard him saying: "In a foreign country I like to do what the inhabitants do. One understands them better if one adopts their customs."

"I've heard," said Franz Kien, "that an Englishman is always an Englishman, regardless of where he goes."

"Oh yes, we're always Englishmen," said Wilkins. "But we try to understand."

Franz Kien looked at the onetime civil governor of Malta, military governor of the Windward Islands, and judge in East Africa. An Englishman who, with expressionless features, studied the ways of the natives. The natives of Malta and the Windward Islands, of East Africa and Munich. This Englishman, in all likelihood, had lost all desire to rule. He was content to sail from island to island on his governor's yacht and settle disputes when asked to do so. A dispute that could not be settled was probably inconceivable to him, Franz Kien thought. It would have been useless to tell him about Dachau.

No, Franz Kien thought, when it was too late, it would not have been useless. On the strength of what he had told him, Sir Thomas Wilkins would probably have submitted a confidential report to his government.

Wilkins handed him a folded hundred-mark note.

"That's too much," said Franz Kien.

"It's very little," Wilkins replied, taking the same tone as when he had decreed that Franz Kien should accompany him to the Deutsches Museum. He gave Franz Kien his card. On it there was only his name, and, in the lower right-hand corner: St. James's Club, London S.W. 1.

"I travel a good deal," he said. "If you should like to write to me, Franz, a letter will always reach me at this address."

Franz Kien never wrote to him. After the war, on his first visit to London, he went to the St. James's Club. The man at the reception desk looked through the register. Then he said: "I'm sorry, sir. Sir Thomas Wilkins died on March 5, 1941."

Franz Kien was sorry too. As he stepped out into St. James's Square, he could see Sir Thomas—as he now called him in his thoughts—skirting the grass plot at the center of the square, turning into Pall Mall, and receding from view. That day in Munich he had receded from view on Promenadeplatz in exactly the same way, a tall old gentleman wearing a light raincoat and carrying a tightly rolled black umbrella. Franz had taken the streetcar home. On arriving, he had again consulted the atlas and tried to imagine the wind which was so strong that in spite of the heat the islands that lay in its path had taken their name from it.

++

My Disappearance in Providence

++

Novel as coded message. Written by T. while held prisoner in that house on Benefit Street. *I put the sheets in a large orange envelope that I found in William's desk, and write on it: To whom it may concern.*

T. left Gardner House on Saturday, October 17, 1970, at eight-thirty in the morning. Since then there has been no trace of him except for his registration card at the Avis Auto Rental Agency on Kennedy Plaza, which shows that at four in the afternoon he returned the car he had rented that day, a Dodge. The clerk at the Avis office had noticed nothing unusual in T.'s behavior; in fact, he could hardly remember him.

T. paid for the car rental with a Diners Club credit card. Consequently, if he fails to reappear, the Diners Club will have to foot the bill. Fraw T., who lives in West Berlin—the T.'s were divorced two years ago—refuses to pay T.'s outstanding debts.

Gardner House, a graceful brick building dating back to the colonial period, is used by Brown University as a guest house. *Imprisoned in the loneliness of a traveling writer, I stayed there for a few days in a room darkened by old furniture, a canopy bed, books and periodicals devoted to the lore, geography and archi-*

tecture of New England. T. was scheduled to read selections from his works to the students and faculty of the German Department on Monday, October 19.

5

T. wants to make it clear that he felt no "presentiment" of any kind when he closed the white-enameled door of Gardner House behind him. What he did feel was *the unexpected cold which, on October 17, froze the Indian summer of the year 1970 to the bones,* as he wrote. *On the eighteenth the maple trees were no longer so red or the oak trees so yellow as on the seventeenth, as I observed when, sitting at the window in handcuffs, I looked out at the garden of Eliza's and William's house.*

6

Shivering, T. walks through the historical beauty of the university area, situated on a hill in Providence—old trees, concrete-and-glass libraries. Should I have him buy a sweater before picking up the car he ordered for yesterday? Unfortunately, he can't summon up the courage.

7

T. seems to think that the emptiness and resulting monotony of the streets of American cities had a good deal to do with his disappearance. *They* (the streets) *are devoid of walking human beings. On George Street and College Street, I passed no one; on Kennedy Plaza, the square in front of the railroad station, which is the center of the city, I counted five pedestrians.*

8

T. is a middlingly well-known (West) German writer. He is feeling disgruntled because he has discovered that in the course of the standard reading tour of the German departments of several American universities he has been seeing no more than the German departments of several American universities. His trip is being financed by the (West) German Goethe-Institut.

9

He has rented the car in order to visit a stretch of coast near the mouth of Narragansett Bay, where, twenty-five years ago, in the summer and fall of 1945, he lived as a prisoner of war. *The desire to visit this place once again has become an obsession with me. To be perfectly truthful, I accepted the invitation to America only in order to make this short excursion.*

10

The car, a brand-new Dodge, had an automatic gear-shift and kept setting itself in motion when I forgot to throw out the clutch. The upper part of the windshield was tinted blue to give the driver the illusion of sailing along under an eternally blue sky. On October 17, however, the sky was blue to begin with, blue over a day swept by a biting east wind.

11

A few weeks later Eliza showed him the portfolio in which she had collected newspaper clippings relating to the (thus far) unsuccessful search for T. It occurs to T. that on October 16 he took two shirts, two pairs of shorts, and two pairs of socks to a laundry on Thayer Street. "You won't need them any more," says Eliza, laughing, and tears up the laundry ticket.

12

T. also left his suitcase behind in his room in Gardner House. Professor Carver, who was deeply upset by his guest's disappearance (accident? crime?) turned T.'s belongings over to the police for safekeeping. T.'s quietly elegant suitcase, made of chestnut brown imitation leather, is now gathering dust in a lightless storeroom at police headquarters.

13

To his astonishment, T., once seated in his car, has suddenly lost all desire to visit the scene of his life as a prisoner of war. He is a man in his middle fifties. At this age one is subject to intense attacks of futility, meaninglessness, indifference.

14

I regretted that I was using this car only in order to wallow in memories. What a pity that it didn't belong to me and that I didn't have enough money to escape from the Goethe-Institut with its help. Then, perhaps, I would have driven to Tallulah or Hannibal, and not to the scene of a past utopia.

15

I left the highway after Saunderstown, and had no difficulty in finding the place where the white barracks of Fort Kearney had once stood. South Ferry Road ends in a gravel path which descends in a rather steep hill to the bay. There is no ferry, maybe there never was one.

16

Along South Ferry Road there were no villas or summer houses as everywhere else in the Narragansett Bay region, but old farms, weatherbeaten frame houses surrounded by scrub oak and negligently harvested fields. They must have been there in 1945, when we were taken to the camp in tarp-covered trucks. As a prisoner, I had lived at the foot of the shore dunes, which hid the countryside, yet strange to say I had always imagined the country around Fort Kearney exactly as I finally saw it on that day in October 1970.

17

After T. has read this passage to Eliza and William on a spring evening in 1971—the Dorrances insist on his reading what he has written during the day to them in the evening—William interrupts him. "I presume that's the difference," he says, "between your past and your present imprisonment. If I'm not mistaken, you know the neighborhood of our house rather well."

18

The site of the barracks where the loudspeaker on the roof of the mess hall woke us up every morning with a Duke Ellington version of "Oh Lady Be Good," was now occupied by a modern recreation center operated by the University of Rhode Island. At this time of year it was closed and there was no one to be seen. The old pier down below was unchanged, as dark brown as ever.

19

I went down to the shore. After an absence of twenty-five years I looked out at the white lighthouse in mid-channel, at the low hills of Conanicut Island, and at the mouth of the bay. I felt nothing.

20

"Poor fellow," says Eliza—*incredible how warmth and mockery can combine in her dark voice*—"should we drive you out there again? Maybe you were just out of sorts." And turning to William: "Good idea! Let's take him on a little excursion to his old camp!"

21

At that time my old camp meant a great deal to me, everything in fact. I had thought that seeing it again would have an enormous effect on me. After all, it was in the seclusion of Fort Kearney, after years of fear and trembling that I decided to become a writer.

22

"No, thank you," T. replies, "never again!" This may be the place for the first flashback: the private circumstances of young

T., then under thirty. Interpolation of his relationship with N., from whom, after his return to Europe, T. never heard again.

23

Thinking of N. on the pebbly beach, I picked up a small seashell; I had toted a large one of the same kind back to Europe in my sea bag as a present for her. But on that day even N. remained as indifferent to me as the place itself. Maybe it was the weather, the ice-cold wind under a blue sky, a sharp-cut day without perceptive.

24

In Fort Kearney, in the germ-free environment of that luxurious prison camp, I also learned democracy. "Democracy," said Professor Smith, "is a technique of creative compromise." The idea appealed to me.

25

I wonder if I should have T. read the items referring to Eliza in his manuscript aloud, for instance, the sentence: *Amazing how warmth and mockery can combine in her dark voice,* or the passages about her in the later chapters. Maybe he skips them when he reads, out of diffidence or out of consideration for William. But it would be better if he could summon up the courage not to suppress them.

26

Naturally Eliza takes an interest in N. and questions T. about her. Consequently, the above-mentioned flashback follows organically from the narrative process. Later on, T. notes in his manuscript that Eliza is the first woman in relation to whom his memory of N. does not create a block.

27

Then I drove out to Point Judith and looked out at the open sea. I remembered the moonlight nights on board the troop trans-

port Samuel Moody. *"The dolphins are attracted by the phos-phorescence of the bow wave," a sailor explained to me, as I was bending over the stern rail during the crossing from Boston to Le Havre one November night after the war was over.*

28

T. eats lunch in a seafood restaurant in Matunuck, then drives slowly back to Providence through autumnal woods and past lakes, returns his car at four o'clock, signs a Diners Club check for twenty-five dollars, and heads for Gardner House, his temporary domicile. On the way, at the corner of College and Benefit streets, he sees the Athenaeum and, finding it open, steps in. Built in 1838, the Athenaeum, one of the oldest private libraries in America, is a small Doric temple, overgrown with ivy.

29

Theodor W. Adorno once said to me that in approaching Proust one sets foot on sacred ground—a rather astonishing meta-phor in the mouth of the always rather timid but never cowardly hero of the *Critical Theory*. What he said of Proust strikes me as applicable to Poe. In any event, I have T. wander about the Athenaeum with such thoughts in mind; it was the scene of one of Poe's amours. The librarian whom he questions about memen-toes of Poe—she shows him the hand-written dedication of *Ulalume*, which appeared anonymously in the December 1847 issue of the *American Review*, to Sarah Helen Whitman—tells him in no uncertain terms that she regards Poe's behavior toward that beautiful, wealthy and respected Providence lady as unspeak-able. Briefly her eyes rest on the narrow, alcovelike niches between the dark mahogany bookshelves that occupy a gallery overlooking the ground floor.

30

The postcard that T. wrote in the Athenaeum and addressed to Bargfeld, Kreis Celle, Haus Nr. 37—*"Can you give me any details about Poe's relations with Mrs. Whitman?"*—is to date his last sign of life. Consequently the Providence police visited everyone living near the library—including the Dorrances—and asked whether on a certain Saturday in October they had noticed a man above middle height, with a pale complexion, gray hair, rimless glasses, and a light-colored raincoat. Under "special remarks," Inspector Osborne added: "A European taking a walk."

31

Eliza promises T. to inquire about the Sarah Helen Whitman episode in Poe's life. Of course I am in doubt whether to have T. include this and other aesthetic digressions in his coded message, but in my opinion T.'s reference to *Ulalume* accounts in part for his becoming the Dorrances' prisoner. *It was night in the lonesome October of my most immemorial year.*

32

After leaving the Athenaeum, I let the smoky-pink sky beguile me, in spite of the cold, into a short stroll down Benefit Street. The white, chocolate-brown, light-blue and copper-red eighteenth- and early-nineteenth-century wooden houses with their classical door frames and gables, their muslin curtains behind coffered windows, and their brick chimneys were just too beautiful. In this street, which looked to me like an ideal corso, I found myself, as I had in all the most attractive parts of upper Providence, totally alone.

33

At the corner of Benefit and Hopkins streets, I caught sight of a house that was not only beautiful, but also mysterious, because the whole of it, including the window and door frames, was painted a red in which black must have been mixed. Even the garden fence was the same color. Whoever lived here had decided to live within a darkly burning monochrome shell.

34

"You see," says Eliza to William, after T. has read them this passage, "I've told you this red repels people." "We only chose this genuine Falunian red," William explained, "because the restorers advised us to. It's a paint that preserves the wood."

35

"It didn't repel me at all," says T. "On the contrary." *I even did something that a New Englander would certainly consider outrageous: I opened the garden gate and went in. Hearing no sound, I started around the house, but stopped to look at the herb garden, which had a sun dial in the middle with the inscription: A garden that might comfort yield.*

36

"You can imagine how frightened we were when we heard you wandering around outside," says Eliza. "We crept up to the window, and I can still hear William saying: 'He looks perfectly respectable.'—'I'm sure he's not from Providence,' I said."

37

Anyone who knows me knows that I don't believe in providence, in so-called fate, but stubbornly insist that every man's life is a mixture of determination and chance. I insert this negative profession of faith in my novel, because I wouldn't want anyone to suspect that I regard my disappearance in a city named Providence, the capital of the smallest state in the Union, as an event of profound symbolic significance. All that can be inferred from the fact that I disappeared in Providence is that I disappeared in Providence.

38

Accordingly, it can be put down only to chance that Eliza Dorrance opens the door and asks T. in to visit the house and join them in a cup of tea. She never saw T. before nor was she expecting him to turn up at five in the afternoon on October 17, 1970. The event is determined by the coldness of the day, the deserted condition of Benefit Street, and a look of connivance exchanged by Eliza and William before Eliza went to the door.

39

Eliza must be in her forties, about five foot six in height, slender (but not excessively so), athletic, clear-eyed, open, and cheerful; her complexion must be very pure and transparent, and she must as a rule wear her hair (what color?) pinned up. In the course of his novel, T.'s libido becomes increasingly concentrated on Eliza. Show that this is not only because T. has no other choice.

40

As I followed Eliza, I remembered how my wife and I had once come face to face with a large Irish manor house, tucked away deep in its park. "If the owner were to open a window now and ask us in," said my wife, "he could commit the perfect murder. No one in the whole world knows we have come to this house on this rainy afternoon on our way from Cork to Limerick."

41

"And yet," Eliza comments on this recollection, "you stepped into our den of murderers without a moment's hesitation." "I must have read too much about American hospitality," T. replies. "Well then," says William, "I'm sure you can't complain on that score."

42

At tea I told the Dorrances about my excursion to the site of Fort Kearney, so giving them a brief sketch of my life. I complained about having to give these academic readings instead of writing—I was just in the right mood for writing, I claimed. I don't know what made me talk about myself so much, possibly Eliza's excellent tea with rum.

43

"Just excuse yourself," said William. "I know Professor Carver well; he won't take it amiss if you call your reading off. No American professor of literature doubts that writing is more important than lecturing."

44

It wasn't until the following morning that we started calling each other by our first names. It never occurred to me to call William and Eliza "Bill" and "Liz."

45

So far the figure of William Dorrance is unclear. What profession should I give him? In any case both Dorrances have inherited money, they are both descended from retired industrialists and live on the income from their capital.

46

William Dorrance is the same age as T., which makes them both about fifteen years older than Eliza. *That evening Eliza wore a dress of thin yellow wool with a brown silk jersey under it.*

47

In the meantime it had grown dark; Eliza had lit the lamp. William said: "I'll show you the house tomorrow, by daylight." This remark aroused no suspicion in me; I merely assumed that I would be welcome to come next day, and, with foreknowledge, I was pleased because of Eliza.

48

Like myself, William was wearing a tweed jacket and gray flannel trousers. But he is not, like me, a pipe smoker. Also he is somewhat taller than I, bony and stringy, with unbespectacled blue eyes (whereas mine are spectacled and brown).

49

For fear that William might regard me as nothing more than a traveling interpreter of myself—I suddenly felt the need of explaining my situation—I said one of my reasons for taking this trip had been to make a little extra money. Calculation of the income of a middlingly well-known writer. With this explanation I unwittingly reinforced the Dorrances in their decision.

50

The Dorrances must not be readers of literature in the usual sense of the word. Nevertheless, T. finds in their house a large collection of fairy tales, legends and myths. Their favorite tales: *The Mine at Falun* (William), *Rip Van Winkle* (Eliza).

51

I was sorry, I said, that I could not invite my hosts to my Monday reading; since they didn't understand German, it would be pointless, they would only be bored. "Your reading," William replied, "will never take place." I looked at him in amazement.

52

Among the Dorrances' motives, I could stress their childlessness. The novel must go into its causes and consequences. Hence, a flashback: the Dorrances' marriage.

53

The strange hypothesis of Isador Coriat and Sigmund Freud concerning the childlessness of Lord and Lady Macbeth. ". . . Macbeth and his wife, both of whom reverse their characters in the course of the drama, were, psychologically speaking, one and the same person: an example of the mythological 'decomposition' which Shakespeare sometimes adopted" (Ernest Jones). Could this theory, which runs counter to all current psychologies of marriage, be applied to the Dorrances?

54

I awoke next morning, Sunday, October 18, 1970, on a kind of army cot, fully dressed and covered with a woolen blanket. Except for my cot, the room was devoid of furniture. The first thing I saw—I must have rolled over on my side in my sleep—was a white-pine floor that had turned gray with age. My wrists were handcuffed. When Eliza came in to see how I was getting along, I said: "If this is a kidnaping, Mrs. Dorrance, I wish to call your attention to the fact that you will find no one willing to pay a ransom for me."

55

"My name is Eliza," she said. Dark early-morning light. She asked me what I would like for breakfast.

56

Maybe the drug (Eliza's tea with rum!) and handcuff motive is silly. Had the Dorrances any need of such crude methods? Mightn't a few words have sufficed to make T. their prisoner?

57

But then the Dorrances would not have been breaking any law. And that would be wrong. The reader must, if he so desires, be able to regard their action as a crime.

58

Besides, drugs and handcuffs are very simple symbols, their significance is immediately apparent to the reader. Most readers tend—and rightly so—to accept the use of such props more readily than disembodied metapsychological dialogue. In a cloak-and-dagger play, cloak and dagger must actually be in evidence.

59

The Dorrances' motives would become intelligible if I succeeded in showing, that is, telling, under what circumstances Eliza Dorrance arrived at the decision to take a prisoner and how she managed to win over her husband as an accomplice. Hence, more about the couple's past. Transposition of analysis into narrative;

narrative is just as true as analysis, but richer in meanings; narrative does not explain, but places the explanation in a setting; narrative does not provide answers but asks questions. All hoary platitudes or rules of thumb, but a writer has to keep them in mind.

60

At breakfast (which we ate together) they removed my handcuffs. In the end they also had to let me take my bath and go to the toilet without them. After that I waited, again confined in steel, to see what they would do with me. I looked out into the garden where the maples were no longer as red and the oaks no longer as yellow as the day before.

61

Why after breakfast did T. let them put the handcuffs back on instead of jumping up and running out of the house? Did William, without a word, set down a pistol on the table beside him? T.'s coded message provides no answer.

62

William kept his promise and showed me the house. Handcuffed, I followed him. At the end of the visit he led me to the room where I was going to live, and left me alone.

63

I have no need to describe the house, because anyone familiar with Providence has guessed long ago that I am using the Stephen Hopkins House, built in 1707, as a model (the red color! Corner of Benefit and Hopkins streets!). Today it is a museum; you can visit it. Stephen Hopkins was one of the signatories of the American Declaration of Independence (1776).

64

For my purposes I merely surround the Stephen Hopkins House with a large garden or small park, because that is where the love scenes between T. and Eliza are to take place. In reality the house has only the herb garden which T. has already mentioned, with its sun dial erected by the American rebel and statesman. Except on the street side, the house is surrounded by the trees of neighboring gardens.

65

They had already adapted the room to my needs. A bed of colonial simplicity, neatly made up with lily-white sheets and army blankets; a large table near one of the windows, on it a sheaf of paper and a typewriter, a rather old Underwood noiseless as I ascertained, and ten well-sharpened pencils in a glass. In one corner, an easy chair and beside it an end table on which lay a package of tobacco—unfortunately a brand I don't smoke—and the Sunday issue of a local newspaper.

66

With some difficulty, I managed to take my pipe out of my jacket pocket, to fill and light it. I sat down in the easy chair and contemplated a still empty bookcase and the pleasantly blue-green striped paper on the pictureless walls. Having assured myself that the windows fronted on the garden and not on the street, I assumed that there would be no point in opening one of them and calling for help.

67

When Eliza knocked, I called "Come in" without getting up. She informed me that my clothes cupboard was outside in the hall. "But it's still empty," she said. "We'll have to buy you a few things. What size collar do you wear?"

68

"Forty-one," I said, "but that won't do you any good." She produced a tape measure, put it around my neck, and took my American measure. Since I was still sitting while she measured my neck, I looked up, from no distance at all, at the upper part of her body which this morning was clothed in a dark-blue blouse.

69

T., who has decided to omit nothing when reading aloud, doesn't dare look at William after acquainting his listeners with this and similar scenes. When T. has finished reading, William only raises technical questions, or goes into problems of a general literary character; his remarks are quite impersonal. Lady Eliza listens graciously to her troubadour's arias.

70

In the afternoon the Dorrances had a call to make and left me alone. They gave me the run of the house, but before leaving cuffed my hands behind my back. I heard them getting into the car and driving off.

71

I went to a second-floor window, looking out over Benefit Street, where there wasn't a soul to be seen. From time to time a car drove by. If a pedestrian had turned up, my only chance of attracting his attention would have been to tap on the windowpane. I tried to open the window, which seemed to be stuck; with my hands chained behind my back I hadn't enough leverage.

72

After a while I gave up. While waiting for the Dorrances to come home, I spent the time standing, walking around, or lying on my stomach on the living room sofa. I wasn't even able to read or turn on the television or pick up the objects that interested me to look at them.

73

Still, it would not have been very hard for T. to pick up some object, an andiron for instance, and smash one of the ground-floor windows. The thin wooden coffering would scarcely have resisted a few kicks. A few minutes later T. would have been free.

74

After supper the Dorrances made me their proposition. I was to remain their prisoner but I would be permitted to write in perfect freedom, with no need to worry about the day-to-day problems and economic considerations, the servitudes, relationships, traditions, and structures that had hitherto circumscribed my life as a writer. I would want for nothing.

75

I asked what they would have done if I hadn't been a writer. "We nabbed somebody once before," said Eliza blandly. "He turned out to be a traveling salesman, so we didn't even take him prisoner, we just let him go." She looked at me and said: "For us you're a godsend."

76

I made my stipulations. They must provide me with two German thesauruses (Dornseiff and Wehrle-Eggers), Kluge's Etymological Dictionary, Heuer's Grammar and the two-volume Encyclopedia of the German Language published in the German Democratic Republic. William carefully noted the titles, and I gave him the address of a bookstore in New York where he could order them. Then they removed my handcuffs.

77

It is safe to assume that the Dorrances did not go calling that Sunday afternoon, but that, sitting in their car at a well-chosen strategic point, they watched the house. If T. had appeared on Benefit Street, it would have been all up with their game. "In that case," Eliza told T. later on, "we would have offered you so much money for your silence that you couldn't have resisted."

78

Consequently, as far as the law was concerned, this is a very mild case of sequestration. A clever lawyer could easily get the

Dorrances acquitted by representing it as a joke. On the other hand, it must be made clear that although T. made no attempt to escape and accepted the Dorrances' proposition, he did not freely choose to be imprisoned, so that his imprisonment is real.

79

Deciding to take advantage of the situation, T. busies himself, as he had long intended to, with the problem of sentence sequences in free association. This activity produces the most astonishing results: for example, he finds himself obliged to move the Wulle Brewery in Stuttgart to Dellbrück, which later, when his pieces are printed in Max Bense's *red* series, elicits an indignant protest from T.'s faithful reader Jürgen Becker of Cologne. At the end of February (1971) he drops this work and starts writing *My Disappearance in Providence*.

80

After the first few readings, the conversation naturally turns to the question of future publication. William, Eliza, and T. all realize that even anonymous publication would reveal T.'s whereabouts. After all, there is only one writer who had disappeared in Providence and is being looked for by the police.

81

In doing the translation necessary for the evening readings, T. consults Eliza; he shows her his English sentences, testing them both for linguistic plausibility and for sound. *When I came to passages hinting at my feelings for Eliza, we read no further; but not for the reasons Dante implied with these words. On such occasions Eliza simply stood up and said she had household chores to do.*

82

When spring came, I spent several hours of the day in the garden. I helped Eliza set out the dahlia tubers and hoed the raspberry patch. I had the impression that she was more interested in efficient gardening than in the beauty of the arrangements.

83

Once when we were standing side by side after tying up a clematis vine and checking over its frail stems, she let me put my arm around her waist. She disposed of the incident with a light, noncommittal kiss, and disappeared into the house. I did not follow her, though I knew William was not at home.

84

William didn't even react to my account of this scene. He merely registered it as though reading a novel. Eliza also behaved as if what she had heard did not concern her personally, passing the tea cups around with no trace of embarrassment.

85

Eliza will question T. about his wife, why they separated, how he met her, whether they have children, and if so whether he occasionally goes from Munich—so T. lives in Munich!—to Berlin to see them. Once again, a part of T.'s story transpires from Eliza's questions. T. is getting a pretty good idea of the structure of his novel.

86

T. dreams that he phones his wife from Tempelhof airport to tell her he has returned from America sooner than planned. Only after he has hung up does it occur to him that the plane he took was lost over the Atlantic. When an airline official informs his wife of the disaster, she says it can't be true, there must be some mistake, because she has just spoken to her husband on the phone.

87

T. will tell Eliza about the poetry seminar he attended with Professor Carver. Thirteen graduate students, among them two blacks. Their assignment: Goethe's revision of two lines in one of his Sesenheim poems. The first version was:

> You went, while I stood looking down
> and followed you with tearful eyes.

In the second, published thirty years later, Goethe had preferred to write:

> I went, while you stood looking down
> and followed me with tearful eyes.

88

I had made an interlinear translation of the two versions for Eliza. She laughed. "Your Goethe must have been a vain man," she said.

89

And then she asked: "How was it with your wife? Did she follow you with tearful eyes?"—And she added, "if ever you leave Providence, I'll make sure you go by the first version."

90

William listens eagerly to T.'s narrative, but he is basically dissatisfied. "It seems strange," he will say one evening, "that living as a prisoner under conditions of the most perfect artistic freedom, conditions that ought to enable you to carry out your most ambitious plans, you confine yourself to a direct treatment of your most immediate preoccupations. You insist on being subjective, it's a pity!"

91

So William wants objective literature. I still haven't managed to define him, but it's gradually becoming clear that he inclines toward the exact sciences. Is he carrying out an experiment?

92

At what point did William's scientific intentions and his wife's —let's say—need of entertainment meet? Hence another flashback. If I avoid the obvious sado-masochistic platitudes, the Dorrances' motives will undoubtedly be my thorniest problem. There can be no *direct* nexus between infantile sexuality and the dream that William and Eliza are trying to realize.

93

In regard to the possible publication of the novel, T. is unable to set the Dorrances' minds at rest, although he promises to preface a statement that would relieve them of all legal responsibility. "It's not that," says William. "The crux of the matter is that we'll have to leave Providence if the story gets out." T. offers to change the names and the scene of action, but he himself doesn't seriously believe in the possibility of substituting Savannah, for instance, for Providence.

94

Though with his choice of the Stephen Hopkins House he has already introduced an element of fiction into the novel! Or could it be that the Dorrances aren't the Dorrances at all? In any case Providence can't be anything but Providence.

95

My desire for Eliza sometimes drove me to leave my door open at night and wait in the darkness: would she come? Maybe she heard the creaking of the door and the ensuing silence. The room where Eliza and William slept was on the same landing.

96

I go out for the first time: to the cigar store. Since the objects I was obliged to leave at Gardner House included my pipes and since those procured for me by William were not to my taste, I insisted on buying a few myself. So one morning in May I made my way to the cigar store at the corner of Thayer and Waterman streets, deliberately taking the route through the campus and stopping from time to time to watch the comings and goings of the students. But I was not recognized.

97

Maybe it was my beard that prevented any of the students from recognizing me. Yes, during the winter I've grown a beard, though I keep it close-clipped. Solemn and bearded, I spend my afternoons in the living room of the dark-red house, reading the paper, watching TV, or listening to the brooding cadences of Paul Gonsalves's tenor saxophone in "Mood Indigo" or "Come Sunday," my favorites in the Dorrance discothèque.

98

Sometimes Eliza comes in, stands beside me and rests her hand lightly on my shoulder. She has just come from the tennis courts in Blackstone Park and is still somewhat overheated. She uses some sort of perfume.

99

"Eliza," I say without turning around. "What?" she asks in her dark voice in which—as I have already written—warmth and mockery are combined. "Nothing," I say.

100

All the same I regard it as most unlikely that Eliza will resist me in the long run. I am one of those who hold that no woman will pass up an opportunity to live with two men instead of one if it presents itself, and since I am not physically unattractive to Eliza . . . But she hesitates, because she thinks I won't be her prisoner any more if she gives in.

101

When the Dorrances have visitors, they have to ask T. to go to his room. They own a summer house on the coast of Cape Cod. "It's off by itself," she says. "But there it won't matter if you're seen with us."

102

In Cape Cod I worked very well. Toward noon I had to close the shutters, because the dunes and the sea began to shimmer. Then I could hear the soft conversation of my wardens, who were sitting down below in the shadow of the veranda: Maecenas and his wife.

103

Now and then T. considers writing his novel from William's point of view. Then it would become the story of a scientific experiment: William's attempt to create conditions of absolute, abstract freedom. The working title of this version, which T. finally rejects, is: "An American Dream."

104

In the warm moonlight nights on the Cape we went swimming in the nude—Eliza's idea. Once as we lay side by side in the dunes, I put my hand between Eliza's thighs. She seemed to like it, for she did not push my hand away, and William expressed no objection.

105

T. has now completed the planning of his novel. A first rough outline shows the following structure:
1. Trip to the U.S.A.
2. Fort Kearney

3. Memories of N. $=$ $=$ of the war
    (First Flashback)
4. Walk through Providence
5. Disappearance in Providence
6. The Dorrances' motives
    (Second Flashback)
7. Experience in captivity
8. The Dorrances' motives II
    (Third Flashback)
9. Experience in captivity II
10. T.'s memory of his wife $=$ of the postwar period
    (Fourth Flashback)
11. Experience in captivity III
12. The Dorrances' motives III
    (Fifth Flashback)
13. Experience in captivity IV
14. Cape Cod
15. Ending.

As usual before writing a novel, T. was exasperated at the thought that such an outline looked like an attempt to confine him to linear narrative and gave no idea of the work involved in blending the various time levels into a single time, the time of the novel.

106

I shall have T. postpone his decision concerning the perspective of his story. Should I make him the "I" of the novel or make him a narrated narrator? Should I make sure that no one accuses me of having invented him and breathed life into him like a God? In other words, should I mask him as *I*, or frankly set him down as *him*, trusting that my readers will not endow me with divine attributes merely because I have used the third person singular?

107

As to the ending, that stumbling block of every novel, T. knows this time what he wants. (Unlike a short story or long short story, a novel should not have a so-called open ending.) The ending will force him to decide whether T. is to write his novel in the Dorrances' house—he thinks it will take two or three years—or in freedom.

108

And so one day T. puts his outline along with a few sample passages into a large orange envelope he has found in William's desk and writes on it: *To whom it may concern.* Of course it would have been more reasonable, and fairer to the Dorrances, if he had simply addressed it to a publisher and taken it to the post office on Kennedy Plaza. But since he is a writer, he relishes the inevitable consequences of his mystification: the police jeeps pulling up to the Stephen Hopkins House, the television trucks, the hearings, the press reports, the interviews, the pictures, in short, the scandal.

109

The only hitch to this plan is that the police—since T. has taken the Stephen Hopkins House as his model for the Dorrances' residence—will search that museum in vain. Consequently T. will have to be somewhere else—maybe in Savannah after all? It is only logical, Roland Barthes will observe in commenting on the incident in a structuralist periodical, that a novelist should make use of a museum for his disappearance.

110

After our return from Cape Cod I have been taking frequent walks in this lovely upper Providence, which in its way is just as self-contained and full of meaning as Dinkelsbühl or San Gimignano. At this stage I can hardly speak of imprisonment. Sometimes, when Eliza hears me leaving the house, she makes a feeble attempt to remind me that I am a prisoner by calling out: "Be careful—somebody might recognize you!"

++

The Cherries of Freedom

++

Deserters are my last remaining hope.

André Gide, *Journal*, May 11, 1941

The Invisible Course

THE PARK AT SCHLEISSHEIM

I don't remember exactly at what time of year the Munich Soviet Republic fell. It would be easy to find out. In the spring, I think. I believe—you mean you think, K. would say, we can't believe in anything but God—all right, I think it was a dark, gloomy spring day when they led long columns of people down Leonrodstrasse on their way to the Oberwiesenfeld where, in the big courtyards of the Bavaria Trucking Company, they were lined up against the garage walls and shot. The ones who were going to be shot had their hands up; because their arms were tired they let their hands curve limply over their heads or gripped one wrist with the other hand. Long columns, irregularly grouped. More and more of them. The others, the men who were going to shoot them, held their rifles at the ready. I looked on from the balcony of our apartment in one of the side streets, but at the time I was too young to understand. "Riff-raff," I heard my father say behind me, for the Soviet Republic was at an end. Then he pulled me away from the window, maybe because he felt the horror of it, maybe because a busybody down in the street had shouted: "Shut your windows! There's going to be shooting!" My five-year-old eyes looked down over the balcony railing, but I didn't know these people were being taken away to be shot, I didn't realize that I'd never get to know any of them. I didn't find out until later, when I was maybe fourteen or fifteen, it must have been about 1928. And then, I remember, what interested me most was trying to figure out how somebody felt who was going to shoot somebody else. Not in anger —no, all the way down this long suburban street on a dark spring day, he was with the other man, he had time to think that when they reached the end of the street he was going to snuff out this other man's life. Anger doesn't last that long. Then what is it that lasts the whole length of a street? The stupidity of self-righteousness? The need to carry out orders? The effects of propaganda? The delusion that some people are mere riff-raff? The pressure of the leveled rifle, which demands to be fired? Or the image of a sagging body that has already inscribed itself on the retina?

In any case I fail to understand why the man with the rifle doesn't stop to light a cigarette, and in the two seconds it takes his match to flare up and go out, whisper to his fellow man, waiting with upraised hands for the death march to reach its destination: "Over there—that street, first doorway! Beat it!"

I admit that in those days, while I was getting ready for my confirmation, such thoughts didn't trouble me very often. The rest of the time my childhood ran off like clockwork. Whenever I think about it, I'm overpowered by the boredom that held me in its grip while I was growing up amid the characterless façades of the middle-class apartment houses of Munich-Neuhausen. Through the glasses that I wore even then, I looked out on a landscape of colorless house fronts, dead drillgrounds, and the red brick walls of barracks. Lacherschmied Field was parched in the summertime, the cries of football players rose faintly to the room in which I sat listlessly over my homework. To this day, when I'm in Munich, I can't resist the temptation of taking the streetcar to Albrechstrasse and, strolling through the streets of my childhood, recapitulate the feeling of listless waiting that surrounded me here as a boy. In the entrance hall of the Wittelsbacher *Gymnasium* there was nothing to interest me but the aquariums that had been placed in the south windows, so that the sun shone through the green water and the gold of the fishes' bodies: I looked forward to Professor Burckhardt's natural history class, not because I was interested in the subject, but because I was drawn to this red-haired, white-skinned man, whose pale-blue eyes, sheltered by thick glasses and bushy white brows, shot irritated glances at the class before he embarked on the day's lesson. But the sensitive intelligence of Burckhardt's teaching was only an interlude in a world that filled me with disgust. I was dismissed from the *Gymnasium* in the middle of the third form; my marks in German and history were excellent, but I have never been able to learn a language by grammatical rules or to understand mathematics beyond the simplest arithmetic, any more than I am capable of following a philosophical train of thought expressed in conceptual terms. The glaring discrepancy between my A in German and my D in Greek convinced my teachers, with their strictly scholastic habits of thought, to suppose that I was willing to learn only what I wanted to learn. It would have been closer to the truth to say that I didn't want to "learn" anything at all; what I wanted was to see, to feel, and to understand.

About a year before leaving the *Gymnasium*, I was confirmed at the Lutheran Christus-Kirche in Munich-Neuhausen. Like all the official ceremonies I have lived through since then, confirmation was for me a thoroughly unpleasant business. As I led the alphabetically ordered procession through the black-clad congregation to the candle-spluttering altar, I tried frantically to summon up a festive mood. I didn't succeed. I knew very little about the sacrament in which I was going to partake, and my response to the pious emotion that seemed to ooze at me from the onlookers was indifference tinged with contempt. Not even when Pastor Johannes Kreppel put the wafer on my tongue and raised the cup to my lips did I experience anything more than the pure mechanics of the act.

This seems all the more astonishing when I recall that I had always looked on Pastor Kreppel, that apostle of the Evangelical diaspora, as a venerable and imposing figure. He was of less than medium height; his light skin had the transparency of wax, a sure sign of spiritual distinction and frail health, and indeed Pastor Kreppel died of pneumonia at the age of fifty; yet his eyes sparkled with life and his features expressed all the firmness of his Protestant faith. He met the most essential requirement of his religion, which stands and falls with the character of the man who professes it. The Protestant revolution set out to destroy a hierarchy that had lost all inner meaning and by giving the sermon a central position in the divine service elevated the office of priest to the highest personal dignity. Later on, I left the Lutheran church and have not joined any other. Have I thus annulled the sacrament of baptism? That is a question which only my own conscience can answer.

It occurs to me as I write that in the last paragraphs I have departed from the direct narrative style I began with, and veered toward the more leisurely reflection, the constructed periods and ele-

gant harmonics, of older schools. Perhaps because I was describing
a period of boredom? I had better make a fresh start.

Pastor Kreppel was not only a pious man but a nationalist as
well. That no doubt is what won the admiration of my father,
who, though religious, was first and foremost a nationalist. My father had the black hair, the aquiline nose, the sparkling gold-
rimmed glasses, and the red, easily inflamed skin of a volatile
man. Though engaged in a civilian occupation—he operated a
small insurance and real estate agency so incompetently that the
family became more and more heavily indebted—regarded himself in reality as the reserve captain he had become when, covered
with medals and wounds, he had returned to Munich from his infantry position in the Vosges Mountains. The moment he set foot
on the station platform, his epaulets had been torn off by revolutionaries. He went home a defeated hero and a dishonored one as
well, and from then on led a semi-military life in organizations
named "Reich War Banner" or "German Renewal." A man who
has stormed the Hartmannsweilerkopf is unlikely to understand
that the great historical decisions are not made in company command posts.

Time and again he sallied forth and returned in defeat. I still
remember the morning when he came home from the turmoil of
the Hitler putsch—after a brief period in jail. That was in 1923.
He became an unquestioning supporter of General Ludendorff.
One night he took me with him to a torchlight parade in honor of
the general. The uniformed men assembled in a wood on the
banks of the Isar and marched in long columns to a square not far
from Ludendorff's house. There they stood for a long time in formation. Now and then the silence was shattered by cries of command. The red and yellow flames of the torches transformed the
night and the treetops into a fist that held the demonstrators in
its grip. I stood at attention beside my father as Ludendorff
passed slowly before us, stopping now and then to exchange a few
words with one of the men. His face with its broad planes made
me think of a lion carved in stone, but at the same time his light-
colored skin and white hair (he was hatless) suggested thought
and sensibility. You had a feeling that for him displacing a division on the map was something more than a technical operation.

This man—who alone of all those on the square was wearing civilian clothes—was an artist of the battlefield.

As my father's political fever mounted, his diabetes got worse and his business foundered. A piece of shrapnel he was still carrying about in his leg began to fester; the wound refused to close, and he was confined to his bed. From my fourteenth to sixteenth year, I watched my father die. I saw the toes of his right foot turn black with gangrene and saw him being taken away to the hospital, where his right leg was amputated. Once again he returned in defeat to our lower-middle-class apartment, where our poverty had become palpable. When I heard the tapping of his crutches, I fled to another room; I didn't want to listen to his nationalist speeches.

I did most of the shopping; we were charging our food by then. One day as I turned into our street, I saw my father hobbling out of the house on his crutches. I saw his loneliness. He stood outside the door, looking irresolutely into space; he didn't notice me. There was something unbearably tragic in his look; I knew he had no money and didn't know where to go. The poor man's friends had dropped him, and we too, his family, had already forsaken him in spirit. He knew there were times when my mother could hardly bear to go on living and that my brother and I didn't share his political opinions. His life was shattered, all his plans had gone wrong, and death had taken root in his body. At that moment, when he thought himself unobserved, his proud, manly face was full of desolation, his eyes gazed sightless past the smooth asphalt of the street into the abyss of the years. His shoulders bent forward over his crutches, he stared at the board fence of the coal dealer across the way; he knew he didn't have a pfennig in his pocket.

Overpowered by the sight, I ran to give him a hand, to help him; I knew that this was one of his first attempts to walk after his amputation. But I was too late. I was still running when I saw him turn deathly pale, drop his crutches, and fall to the pavement. He lay very still, in a deep faint. His face was waxen yellow; the sadness had gone out of it, and only exhaustion remained; it was the face of a man who had destroyed himself by giving himself heart and soul to a political idea. My father had no money because he had made the defeat of Germany his own.

He never recovered from that fall. His leg stump hadn't healed properly; the wound broke open and incurable gangrene set in. His death agony, in which excruciating pain alternated with morphine delirium, went on for two years. At night, in the midst of his desperate moans, I often heard him pray. He prayed in the words of the old hymn: "O Haupt voll Blut und Wunden," or he would sing the melody from the St. Matthew Passion in a harsh voice tinged with unbearable torment. In those moments Pastor Johannes Kreppel won out over General Ludendorff in my father's heart. Then I heard my mother turn on the light, get out of bed, and prepare one more morphine injection. My father was the kind of man who could perfectly well have put himself out of his misery. But then he wouldn't have died as a "hundred per cent war invalid," to use the language of the welfare office, and my mother wouldn't have been entitled to a pension. So he chose to be tortured to death under the scourge of a grain of sugar that his blood was unable to eliminate.

As for me, I escaped whenever I had time. I often took my bike and rode out to Schloss Schleissheim, which was only an hour from Neuhausen. I could have gone to Nymphenburg, which was a good deal nearer, but preferred Schleissheim. There were never many people. The castle, which was nothing more than a large, run-down but still festive-looking house, rose white above trees of a Bavarian village square. You turned left and entered the park through a gate in the iron fence.

No comparison, of course, with the view I was to enjoy later on from the terrace in Versailles, where beyond the ponds and silken lawns of the foreground the whole of France lay at the king's feet. Here there was nothing but a moderate-sized flower garden, curved petunia borders, and the broad allée with its ancient trees and oak and boxwood hedges, which ran parallel to the moat and led to the little belvedere at the neglected far end of the park, a mere pavilion, with nothing in it except for a few dark paintings of hunting scenes. Strange to say, that secluded park with its white *Schloss* and modest flowerbeds gave me a feeling of enchanted infinity. There sitting on a bench, I found what I looked for at the Pinakothek on Sunday mornings (when the admission was free), in the green gloss of El Greco's "Madonna," in the gray and pink of a Filippino Lippi "Annunciation," in Canaletto's

crystal-clear dream-Venice—the perfume of art. The pearly whiteness of the *Schloss* entered into me as I read Verlaine or Rim-
baud. I dreamed again of the unknown woman who had so often
stood before me in my dreams, the flowers taught me the vowels
—A black, E white, I red, U green, O blue. I was on my way to becoming, as they say, a self-educated man.

Forgetting those who had died in the revolution, the boredom
of Neuhausen, the misery of school, my declassed petit-bourgeois
family, even my father's groans, I began my own life, entering the
park of literature and aesthetics through the gates of puberty and
Schlossheim Castle.

SPILT BEER

Not long ago I saw one of those Italian movies (*Neo-Verismo*) and had a vision of what our life will be like. Mostly at night, improvised rooms, bricks, quick fires made from wood scraps, wide, tattered jackets, shawls, small pistols, a battered gramophone, Bartok's *Concerto for Strings, Percussion and Celesta,* and Duke Ellington's "East St. Louis Doodle Doo" (a Negro whistling as he walks through the St. Louis slums at night). Jerry, the ten-year-old, stands guard, Lisa opens a can of milk from the latest burglary and prepares a bottle for the ragged but clean little baby in the corner. Luxury: when you break into a house with a library in it, you take one or two books, maybe Hemingway's *Death in the Afternoon* and Huizinga's *Waning of the Middle Ages,* you don't bother with the rest. Love: a glance or two suffice for recognition, but then tenderness, the best things in life are Topas's chestnut-brown hair and her face in the light of the oil lamp, and walking hand and hand with her, gazing at the church of Saint-Julien-le-Pauvre, still relatively upright and so charming in its nest of tumble-down buildings. In general: an alliance between sensitive souls and tough underworld intelligence—a silent, anarchistic free corps. The necessity even now of forming cells in preparation for things to come. "Consider the darkness and the great cold in the valley of lamentation."

Ah, Odysseus lashed to the mast, listening to the song of the sirens. And we, on our odyssey through the century, surrounded by the music of heart-shattering ideologies. The height of treason: to let yourself be untied.

Stick to the mast, through the night of rain and catcalls. . . .

Some beer had been spilt, it made a puddle on the dark-brown table top. I was careful not to get the *Red Flag* I was reading wet. The signs on the walls advertised Paulanerbräu. The comrades were sitting around the table, talking in an undertone and listening to the sounds from the street.

I didn't like beer puddles; they had no connection with the neat volumes of Lenin and Upton Sinclair that I bought every month when I had made a bit of money. It was depressing to sit here waiting. Heini Suderland, who was then of the Neuhausen section of the CPG and a member of the district committee, had stopped playing *Red Wedding* on the piano. He was reading a pamphlet, holding it up to his half-blind eyes. The light in the Volkartshof tavern was dismal. Most of the comrades were badly dressed, but they had good faces and each one had his own character. I had just finished reading Lenin's *Materialism and Empirocriticism*; everything was perfectly clear to me: motion was mere matter and there was no God. Everything fitted into the picture except the beer puddle and this dismal waiting.

When the door opened, a gust of cold air blew in. By then, early in the winter of 1933, we were almost illegal. Six months after my father's death I had joined the Young Communist League. While he was still alive, I had kept Münzenberg's excellently turned-out *Workers' Illustrated* hidden under my mattress. I went into Communism with the eager delight of one setting foot for the first time on a virgin continent. To me it was something absolutely new and different; here I breathed in the wild fragrance of life. Communism helped me free myself from my petit-bourgeois surroundings. The word revolution fascinated me. With the speed of sudden illumination I swung from my father's nationalist doctrines to the ideas of socialism, the love of mankind, the liberation of the oppressed, international solidarity, and militant defeatism. It began, as I say, with the *Workers' Illustrated*, which I bought at newstands, and Upton Sinclair's novels, which I ordered through the publishing house where I went to work as an apprentice after leaving the *Gymnasium*. My reading matter plunged me into a bath of utopia; I believed that man could be changed and the world made better through rational acts of will. But in reconnoitering the new terrain, I came to see, if only vaguely, that the purely rational and humanitarian arguments for socialism put forward in the West by liberals such as Rolland, Barbusse, and Sinclair were superficial. I dimly perceived what had happened when, drawing on Hegel, Marx and Lenin replaced mechanistic by dialectical thinking. My brother, who was physically and in every other respect very different from me, dreamed of a synthesis of "Prussianism and socialism," of the German and Russian spirit. He was one of those young activists who knew every word of Karl Radek by heart, who rejected all compromise, called for total solutions, and failed in their sociological ignorance to suspect that their radical formulas would provide the petit-bourgeois masses with the slogans and methods of their own simplist revolution.

But I was proud of my intellect and its power to draw distinctions with passionate coldness. I located the one Communist bookstore in Munich, a small shop on Humboldtstrasse. There I bought on credit, the numerous theoretical works and periodicals of the Third International, and made my first Communist acquaintances. I had no further need to be convinced, my mind was already made up. I merely confirmed my convictions by immersing myself in Varga's dry-as-dust writings on economics, Bukharin's *Dialectical Materialism*, and the decisions of the Central Committee. My teachers at the *Gymnasium* would have been amazed to see how receptive I had suddenly become to scientific method. But if this science had been mere science, it would not have attracted me. My tactile sense was stimulated; my whole nervous system responded to the fascination of a new, realistic scholasticism imbued with the spirit of the revolution.

I became a party functionary. At the age of eighteen, despite my petit-bourgeois origin, I became organizer of the South Bavarian Young Communist League.

I was full of hope. Exactly what I hoped for, I don't remember. Like millions of others in those years of world economic crisis, I was unemployed, but I wasn't inactive for a moment. Chalky-pale, my comrades and I left the dark back rooms where we mimeographed our leaflets and stepped out into the warmth of summer days. Our conferences and meetings were endless, but the owners of the taverns where we held them were themselves party members and let us sit there all day, ordering no more than a pint of beer and eating our own bread. How much better our speeches and debates must have been than the reality we created! For around us the world grew darker and darker. Already the shadow of defeat was creeping up on us. At meetings of the district committee I was often overcome by melancholy. I looked at these men who, while discussing the practical business of the day—meetings, demonstrations, strike agitation, leaflets—expounded acute and profound analyses of the situation. If I had been gifted with second sight I would have seen the proletarian death that the tubercular city councilor, a former shoemaker, spat into his little bottle after a violent coughing fit; or the hostage's eye-for-an-eye death that would send the former lathe operator and then party secretary Josef Götz to the isolation cells of Dachau after Hans Beimler, the party organizer, escaped from the camp. But now Beimler sat among us with his hard machinist's face, suspecting no more than I did the soldier's and revolutionary's death, spewed from a Moroccan machine gun, that would overtake him some years later as commander of the Thaelmann Brigade in Madrid. We sat on the hard chairs of the party bureau in a wretched building on a courtyard off Ringseisstrasse in Munich, conversing in soft, deliberately passionless voices, in a jargon charged with the cold passion, which hardly anyone but ourselves could understand: Lenin had created a type, and to that type we belonged. For the small, isolated Bavarian party, far from the struggles of the Berlin central committee, had remained a Leninist party of the purest water.

At the age of seventeen I came in contact with workers. The intelligence they emanated was such that to this day when I see a dough-faced businessman in a double-breasted suit sluggishly grinding what he calls ideas between his teeth, I am suddenly reminded of Hans Beimler's frayed leather jacket.

But what happened wasn't the revolution. We stared as though hypnotized into the cruel cobra eyes of defeat. That afternoon we were waiting for a rally that the SA had announced. We ourselves hadn't staged a demonstration in a long time. For a while there had been short illegal shock demonstrations, but the Central Committee had forbidden them as "sectarian." I was surprised when Gebhard Jiru poked me in the ribs and asked:

"What do you say we do something?"

I understood him immediately. Jiru was a Czech but spoke Bavarian like the rest of us. Dark-haired, well educated, shrewd, and lively, he was the political leader of our youth organization. We knew each other well.

"We're not supposed to," I said.

"Go on, what difference does it make?" We couldn't stand the inactivity any more.

We notified the boys and the two or three girls in whispers. At a signal we all ran out, formed ranks of three, and marched down the street, waving a red flag and shouting slogans such as: "Workers, fight the November decrees!" "Join the CPG, the party of the working class!" and "Down with the Hitler Fascists!" In about ten minutes we heard the wailing of police sirens, and we scattered.

I see myself panting in some doorway. The earth had swallowed us up and the Brüning-Papen police didn't succeed in arresting anybody. Practice in evading the police is an indispensable preparation for the world of the future. Familiarity with the intricacies of house entrances and the layout of factory yards, the art of disappearing in stairwells, the use of the cover provided by parks, can be a matter of life and death.

But when we got back to the tavern half an hour later, Suderland said reproachfully in his muffled voice: "I don't want any more of this monkey business." And added: "You haven't got a mass base."

"At least we showed 'em we're still here," said Gebhard Jiru.

"But you're only endangering the comrades," said Suderland quietly, without much conviction. We said nothing: none of us realized that the danger was not in those dark streets where we moved like hunted animals. Gebhard himself didn't know the answer yet, though he too, like Comrade Suderland, was to die in Dachau later on.

We sat some more and ordered beer. When the SA attacked us, we'd fight. But only a few of us had really fought, physically, I mean. I discussed the Hegelian dialectic with Schmeller, a music student. The formula thesis-antithesis-synthesis was easy to understand. One need only adduce the example of the egg. Armed uprising was the bursting of the eggshell.

Suddenly it seemed quite clear to me that we would never again sit so calmly in the Volkartshof, with its Paulanerbräu posters on the walls. Never again would Suderland explain the latest decisions of the Central Committee, or the more eloquent functionaries stand up and speak, one after the other. Children were coming to the outside bar with pitchers in which to take home beer for supper. While outside the cold winter wind blew around the corners of the working-class houses, I read tidings of death and loneliness in puddles of spilled beer. But I was still waiting for a herald who would proclaim aloud that now we would fight in earnest.

At that moment we heard hurried steps outside; the door opened and Bertsch appeared. We jumped up; Long Hans Bertsch's face was covered with blood. "The SA!" he shouted. He had a head wound and the blood was flowing down over his gray, threadbare winter coat. Bischoff, who'd had a good deal of beer— he was said to be the district leader of the illegal Red Front fighters—yelled: "Follow me!" A few of the men took iron rods and brass knuckles from their coat pockets and ran out into the street with him, though Suderland shouted: "Don't move!" Bertsch was a metal worker, he'd been unemployed for two years. He stood slumped over the bar. His face was chalk-white and blood-red. It was a dark, dingy room with beer puddles on the tables, a workers' tavern in Munich and headquarters of a Communist unit. Before we rushed to Bertsch's help, his eyes seemed to look through us at the windows, behind which night was falling on the streets of the years. It was the same look I had seen in my father's eyes when leaning on his crutches he had stood for a while irresolute outside the house door, before collapsing.

Did I still make attempts at escape as I had then, on days when my father and Neuhausen were more than I could bear? I worked occasionally for the agency that distributed the Communist press. I gave my mother the money but kept two or three marks for myself. Thus provided, I packed my knapsack and started off on my bicycle. To the Kesselberg road, for instance. Behind it lay the Karwendel range. I rode on along the foaming light-green Isar, where above Wallgau rose enormous limestone cliffs, glittering painfully under the baking blue sky. On those trips, which I always took alone, I came awake to the possibilities of life, aware that behind the life I was living just then a thousand other lives were waiting for me. I reached Mittenwald in the rosy half-shade of evening, the mountainside that rose from the meadows glowed in the setting sun. There I slept. In the morning I climbed the steep wooded slope. When I came out of the woods, I was on the talus of the western Karwendel peak. A boy of seventeen. How long does a man live? Maybe thirty, fifty, seventy years. In that time I'd have to see jungles and deserts; I'd have to see the Himalayas from Darjeeling and the towers of Manhattan. Why else had I been born into the world? I sat down on a gray stone and looked down into the Bavarian Valley and the receding shadows of the mountains. Silence except for the shouts of mountain climbers on the Zwölferspitze. To go away, I thought while rummaging in my knapsack for bread, farther and farther away, to leave everything behind, to visit new mountains and plains, and the ocean, which I'd never seen.

But that night, with the white moonlit mountain wall behind me, I rode back to Munich and the party.

FISTS IN MY POCKETS

The masses in the streets around the Munich Trade Union House on a day in March 1933—something in me always rebels against the word "masses," because I suspect there's no such thing. Despite all efforts to define it, "masses" is merely a word, taken from the jargon of conservatism. When I say: "the masses," I see myself alone in their midst; my mind hovers over them, my lips curl in a smile of contemptuous wisdom. Yet if they exist, I'm a part of them. A few years later, on November 9, I was standing on Briennerstrasse in Munich when Adolf Hitler drove by at the head of a column of cars, on his way to Odeonsplatz from the headquarters of his Blood Order. His path was lined with human walls, cheers spawned cheers, and when I saw his white, sponge-like face with the black forelock and cowardly, treacherous smile, the face of a pale, bedraggled sewer rat, I too opened my mouth and shouted: "Heil!" When the crowd dispersed, when I was an individual again, with space around me, I thought—and I'm still of that opinion: you've just cheered a sewer rat. But then I managed to stroll around Lenbachplatz and lose myself in the windows of the bookstores and antique shops, to get back into my real life and be alone.

For those who like to talk about the "masses," I have yet another story; let them draw their arrogant and contemptible inferences. On that day in March 1933, when the Trade-Union House was occupied by the SA, the streets around the building were crowded with workers. I don't know who had mobilized them; possibly the shop committees. Or perhaps they had come spontaneously, in response to the rumor that was going around the relief offices. They stood there in silence, taking up the whole sidewalk. From time to time a column of SA men marched past in the roadway. Not a sound could be heard from the crowd; they seemed to

be waiting for something. Hours passed. Fewer and fewer of the
enemy came by. In the gray light of the March afternoon we
looked out at the empty roadway. Then an SA man on a motorcycle approached from the direction of the Trade-Union House. He
was wearing a brown shirt, black riding breeches, and a black
crash helmet. For some reason he suddenly lost control of his motorcycle, skidded, and fell to the ground with his machine.

That would have been the moment for an uprising that might
have given Germany another face. I stood with my arms pressed
against my body and felt my fists clenching. One little gesture,
one single shout would have set us all in motion: a hundred fists
would have rained down on the SA man, the workers would have
stormed the occupied building, rifles would have barked, bodies
would have fallen, but doors and windows would have been shattered, and the end would have been conquest, victory, a successful
action. Of course it would have been a small victory, a quickly ob-
literated conquest, soon blown away by the hurricane of defeat—
but it would have sufficed to transform the coup d'état into a
bloodbath visible to all and destroy the semblance of "law and
order."

But I didn't shout. Nor did anyone else. The SA man stood up,
brushed the dust off his clothes, and set up his motorcycle. He
looked it over; it was still in working order. He straddled it and
stepped on the starter; the engine sprang to life and slowly he
rode down the street. You couldn't tell by his face whether he had
any inkling of the threat that had faced him in those moments.
That was a signal; we dispersed. Each of us was alone again.
There were no masses. There may have been masses at some time
in the past, collectively directed phalanxes of the will, tidal waves
of history, the raw material of uprisings, the seething lava of revolution. But the appeals of history have gone up in smoke. Nothing
remains but individuals, occasionally compressed into crowds by
chance or coercion, momentarily subject to psychotic states of
jubilation or fatalism, but then returning home alone, sitting in
rooms, listening to the radio, the clatter of dishes, the wailing of
sirens, praying or silent as the bombs crash down, sensing the
timelessness of history, thrown back on the fear that they must
bear alone, that no one can relieve us of.

That night the radio broadcasted the news of the Reichstag

Fire and Goering's speech announcing "stern measures." I was standing in the street with Jiru and a few others, talking about what we should do.

"I'm not going home," said Jiru.

"I'll take my chances," I said.

Jiru shrugged his shoulders. "They'll come in the morning!" We all knew it. He didn't tell me to hide. We'd been talking about illegality for years; now it had hit us like a bolt from the blue. We had no arms. The Young Communist League had some thousand members in Munich. Tightly organized, supplemented by party cadres, and suitably armed, we could have turned Munich into an inferno in two hours. I'm accusing no one. We were the victims of the deterministic philosophy that denies freedom of the will. We talked and talked about not having a mass base, and it never dawned on us that the workers would have followed us if we had resolved to act. The enemy marched. We waited for the order to take action. No, we didn't even wait; we knew the party wouldn't issue any order. Not the Communist Party, not the Social Democratic Party, no one. The republic had long been dying, now it was dead. It had died because the bourgeois center had let the enemy dictate its topics of conversation, and because the Social Democrats had debated with the bourgeois center about the enemy's arguments. Above all, it died because the Communist Party denied freedom of the will, the freedom of human thought, man's capacity for choice. No one could elucidate the laws of dialectics as brilliantly as the Central Committee of the Communist International. Its historical forecasts had the precision of clockwork. But no one was as incapable as the Communist leadership of recognizing that the dialectic of history is made by human beings.

Of all political movements none is more penetrating in analysis and more pathetic in action than Marxism. At the crucial moment, the Marxist continues to eye himself in the mirror to see if his action is "correct," if it's consonant with the laws established and handed down by the Central Committee. True action calls for the spontaneity that brushes aside old lessons and lifeless rules, that overflows all barriers and creates new history. The Communist Party has chosen the opposite course, fixating its con-

sciousness on bureaucracy and terror, transcending all consciousness in a cold dream of power.

Late in the night of March 7, 1933, on Kaufingerstrasse in
Munich, surrounded by the battle songs of the SA, we lived the
death agony of the party we had joined because we thought it was
spontaneous, free, vital, and revolutionary. At that time we had
no way of knowing that the party which would later rise from its
ashes would be a very different one: endowed with the enemy's
guile, but still without his free will. (Nor did we foresee that the
enemy too would be defeated because he curtailed freedom; not
ours—that is not what defeated him—but his own freedom,
which it confined to "Aryan man" and hedged about with biologi-
cal laws.)

Then we shook hands and I went home. I never saw him again.
I slept a few hours and woke up with a start at about six in the
morning when the police rang the bell and pounded on the door.
While I went to open, my mother threw the membership lists of
the youth organization in the stove. They found nothing of any
importance. They confiscated some of my books. With a glance at
my little white bookcase, the inspector shook his head and said:
"How can an educated man be a Communist!"

I felt obliged to say something and was winding up for a little
speech when the inspector, not one of the newly appointed National Socialists but a long-time servant of the Republic, said:
"Keep your trap shut or I'll brain you!"

One on either side of me, the inspector and a uniformed policeman led me through the morning darkness to the police station. I
accuse no one. Though I was organizer of the Young Communist
League, I had not provided myself with a place to hide. I was very
young, I find some justification in that. None of us youngsters had
given any thought to borders. We had never been outside Germany. Absurd as it may sound today, the idea of escaping abroad
never entered our heads. We let ourselves be caught like so many
rabbits.

My piddling three months in the concentration camp was nothing compared to the twelve years many of my comrades spent
behind the barbed wire. In May 1933, I was released from
Dachau; my mother had besieged the Gestapo with my father's
testimonials, and in recognition of his services to the nationalist

cause, they had let me go. When I was arrested again six months later, my mother's charm and determination—she has the irresistible social grace of an Austrian woman raised under the old monarchy—saved my life. In September 1933, a secret Communist printing press was discovered; I had nothing to do with it, but my name figured on the raiders' list. My illegal party work had been confined to receiving the couriers sent to Munich by the Central Committee and directing them to a secret address of which I had been circumspectly informed, through intermediaries.

As I lay on a wooden bunk in a large, stinking, overcrowded cell at police headquarters, in the hours after my second arrest, I was taken with a fear I had never known during my months in Dachau. There were some twenty or thirty men in the cell; no one spoke much; a few had been brought in from Dachau for questioning. They were uncommunicative when I asked them what the camp was like these days. One of them asked me: "Is this your second time?" When I nodded, he said: "You can expect the worst!" I withdrew from the group, I didn't feel like talking or listening to anyone. I was terrified. I lay on my bunk and prayed.

I thought of my days in Dachau. I saw the long cement barracks; sometimes after roll call SS man Waldbauer had come in to pick up the letters he secretly mailed for us. He told us not to worry, things wouldn't be so bad. That was before Willi Franz, tall, lean and hard as a rock, a famous mountain climber, hanged himself. He played chess so badly that I beat him without difficulty. We always put the board on a stump outside the barracks. One morning they shaved our heads. That was one up for the pessimists who said we were in for a long time. A young Jewish comrade had been barbered in a different style; through his thick black hair they had shaved three stripes from his forehead to the back of his head. We looked at each other's bald heads and teased each other. We hadn't understood our situation yet.

After they shaved our hair, I remember SS man Steinbrenner made us goose-step past a group of his superior officers. One afternoon the news went around that Hans Beimler had been brought to the camp. That same day a shipment of a hundred Jews from Nuremberg had arrived; they were just making themselves at home in their barracks. The Jews wouldn't be there long, we thought. They were all businessmen, doctors, and lawyers—bourgeoisie. It was unthinkable that they would be kept with us. Up until then, there had only been Communists in the camp. The Jews looked out of their barracks windows. They were quiet and were wearing good suits. At six o'clock two of them were called out to carry water. Steinbrenner appeared in the doorway and shouted: "Goldstein! Binswanger!" They had to pick up a water barrel and follow Steinbrenner outside the gate.

That evening was the first time we heard shots connected with us. We were all standing against the same wall as Goldstein and Binswanger. The shots rang out while we were sitting on planks between the barracks, eating our evening soup. We stopped talking but finished the soup. Only the Jews stopped eating; they weren't as hungry yet as the rest of us. Goldstein and Binswanger didn't come back, though we waited and occasionally asked about them in whispers. Next morning we were standing in formation. The SS men in their long gray coats looked like statues in the dark, foggy April morning. A voice passed over us: "Shot while trying to escape." We never saw the bodies.

I remembered all this as I lay in the big cell after being arrested the second time. But the unreflecting stoicism of my first stay in Dachau had left me. Then I had never been afraid, though they had put me in the punitive company. Membership in the punitive company gave us a kind of halo. We felt ourselves to be an élite. That day I'd have said anything my questioners wanted me to say. They wouldn't even have had to beat me. I never was beaten; in that respect I had incredible luck.

(I only hope my luck holds out in the camps the future may hold in store for me, for us. I'm touching wood three times, I'm superstitious.)

The inspector who questioned me contented himself with checking my alibi about the printing press. When I stepped out of police headquarters into the light of the setting September sun, which wove a silvery spider web around the gray Renaissance façade of the Michaels-Hofkirche on the other side of the street, I knew that my activity in the Communist Party was at an end.

In the years that followed I tried to forget the whole business. In Dachau I had met a man who spoke to me in whispers about Rilke and knew lines from the *Buch der Bilder* by heart. Rilke brought back the feelings I had known at Schleissheim, feelings that I had briefly indulged on my bicycle trips to the Karwendel Mountains but had repressed or forgotten while discussing strike strategy with the young workers at the Augsburg textile mills or the Bavarian Motor Works.

I held small white-collar jobs and on Sundays took bicycle trips to Rott am Inn, Ettal, Wies, and Diessen, where I visited the interiors of baroque churches. I took my moods from Rilke and wrote Rilkean poems; a persecution mania that I myself was unaware of threw me into a deep depression. I hated my work, day after day over the ledgers of a small publishing house, and ignored the society that the totalitarian state was building up around me. The escape I chose was art. All in all, my artistic occupations were meager. Since an art connected with the society I lived in was impossible, I studied the façade of the Preysing Palace and the arrangement of vowels in the *Sonnets to Orpheus*. I paid a high price for my emigration from history; higher than the price I paid while living in history with the Communist Party. I forgot the revolver Brigade Leader Eicke had threatened me with if I should ever again show my face in Dachau, I really and truly forgot it. Instead of thinking about revolvers, I rediscovered my lost soul in the contemplation of Tiepolo's glazes. I reacted to the totalitarian state with total introversion.

Kierkegaard would have called my way of life an aesthetic experience; a Marxist would have spoken of a relapse into my petit-bourgeois background, and a psychoanalyist of a psychosis induced by the traumatic shock of the fascist takeover. Explanations after the fact never hold water. I mention my state of introversion only for the benefit of historians concerned with the sociology of modern dictatorship. Some of them confuse it with the older despotisms, Czarism, for instance. They disregard the role of technology. The new system with its total planning and all-embracing mechanisms of terror and propaganda cannot be combated with religious, humanistic, or socialist weapons. Seen in the light of the Gestapo or of the Reich Ministry for Popular Enlightenment and Propaganda, the revolutionary printer of leaflets or thrower of bombs is a pathetic figure out of the nineteenth century. What actually undermines the system is the very technology that creates it: little by little the cogs break down or disengage. Thinking in terms of masses, that is, of more or less expendable work units, the dictator or dictatorial management provokes a fragmentation of the people. In their isolation, the worker at his machine, the engineer over his drawing board become deaf to the totalitarian appeal, and the consequence is a gigantic wave of implicit sabotage, directed by no one. In the last years of the dictatorship, Germany was an enormous machine composed of wheels that revolved in the void and failed to drive the transmission belts which the dictator was trying to propel history.

And what a miasma of feelings, ideas, opinions! The soul shriveled for lack of air. In my case the consequences were art history instead of art, calligraphic experiments, Rilke, hours spent gazing against the light at blue-shimmering churches and palaces in Munich or Rome. I saw the world from the Promenadeplatz to Piazza Navona, from the Asamkirche to San Miniato al Monte as a vista, projected into the distance by the greenery of some park and stripped of its contours by a strangely diffuse light, a flaneur's illusion. But there were also great moments: the magical white of the walls of Santa Maria in Cosmedin, the view of the Umbrian mountains from the hill on which Orvieto is situated. Musical elements entered in: from the glittering black of a revolving disk imprinted with sound rose beaded syncopations pounded out on two pianos, my first intimation of jazz. I explored libraries and rummaged through secondhand bookstores, looking for impressionist authors; but when I dropped in on old Herr Fritzl, who daydreamed aloud and showed me his collection of the Romantics, I reached out, not for E. T. A. Hoffmann's *Golden Pot*, in which nourishing food was cooking, but for lyrical tidbits. Still, I was on the trail of art, I knew the meaning of art when I saw *Cymbeline* staged at the Kammerspiele, directed by Falckenberg, a magician who lifted poetry into the daylight from the well of fantasy. When I saw the two lovers lying on the stage and listened to their dream dialogue, the elements of my being merged into a deep and fearful life-feeling. And even now, when I go to see a play, it comes to me in the seconds before the curtain rises that I shall have to die some day.

I have just been imitating my style of that period. There were antidotes, however, and now and then I was given an injection. Someone took me to see Dr. Herzfeld, a tall, willowy man with black hair, a hooked nose, and sparkling eyeglasses. On occasional evenings he read Shakespeare to a small circle of friends. A wholehearted admirer of the Schlegel-Tieck translation, he hated and was at the same time fascinated by Goethe. On my first visit he read *Antony and Cleopatra*, acting out the parts with great restraint and stressing certain formal elements of the work, which glittered like the skin of some tropical beast. Here for the first time I came into contact, not with aesthetics but with the tension of art; it troubled me and aroused a mood of mingled impatience and disgust. Spleen. Herzfeld embodied the type of German romantic, half Oriental Jew, half the Prussian officer he had been during the First World War. A German artist, anything but a bohemian. His masters were Shakespeare and Kleist. The Prince of Homburg was his valiant cousin. He himself wrote fairy tales that he kept rewriting; each version was more spare than the last; ruthlessly he stripped away all "atmospherics," so that the figures stood out more and more clearly, projecting themselves into the very heart of his fables. Masterpieces. What has become of them?

"Rilke?" he said with a contemptuous laugh. "The inventor of the subjunctive!" When I objected, he questioned me: "Now tell me, what have you read? *The Elective Affinities*? No. *The Italian Journey*? No. Brentano's *Godwi*? No. Mörika's *On a Winter Morning before Sunrise*? No. The correspondence between Goethe and Schiller? No. Ranke's history of the reformation? No. Start with that! Read all six volumes from beginning to end. And then the *Popes of Rome* and the *History of France*. That will give you an idea of what great form means!"

He never told me to educate myself. He only thought it necessary to acquire standards. When I sent him my poems, he wrote: "Don't forget that Goethe wrote at the most twenty, and Mörike perhaps five, really perfect poems. At your age and at your stage of development, you can't hope to produce anything perfect, because the eggshells of undesirable teachers, such as Rilke, are still clinging to you. All your poems show a lack of discipline and work, hence of ability. You may say that in this wretched world you have no time, that you're consumed by your work. That is undoubtedly true, but such an answer is not valid from the standpoint of art. You must learn and you must work: *how* you do it is your affair. The essential is *that* you do it. To indulge, as you do, in pure poetic effusion is very dangerous, though of course it would be equally dangerous to lose your capacity for effusion. But with effusion alone you can hope for nothing except, if you are very lucky, to turn out a masterpiece by accident. If you wish to perfect yourself and produce a work that will be excellent even in its lesser parts—and that is what distinguishes a true work of art from the mass of literature—you must not scorn on occasion to support feeling with so-called artistic intelligence, and that means eating from the tree of knowledge, the bad with the good."

Classical doctrine, pronounced by a Romantic who himself suffered under it but suffering mastered it.

And so I opened Ranke without closing Rilke. But then I too left the baroque mountains for the primeval plains, the semi-artistic atmosphere of a publishing house for a factory in Hamburg. Housed in a red brick compound consisting of a modern office building and an older factory building, the plant manufactured photographic papers. I worked on the top floor, writing advertising copy and doing layouts including a drawing or photograph of the article advertised. I tried to keep my ads simple. This was difficult, because the directors insisted on putting in everything imaginable: a description of the packaging, a reproduction of the trademark, boxes and bold lettering for emphasis. I was happy when I succeeded in putting through an ad that consisted exclusively of copy and picture and thanks to a proper balance between occupied and unoccupied areas made an impression of repose. Of course repose itself accomplishes nothing; a good ad has to put its message across. The directors evidently believed that content, the underlying quality of the article advertised, was more important than form. They were right. Except that they never succeeded in formulating this idea. For all its brilliant advertising, even National Socialism was unable to keep its consumers satisfied in the long run.

The laboratory was next door to my office. I became good friends with Albert, the technical director; he was pleased with my intellectual interest in the practical problems, though it sometimes made him smile. The laboratory was a small one, with only three or four technicians, but it was the brain center of the plant. I spent all my idle moments there, and it was there that I learned the essence of scientific research: never to take a finding as final, but to question each new finding over and over again. The testing was endless. When Albert worked out a new emulsion formula, innumerable sensitometer strips were checked before it was accepted or rejected. I watched the strips being developed, and time and again, when the gradation struck me as just right, Brandt, the tall, blond chief technician, showed me that I was mistaken.

The scientific atmosphere appealed to me, the white smocks, the test tubes, the chemical substances, the darkrooms bathed in red light. No question was answered, least of all the question at the heart of the photographic process; why silver crystals are split by the light that strikes them. But while watching these men as they dealt with partial problems, such as how the size of the silver bromide grains affected the sharpness of the photograph, the distribution of silver in the gelatin coating, or how the consistency of certain compounds determined their power to reflect or admit light, I soon realized that every problem, even when seemingly solved, had within it an insoluble core, and my insatiable curiosity found a life-giving ferment in this residue of unexplained and not fully understood phenomena.

My observations led me to meditations which I discussed with Albert. Didn't the behavior of silver show that there were substances that could absorb foreign elements acting on them from outside? All other known substances absorb light quite unconsciously and passively, and transform it into free action: into the flowering of a plant or the oxidation of a stone. Silver, on the other hand, with its conscious representational activity, loses its own nature and ceases to be anything but the passive carrier of an image. Did it not in this way differ from the magic of polished glass surfaces, from the formlessness of watery surfaces, which are always able to efface the images mirrored in them, whose magnetic charm consists in the illusion of true self-sacrifice, while the selflessness of fixated silver is expressed in the outcome of the process, as characterized by the word "negative," to wit, the dullness of photography?

And drawing on the symbolism I had derived from the literature of those years of stagnation, I pointed at the Elbe, which simmered gray and endless below us, incapable of reflecting anything. Albert and I were sitting on the terrace of a restaurant in Blankenese.

He laughed. "From a scientific point of view that's nonsense," he said. "The silver doesn't do anything at all. We do something with it. Always these lofty problems! If you had any real interest in science, you'd ask entirely different questions, much simpler ones. Do you know, for instance, why the dirt comes off your hands when you wash them with soap?"

He was right, I didn't know. From that day on, I repressed all stirrings of symbolism. What is symbolism but the bourgeois aesthete's solemn announcement that some things symbolize others? This means that. But it can also mean something else. And so concepts are distilled from life. The owl is a symbol of wisdom. And so, when we are too lazy to try to be wise, we talk knowingly of owls.

Meanwhile the scene became emptier and emptier; more and more, time lost itself in a murky light. Albert died of heart failure during a tennis match; in the morning he had been told that as a half-Jew he would have to withdraw from the business he had founded. On a bright sunny day, with a sea breeze blowing in across the Alster, he collapsed on the Harvestehude courts. 1938. After that I lost all desire to potter around in his laboratory. I went to the sea, at last I saw it, glaring blue behind the giant red towers of Wismar, opal-gray beyond the Husum dikes. I watched the Halligen ferry chugging out of the harbor that smelled of wood and tar. Time had ceased to exist. For me. Over the horizon, far to the west, a cloud dispersed in the sky. I wedged my book under my arm and walked along the dike, farther and farther from the last houses.

The Deserter

COMRADES

Almost exactly five years later, in the spring of 1944, my life finally neared the point toward which, unbeknownst to me, it had long been tending.

This was perfectly clear to me as I stood on a bridge, smoking. The cypresses behind which the last vehicle of the second squadron, a Peugeot truck, had vanished, were blacker than the cloudy crowns of the chestnut trees. But the road was white, flooded with moonlight, and the countryside, the southern stretch of the Arno plain, was shimmering ash, moon-ash. The stones in the dry riverbed were chalky pale.

I had hooked my mud-spattered steel helmet to my belt and taken my carbine off my shoulder. My pipe glowed; it was alive. In the distance I heard the faint, steady rumbling of the columns on Via Aurelia, the coast road. The squadron would be arriving soon. The lieutenant had brought me back here after it had been decided where we were to camp the next day; then he had dashed away southward on his motorcycle. Because I spoke some Italian I always had to ride ahead with the lieutenant; then I would show the squadron the way.

A night will come, I thought, when I'll be alone, with no need to wait for anybody. Alone at last. Alone and free. Beyond the reach of law and order. Swallowed up by the night and the wilderness of freedom. Moving cautiously through grass, between trees and cliffs. Clouds overhead. Voices in the distance. Anxious listening. When the danger was passed, I'd walk on at a leisurely pace. Flowers. Sleeping in freedom on a hilltop, surrounded by broom. Flowing brooks. Peering through the silence like an animal. A night, a day, a second night. Who knows? Nights and days of freedom between captivity and captivity.

It sounded romantic, but it was all very clear and simple. I had to get out. I first knew it for sure as I lay hidden in the heather somewhere near Randers in Jutland, observing the approaching heavy artillery at the divisional maneuvers in March 1944. To lie there thinking about it gave me a wonderful wild feeling. Denmark was a good place for such decisions; as I sat in the café in Aalborg with the rain splashing down on the street outside, as doing sentry duty during maneuvers I looked down at the lake that lay like a sleeping cow between the silent slopes of the heath, freedom appeared to me in the shape of a blond girl or a soaring hawk. But it didn't even have to have a shape—in Denmark freedom was simply there.

I also remembered a fall evening three years before, in 1941; the thought of escape had come to me on a troop train in Thuringia. Huddled in the doorway of a cattle car, I had looked at the big red farmhouses that passed by in the waning light. Get out, I thought, disappear into the country, rent a room in one of those farms or at an inn, and just stay on, an unknown stranger among strangers. Nameless. In uniform, of course, it couldn't be done. In short, an idea taken from books. Impracticable. In the lonely coves along the coast of England there used to be inns where strangers turned up exchanged exotic coins, and gave themselves names such as "The Old Buccaneer," "The Blind Man," or "Black Dog." Countries and times in which a man could live without giving his name. In 1941 in Thuringia that was out of the question. Trees already bare, trees still mantled in color, sailed by in the Thuringian autumn. And then the thought had left me.

But in Denmark it was back again beside me, whispering, a shadow that I covered with my body as I lay in the heather on the lookout for approaching tanks. And when I picked up a pebble on the beach at Hobro and threw it into Mariag Fjörd, it sang the words "desertion" and "freedom" before sinking into the waves.

But that night on the Arno plain the thought had no further need of words. It was silent. It had taken body in the night, in the bridge, in my pipe. Things don't speak. Things are just there.

It was all perfectly clear and simple.

I heard them coming in the distance, voices, laughter, a shout, the clatter of weapons and wheels. A staff sergeant riding in the lead called out to me: "What's the story? How much further we got to go?"

The squadron came to halt behind him. The staff sergeant was drunk, the buck sergeant beside him was drunk. The signal squad behind them, to which I belonged, was sober.

"Fifty kilometers," I said. "We're coming to Via Aurelia now . . ."

"Shit!" he grumbled. "Fifty kilometers! Who is this Rosalia?"

"The coast road. We'll be camping outside a village called Ravi. The MPs will show us the detours around the bridges. The bridges are all in the drink."

"That's lovely," he said, suddenly sober. "What's become of our Air Force?" He gave the signal to ride on. "Get your bike out of the truck and come up front."

The men had taken off their steel helmets, unbuttoned their jackets, and rolled up their sleeves. I could see their faces and hair as they rode by. The night made their hair dark and their faces uniformly light; only an occasional head of blond hair shimmered in the moonlight. They rode on at an even pace, but now and then one of them had to brake because he had been going too fast. Their faces were apathetic and their eyes stared straight ahead, but they didn't look tired. The corporals and sergeants were drunk, they pedaled fast but unsteadily, weaving from side to side of the road, always retrieving themselves just short of the ditch. The privates left regular intervals between themselves and the drunks, so that the column was never broken.

I was fed up with my so-called comrades. They literally made me want to throw up. The worst thing about them was that they were always there. Comradeship meant you were never alone. Comradeship meant you could never close a door behind you and be alone.

Most of them had believed in Hitler's victory until two days before, until we had detrained in Carrara and heard that the division was being sent to the front in five night marches. At that time the front was still south of Rome, and the enemy—theirs, not mine—was about to break through at Nettuno and Cassino. But we didn't know that. All we knew was that we'd had to detrain in Carrara, north of the Arno, because the railroads between there and Rome were no longer in working order. We knew we couldn't travel by day, not on any road in the Italian peninsula, because the enemy—theirs, not mine—was in control of the air

from Bolzano to Syracusa and no German plane dared show itself
in the Italian sky in the daytime.

The strategic situation of the twentieth and twenty-first divisions of Air Force Infantry was this: Semi-motorized, equipped
with heavy artillery and tactical artillery, they had been meticu-
lously trained for a year in Belgium and Denmark with a view
to a war of movement. They were made up of young men who
believed in their mission. Now they were being thrown into a theater of war where the Western Powers had just made a successful
break-through. By the time they appeared on the scene, the generals in command of the southern front knew that Rome and central Italy were lost. I don't know what tactical mission Field Marshal General Kesselring originally had in mind for the two
divisions; possibly he was even thinking of an offensive (which
would never have entered his head if he had had any sort of air
reconnaissance), but by the time they arrived in Italy he had no
choice but to use them to cover the retreat of his main forces. For
that reason he held back their precious heavy and medium-range
artillery at the Arno, and only sent squadrons of "mounted" infantry, equipped with carbines and light machine guns, southward
in forced night marches. By so doing he lost two of Germany's
few remaining full-strength divisions, in three days, for the southward moving troops were caught between the prongs of an American armored division (home base: Texas; emblem: a red bull's
head) advancing on Viterbo and Grosseto and—hardly a shot was
fired on either side—simply engulfed.

I'm not finding fault with Field Marshal General Kesselring.
On the contrary: his blunder saved the lives of most of the two divisions' men. Still, in view of the situation on the southern front,
he ought to have gone to General Clark's headquarters and tried
to negotiate a cease-fire. (The only German officer who declined
to receive the title of field marshal from Hitler was General
Ludendorff. But he—as I have said—was an artist of the battlefield. He was still wise enough to know when a campaign had
been lost.)

A change had come over my so-called comrades since their arrival two days before. This I sensed as they rode by me in the pale
moonlight. During the march they were apathetic, drained by
fatigue; nevertheless, they thought about the heavy guns that had

been left behind somewhere near Pisa. They were fine new guns; the men knew that now there would be no brilliant maneuver-style offensive spearheaded by tanks. They had changed to the point where, lying in their sheltered daytime positions, they looked up at the northward-bound squadrons of American planes with a kind of aesthetic admiration. I don't know if they still believed in victory. In any case, they were still willing to fight for it.

Was I to refrain from deserting on their account? Was I to stand by my outfit out of comradeship? Ridiculous. They made it easy for me to leave. In the midst of my comrades I went about with a magnificent anarchistic feeling. I knew they were heading for destruction in one form or another, and I knew I wouldn't share their destruction: either I'd come through or I'd meet with a private form of destruction that would be all my own. There wasn't one of the "comrades" that I could talk it over with —how could I be sure they wouldn't report me? This was something I had to do on my own. If I could have taken at least one of those young men into my confidence, the circle of pride around me would have been broken. As it was, I had this wonderful, arrogant, anarchistic feeling. I took it on myself to judge the conduct of Field Marshal General Kesselring as well as the attitude of the plain soldiers around me. I regret to say that my feelings in the matter have remained unchanged. My view of the situation was the sounder.

I have a very poor memory for names. Consequently, I can't give the names of several soldiers whom I ought to mention at this point, because their disagreement with what I have just said was deep-seated. Actually, it is I who am stating this disagreement —they themselves would say nothing—the corporal, for instance, who never said a word and never expected thanks when with a few touches he gave my field pack, which had always cost me a bitter struggle, its regulation shape. Still, I had long talks with a soldier by the name of Werber, a member of my signal squad who was planning to study after the war. We talked about literature and art, and to the best of my ability I gave him succinct lectures on the art of the regions we rode through at night. He was open to slight deviations from the rules. One morning when the exhausted squadron had broken down into small groups, he pointed to a mown wheat field where the grain had already been stacked.

"Why wouldn't we stop here and get a few hours' sleep?" he suggested. "We'll catch up in the morning."

"What about the planes?" I objected. "We can't show ourselves on the road by daylight."

"Go on," he said. "There are only two of us. We'll get through."

We lay on sheaves, covered ourselves with more sheaves, and fell asleep instantly. It was about ten when we awoke from a restless sleep; we both had slight headaches. We blinked up at the sky and heard the roar of engines, but far in the distance; there were no planes in sight. We picked up our bicycles and started off. The sun drove us forward with blasts of heat. The road was deserted. We were on the Maremma plain. We came to a river with an emergency bridge over it. Just then we heard the planes. We couldn't see how close they were, because tall trees cut off the view. "Get down off the bridge!" shouted an engineers soldier, who was on guard. We pedaled as fast as we could. Then we saw a string of Lightnings, and threw ourselves in the ditch. We unhooked our steel helmets from our belts and covered our heads with them. We breathed in the smell of moist earth and grass and thought: If only they don't see our bicycles. But the planes—I mean the men who were in them—were interested in the bridge, their bombs fell on the stretch of road on the other end. We saw fountains of smoke and earth, a whole line of them, and gasped with relief. We lay in the ditch for a long while after the danger was past. The heat had thrown us into the apathy of exhaustion, we enjoyed the forced rest. After a while Werner grunted: "Come on! Get up!" and we dragged ourselves to our feet.

So there were comrades after all. I could talk to them about art and take cover with them in ditches. They helped me to fasten my pack and repair my bicycle, lent me muzzle protectors and joined me in wangling extra rations. We did sentry duty together, and together we drank whatever wine we could scare up. (It was rare by then; the armies had drunk Italy dry, and who has wine for a defeated army?)

Maybe—it has occurred to me since—I should have attempted the seemingly impossible, tried to win one of them over to my side and persuade him to come along, put my trust to the test and planted the thought of freedom in at least one man's heart. Werner's for instance. The day after that ride through the Maremma, I started on my flight, and it so happened that Werner was watching me. He saw what I was doing, probably suspected what was up, and said nothing. Should I have broken in on his silence with words? His face closed as he watched me. No, at best I'd have drawn him into an action that wasn't his. He'd have borrowed that action from me.

I hope I shall always refrain from any attempt to convince people. One can only try to show them the possibilities they have to choose from. Even that is presumptuous enough, for who knows another man's possibilities? Another man is not only a fellow man, he is also *other*, someone we can never know. Unless we love him. I didn't love my comrades. That's why I never tried to convince them of anything.

Nor am I trying to convince anyone now. That is not the purpose of my book. Its sole purpose is to show how at a certain moment, pursuing an inevitable course, I chose the act that gave my life meaning and from that moment on became the axis around which the wheel of my existence has revolved. In this book I am merely trying to tell the truth, an entirely private and subjective truth. But I am certain that every private and subjective truth, if it is really true, contributes to man's knowledge of objective truth.

I am not suggesting that I had any such thoughts when I saw the column pass me by, stopped the kitchen truck, and asked them to hand me down my bicycle and field pack. One of the kitchen men handed them down. Then I stood for a moment alone on the road, fastened my pack to my baggage rack, and checked the tires. No, I had no such thoughts, but I had my anarchy feeling, my Jutland heath, Thuringian autumn, and Italian moonlight feeling. I thought of the wilderness, of clouds, of voices in the distance, of anxious listening, of sleeping in the open on a broom-covered hill, of peering through the silence like an animal, of the second of freedom between captivity and captivity.

In addition, my political situation was clear to me.

They had stifled my revolutionary youth. They had shut me up in a concentration camp. I myself was released with nothing worse than a black eye, but not so the comrades of my youth and of a revolution which in essence and intention had been a pure youth and a pure revolution. They had killed Gebhard Jiru and Josef Götz and Willi Franz and Josef Huber in Dachau and Hans Beimler in Spain. Those names can stand for the whole elite of the German Communist Party, whom they killed, while their own elite, the elite of the National Socialist Party is still alive. Aside from the *apparatchiks* nothing remained of the Communist Party but a few members of the elite. Those few fell in Spain and—God help us, for no one else will—in Russia. Thus the Nazis destroyed the Communist Party, transforming it from a party of freedom and revolution to a party of *apparatchiks* and of blind faith in a leader, a party that fought with fascist methods. This, to be sure, was possible only because the party had previously adopted a doctrine that denied man's freedom of choice. But it was National Socialist terror that lent this false doctrine a semblance of truth and made the living forces within the party bow to the terror of their own dogma.

I couldn't love my army comrades because I loved my party comrades who had been killed by those for whom my fellow soldiers were fighting. (This was one way of keeping faith with my Communist comrades.) By destroying the party, they deprived my youthful struggle of its meaning and drove me to introversion. For years I lived on the island of my soul, as though glued to a toilet seat. All I had in the world was art and my private life, and those they took away by drafting me. Take up arms for them? Fire on the soldiers who might be able—a glimmer of hope—to change my whole life? The very thought was absurd.

From my political situation I drew the logical consequences. I had no idea that six weeks later a bomb would explode not far from Hitler. My private little July 20 took place on June 6. I grabbed the freedom which even the astute General Speidel—father of the new, postwar German divisions around whom libertarian speeches and actions in contempt of all liberty have clustered like a legend—which, I say, even the otherwise commendable General Speidel denied when he wrote in his book about the invasion: "It was clear to him" (General Rommel) "that only the supreme military commander had the power, right and obligation to take such an action" (i.e., to propose an armistice to the Western Powers, in other words, to desert) "and not an individual soldier or officer, who could not possess the requisite high insight."

Though only an "individual soldier," I did possess "such high insight"; I was quite willing to shoulder the metaphysical and even the rational responsibility. In addition I had my wilderness feeling. To use a metaphor that has been run into the ground in military circles, the idea of desertion sprang full-blown from my brain as Pallas Athena sprang from the head of Zeus. In other words: I had made up my mind to run away. It was perfectly simple.

But would I succeed?

I checked my bicycle tires. Nothing wrong. I started off. The rolling of the wheels under me gave me a pleasant feeling. The squadron was moving pretty fast and I had to pedal hard to catch up. When the column reached the coast road, I was abreast of Werner at the head of the signal squad.

On the highway, on the Via Aurelia, the great retreat came foaming through the night. Under the full moon the Via Aurelia was a glittering silver shield. Only nights can be so bleached-bone pale, to bleached-bone bright, curtained in moonlight, flat, traversed by great shadows, but deep: deep blue in the deep blue acacia-scented foliage.

Swathed in dust and moonlight the acacia-scented campaign sped along the highway, along the Via Aurelia, in the thunder of the columns, in the wild, rasping clatter of caterpillar treads, in the flying hair of the men standing in the hatches of the tanks, in their flying moon-blown hair and darkly northward-looking faces, in the dust-stifled cries of command, stifled by the dying triumph of the dust clouds, by the moon-pale dying dust-cloud triumph of the defeated southern army.

"Tiger tanks," said Werner as the ghost-army sped by. He nodded his head with its pale moon-and-dust face, with its black nose and chin shadows, nodded into the high moon.

"Tiger tanks," he said amid the modest clatter of our squadron. And I: "Heavy artillery." And he: "Motorized infantry." And I: "Anti-tank guns." And he: "Engineers." And I: "Artillery." The steel helmets dangling from our handlebars tinkled, quietly our wheels rolled, as ghostlike, amid the fragrance of the acacias, beside the glittering sea, our detachments approached the darkly rumbling columns of the retreating army.

"They're pulling out with everything they've got," said Werner.

"This war down here is a great thing," I said. And I thought: What a pity! It was a magnificent war. I'd have given a good deal to take part, once in my life, in such a great and magnificent war.

But under the circumstances my thoughts fell flat.

FEAR

On the second morning after that night I was shaving in the courtyard of a villa near Piombino, in whose gardens we were spending the day, when the lieutenant came out with his toilet articles. I attempted a salute, but the lieutenant muttered: "At ease," and prepared to wash. Our water flowed into a large, damask-yellow marble basin from a griffin's head embedded in the wall of the house. We were alone in the courtyard.

"Where did you learn your Italian?" he asked me. He was a small, dark, wiry man, handsome and dangerous. As we were about to leave Denmark, he had made us a speech, which he concluded as follows: "For any of you that disobeys orders in the face of the enemy I've got six bullets in my revolver." That was Lieutenant Meske.

"I was there a few times in peacetime," I said. And instantly I thought: Not a word more. No use showing the bastard that I've seen more than he has.

"Have you heard," he asked me, "what the English did to the Italian deserters in North Africa? They cut the seats out of their pants and sent them back again." Without really waiting for an answer, he added: "Those Italians will never learn to fight."

The sound of the thin stream of water was interrupted now and then when the lieutenant held his head under it. While shaving my chin, I watched him intently out of the corner of my eye. After a while he said: "As soon as we're back in rest quarters, I'll put you in for corporal."

I've done it, I thought. My camouflage was in order. "Thank you very much, sir," I said in a loud voice. The lieutenant nodded.

After putting my shaving equipment away, I strolled off into the park. There were enormous cypresses, of a size I had seen only at the Villa d'Este, great, greenish-black pillars through which the sunlight seeped silently. Laurel trees were growing along the paths, and the wall was covered with thin black branches of long-faded wisteria. The soldiers lay sleeping under the trees. A faint breeze played over their sleep, a light Italian-garden sleep. When I stopped, propped my arms on the wall, and looked out over the countryside, I first saw the silvery leaves of the olive trees that covered the hill, and then the dust-white ribbon of the deathly still road. In a space between the hills to the left the sea was visible, a dull-blue, lonely sea, that looked as if the keel of a ship had never furrowed it, a slate-colored, insidious, end-of-the-world sea. Flying in from the sea, a squadron of silver-glittering east-bound planes—I could hear the throbbing song of their engines—met a flight of twin-tailed planes headed north. Without touching, the mechanical masters passed each other at medium height and flew on over the waving deserted wheat fields, over the terror-stricken, lonely-brooding pines that broke the endless expanse of the wheat fields, and menacing, far in the distance, vanished over the olive groves that had returned to the Etruscan wilderness of their past.

That region lent itself to feelings of fear.

Of course I had still another reason for deserting: I had no desire to "push up daisies," as they say in the Army. Yes, I prefer to call it the "Army" or "armed forces"; anything but *Wehrmacht*. *Wehrmacht* is just the kind of word a feeble-minded rear-echelon hero would make up. Besides, it's historical nonsense, considering that once the enemy began to fight in earnest the so-called *Wehrmacht* (Defense Might) produced nothing but "strategic withdrawals" and movements to "straighten our lines," or at best offered "stubborn resistance"—in other words, was defeated and put to flight. What Hemingway said about General Montgomery is much more applicable to the *Wehrmacht*: "Monty was a character who needed fifteen to one to move, and then moved tardily." It was neither a "defense" nor a "might," but merely a conglomerate of millions of reasonably brave men who felt it in their bones that all in all there was no sense in fighting. When they did fight (and often they fought well) it was under compulsion or in order to save face, because once the total idiots on the other side triumphed and inposed the formula of "unconditional surrender," it became necessary to save face. The German soldiers saved their face, but in the last war there was never a "*Wehr-*

macht," only millions of armed men, most of whom hadn't the slightest desire to fight. The outfit I was assigned to was a rare exception. And it was an ironic caprice of history that just such an outfit should have been captured almost to the last man.

Yes, "almost." I at least would be missing when the division surrendered. I had no intention of surrendering unconditionally, as a body of troops is expected to do. I would give myself up of my own free will, so reserving the right to state my conditions. (Naturally I don't mean that I would demand special treatment as a prisoner; I am referring to political conditions in regard to the postwar period.) Obviously Meske's story about their cutting out the seats of men's pants was nonsense. I had read their leaflets. They guaranteed good treatment and release soon after the end of hostilities. That too was propaganda. You couldn't count on it. And the pants-seat story was counter-propaganda. I had made up my mind to desert because I wanted to perform an act of freedom, an act situated in the no man's land between the captivity I came from and the captivity into which I was going. I wanted to give myself up because by so doing I would recover the right, which I had acquired in the past, to demand conditions. I wanted to give myself up because it would have been absurd to fire so much as a single shot at any enemy who could never be my enemy. The foxhole I could have fired from didn't exist.

Besides, as I've said, I wanted to give myself up because I was afraid of being shot at and dying a meaningless or meaningful death.

It would be possible to delete the last paragraph and explain that I was actually being very brave, since I was exchanging the danger of death in combat for what was probably the much greater danger of being intercepted by the military police and instantly executed. Then my book would become a nice little record of heroism.

The only trouble with such a record is that it wouldn't be true. Naturally, while maturing my plans, I weighed the risk of being caught. But not for a moment did my thoughts about the military police take the form of fear. My project filled me with a courage that had never passed through the phase of fear. To be perfectly truthful, my mood, in face of the risk I was taking, was one of grandiose nonchalance.

I didn't even stop to ask myself whether, when it was all over, I would feel like the horseman who, totally unaware of the danger, had crossed the ice on Lake Constance.

On the other hand, the thought of entering the combat zone, the zone of absurd bloodshed, aroused in me the instinctive distaste that we call fear. By this I mean that I wasn't seized with panic terror. Most cases of desertion, especially such planned mass desertions as that of the Italians in North Africa, have been inspired by the will to live rather than the fear of death. I am convinced that only an irresistible love of death can drive a man to kill himself. A man who deliberately risks his life in combat must have resolved to die, for he cannot count on survival; he is a potential suicide. (I am not speaking of the beasts who fight because they want to win, that is, to kill the enemy; they are potential murderers.) As Schiller observed, the soldier's glory is his ability to look death in the face.

And the deserter's glory is his ability to avert his eyes from death, from the Gorgon's head that does not make us free and able to act but turns those who look upon it to stone.

Only once in my life have I been seized with mindless terror, in the fall of 1933, in the Munich Gestapo prison after my second arrest. Terror comes to a man from outside, whereas fear is an integral part of him. Like courage, it is implicit in his being. Between fear and courage lie two other elements of man's nature, reason and passion. They preside over the decision he has to make between courage and fear. In the fraction of a second that precedes the moment of decision, the possibility of absolute freedom essential to every man becomes a reality. In the moment of action itself he is not free, for in action he reconstitutes the old field of tension within which his nature moves. It is suspended only in the fleeting moment between thought and action. We are free only at certain moments. Precious moments.

My book has only one purpose: to describe a single moment of freedom. But I do not contend that man's potential greatness is realized only at such moments. I can conceive of a life in which freedom is never experienced, but nevertheless asserts its full worth. A man achieves his worth by looking upon courage and fear, reason and passion, not as antinomies, one member of which must be destroyed, but as poles in a single field of tension, which is himself. For how can deadly hostility prevail between two elements which are both so patently a part of human nature that if one were amputated the soul would inevitably die? How many living corpses are there who—though ever so alive in body—died at the moment when they plucked fear or courage, reason or passion, from their hearts? Freedom is only a possibility; the man who can transform it into reality is fortunate—the essential is to preserve the capacity for freedom.

(I hold, accordingly, that a philosophy which takes account of man's fear and care, but has nothing to say of his carefree moments, his courage and spirit of adventure, is hostile to freedom. Staring at the Gorgon's head of death, it will turn to stone.)

Open to freedom, the qualities of our nature are suspended in mood. Without the fresh winds or sultry weather, without the oil smog or the woodland feelings that our moods bring us, courage and fear, reason and passion would languish and die. Mood is the air that surrounds us, an ethereal and at the same time aesthetic element. The park at Schleissheim. Our susceptibility to mood is the source of art.

Art is not the business of the Muses who are able to write, paint, or play the guitar; it is the feeling that comes to us from the rusty iron railing we hold in our hands as we stand on our back balcony gazing at the windows across the court and listening to the faint clatter of Frau Kirchner washing dishes on the ground floor.

Art has nothing whatever to do with technique; if it had, textile manufacturer Reinhard of Krefeld wouldn't be able to form precious, crystal-clear ideas while listening to Wilhelm Furtwängler direct the *Freischütz* overture in his insufferably dignified and passionless way.

And while a painter and an art critic are arguing about representational and abstract art in the touchingly, depressingly poverty-stricken gloom of a studio in Schwabing, a few steps down the street some children, whom a man by the name of Richard Ott has given paper, paint, and brushes to play with, are expressing the mood from which their lives draw nourishment.

When we give ourselves to mood as the life breath of our spirit, we are all geniuses. All men are either geniuses or living corpses. A classification on this basis might usefully be undertaken in the next census.

The Muses, on the other hand, are symbols, that is, an ersatz for reality. They are the pin-up girls of symbolistic, aesthetistic writers, painters, and composers. In the form of prints made from Platonic originals, they grace the walls of our aesthetes' aesthetic rooms, while the consummately museless engineer Dick Barnett— no one is interested in knowing this great artist's real name— designs the F 94 jet fighter in the offices of the Lockheed Aircraft Corporation, Burbank, California.

His work is based on careful calculations, in other words, on his reason, but only passion can create so pure a form, a form that vibrates with Dick Barnett's secret struggle between courage and fear, and gives us the feeling that Dick Barnett was balanced on the razor's edge when he created it. One little false move and he would have come to grief. One false turn of Barnett's mind, and the F 94 would not be the perfect work of art that it is. And in addition, though Barnett is quite unaware of it; the moods of Burbank, California, the particular red of the gasoline cans at a service station that he passes every morning on his way to Lockheed, or the curve of his wife's neck under a street lamp when they got out of their car yesterday on their way home from the movies.

Millions of moods, the life breath of our nature—this ethereal, volatile element in which our nature is suspended comes from nothingness or from God.

I've sketched my image of man. Reserving the right to make changes. I'm not a philosopher. The writer's function is description. I haven't interpreted man as philosophers do but described him. I've described man because I've got to describe my fear. Our fear. The fear embedded in all of us, that we mustn't destroy if we wish to remain alive.

For instance, my fear four years earlier, at the beginning of the war, in the dense, marshy woods at the foot of the Limburg, a few kilometers north of Breisach on the Upper Rhine. Every day the French artillery fired a certain number of shells at an observation post on the Limburg. I was with the engineers at the time. When the shells began to whistle overhead, I was sitting in the woods with my squad. We'd never heard that sound. Actually it was harmless, nothing at all compared to what came later, in the nights when the bombs rained down on the so-called homeland. But precisely because the danger was so insignificant, I was able to observe the phenomenon of fear closely.

It began with our waiting for the cork-popping sound of the French guns, apparently situated at the edge of the forest on the other side of the Rhine. It increased with the song of the approaching shell and finally thrust its knife blade into our hearts when the shell seemed to stand still for a moment over our heads. That was the moment when our veteran sergeant stopped explaining that a shell you heard coming was harmless, the moment when I abandoned my convulsively lyrical immersion in the image of the Rhine that lay before me, detached my gaze from the willows with their silvery leaves, from the wrecked ship caked with white clay in the yellow, still water, from the heat and silence—a gaze I had practiced with a view to holding it fast in the second of fear—and stared instead at the muddy tips of my boots which stood on the ground, touching the blade of my pickax, and seemed to be separate from me, though my feet were in them.

Later, in an atmosphere of swarming gnats and green heat we got used to it. But then no freedom was possible, no interruption, even for a fraction of a second, of the tension between fear and courage, because if we wanted to stay alive we had to hold onto our fear.

Yes, in the spring of 1940 on the Upper Rhine, freedom had vanished from the world. Desertion was impossible and I didn't even want to desert. There was no way of crossing the Rhine with its furious current, and even if there had been I would have run into an army doomed to defeat. But it was bad that I didn't want to desert at that time. I had fallen so low that I thought a German victory possible. I thought the sewer rat had a chance. Whenever I think of it, I spit at myself inwardly. But at least I had an instinct that made me hold onto my fear. If I had overcome and destroyed it, if I had let courage triumph over fear, my spirit would have been blunted, I'd have become the dull-witted soldier the sewer rat wanted me to be.

Through the ensuing war years I managed to save not only my courage but my fear as well, until it came time for me to escape. I would never have summoned up the courage to escape if I had not been as cowardly as I was brave.

I was cowardly and brave that day on the hill at Piombino, as I looked out over a terror-stricken landscape traversed by mechanical monsters, and again on the day—the second after we bivouacked on the hill—when I was cautiously riding across the Maremma plain with Werner.

At noon we saw Tarquinia on its hilltop. High and cyclopean rose the gigantic Etruscan freestone walls on which the castle of the Margravine of Tuscany was built. The road twined upward in endless serpentines. The sky above the shadeless road was leaden white. The air was so hot that we had only the barest intimation of the sea, which ought to have been palpably visible from that height. But all we could make out in the steaming glow was a vague mist; the presence of the sea was revealed only by a patch of storm-cloud, slate color in the west, merging with the harsh, killing whiteness of the raging light. It took us two hours to cover the three kilometers from the foot of the hill to the town on top. As we were resting under the trees on a small square, the planes came back. They approached from the sea, we saw them in the distance, hundreds of them. Their slow, inexorable flight reminded us of our fear. There was no cover, all we could do was crouch down behind the trees like mindless cowards and sweat it out. The bomb bays opened, we saw the small bombs tumbling out in clusters, falling in spirals through the white spirals of seething sunlight; their nerve-shattering sound, a clattering of tin buckets, magnified the shrill heat of the sky. But we were not in their path, they fell somewhere in the country outside Tarquinia.

If I'd been all courage at that time, I'd have stayed calmly where I was instead of hiding behind a plane tree, and I wouldn't have noticed the pale-green and silken-grey spots, as fluid as water color, of which the tree was composed. As it happens, I can still lift those spots out of my unconscious, water-color moods to which I gave my soul, because the deserter's glory is his unwillingness to die a meaningless death. One day I'll know when it's time for me to die or when death holds meaning for me. Then I knew it wasn't time for me to look death in the face, so I averted my gaze from the bombs and hid it in the trees.

A battalion courier posted in the town told us our squadron was assembling at Monte Romano, twenty kilometers southwest of Tarquinia. The road now led inland, and we covered the final stretch quickly and in silence; we had got used to the heat. It was a lonely countryside; along the twining road there were isolated farmhouses, their walls up to their flat, shingled roofs covered with roses; the wild poppy red of the untilled fields screamed into the white fire of the firmament.

Not far from Monte Romano, the lieutenant appeared on his motorcycle. He stopped and shouted: "The Tommies are in Rome! Get back to the outfit! Hurry, hurry! We're breaking camp at midnight, tomorrow we meet the enemy!"

Asshole, I thought, you hurry, you go meet your enemy. You with your six bullets in your revolver, I only hope you get yours quick! You can't wait, can you? Maybe you won't notice that I'm gone.

Tomorrow's the day, I thought.

THE OATH

It all went off more smoothly than I'd expected.

That night I was on sentry duty from ten to twelve. That meant I wouldn't have to start up cursing from my first slumber when they woke the squadron on the stroke of midnight. Naturally we were all drunk with sleep, and after the first excitement we fell back into our chronic torpor. At first we rode on winding, hedge-lined paths, where our wheels often stuck in the inches-deep dust.

The moonlight wasn't as bright as it had been on the preceding nights. Near Vetralla we reached the Via Cassia; it was jam-packed with columns retreating toward Viterbo; they moved at a snail's pace and finally stopped altogether. What would become of them when the planes came at daybreak, which was not far off? We were the only unit moving in the opposite direction; jeering shouts came to us from the columns: "Where do you think you're going?" with cutting emphasis on the "you." And when some eager beaver shouted back: "Up front," the response was laughter and catcalls. Unlike the generals, the soldiers had accepted their defeat.

The stalled columns left us only a narrow lane on the right side of the road. At dawn we turned off to the right onto a white road. For the first time we were moving in broad daylight, but the planes hadn't turned up yet. In the light I began to feel less tired; my fatigue gave way to what I call my "window-pane feeling"; at such times I seem to see the world through glass. We passed a blue lake, which appeared to us through a garland of slender balsam poplars.

The road went from bad to worse; in places it was covered with jagged stones. When we came to a downgrade, I purposely neglected to brake and coasted full speed over the stones. I felt the air seeping slowly out of my rear tire, and a moment later I was riding on the rim. That does it, I thought. And: That was an inspiration.

"Flat tire!" I shouted. Then I veered to the left and got off. Werner who had been riding beside me followed me. When one of us had a breakdown, squadron regulations required the nearest comrade to help him. The staff sergeant who was in the lead turned around for a moment and called out: "Catch up as fast as you can! Destination: Vejano." As usual the lieutenant was up ahead somewhere on his motorcycle. Making a show of haste, I stood my bicycle upside-down, while the squadron raced by me.

I looked after them until the last rattling, glittering bicycles vanished around a bend. The cloud of dust that followed them fell back on the silent road.

It had really gone off smoothly. The only problem was to get rid of Werner in a hurry.

He bent down over my rear wheel and started looking for the leak. "It's these sharp stones," he said. "There are probably a lot of small holes. We'll need a pail of water. It's going to take a long time."

"You go on ahead," I said. "I'll manage. Why should you waste half the day on account of my bike?"

"No," he said. "That's no good. I can't leave you here."

I saw he was uneasy. He wanted to get back to the outfit. He thought the squadron would soon be at the front—we actually imagined that there was something resembling a "front" up ahead —and that he would be absent. Whether he was really so bent on getting to the "front" I don't know, but in any case, though he sometimes had spells of independence, he wanted to stick with the outfit.

Suddenly I saw that he was looking at me suspiciously.

"Would you be wanting to sleep again?" he asked. "You can't do that today. Today we've got to stick with the outfit."

"What do you take me for?" I said in an injured tone. When you lie, you've got to do it properly. "Do you really think I don't want to be there when the fighting starts?"

"Well, you were never very enthusiastic," he said. So he had noticed something. With a little more imagination he would have known what was what. As it was, he could only suspect that I wanted to catch up on my sleep. I had nothing to fear from him.

"Do you really think you can manage by yourself?" he asked. I sensed his impatience.

"Of course," I said. "I'll scare up some water. There are farms all over the place." We were both lying; we knew the peasants had all fled and were living somewhere in the back country, where they had built carefully camouflaged thatched huts. And the wells on all these farms had gone dry.

Werner was still eying me suspiciously, but in his thoughts he had already left me.

"All right," he said. "Then I'll be going. I'll tell them you're working hard."

"Sure, go ahead," I said. "I won't be long. I'll be with you in an hour."

He climbed up on his bicycle and rode away. We hadn't shaken hands, but all the way to the bend he kept turning around and waving at me. I waved back. There was a kind of joy in our waving arms, a desperate, definitive joy. Then there was only the empty road, empty and white and still. I let my arm sink down. I was alone.

Both in my book and in my life, Werner is a pallid figure. I remember him only dimly. He was broad rather than tall, but he wasn't exactly short; he had a full, pleasant face under smooth, ash-blond hair. Three years after the war I received a letter from his father, asking if I knew what had become of him; he himself had had no news since the summer of 1944. So good old Werner had been killed, but I couldn't tell his father where, because I never saw Werner or the squadron again. Did it happen right after he left me? Was it partisans or planes? Was I the last living soul he spoke to? That's unlikely, because the squadron was only ten minutes ahead of us, at the most. It seems more likely that he got lost and fell in with a group of stragglers trying to make their way back to the German forces. In bands of that kind there were always a few idiots who started shooting when the enemy—their enemy, not mine—sighted them; then there were fireworks and they were all shot to pieces. In the end the peasants buried them, because at that stage of the game the Americans or French or Poles or English or Moroccans had no time to waste on the dead.

I often wondered, not that day on the road in southern Umbria, but later as a prisoner and in the years after the war while reading letters like the one from Werner's father, what it was that bound Werner and most of the others. Bound them so firmly that they never so much as dreamed of doing anything but stick with their outfits. What made Werner's face dim and pallid was this "sticking-with-the-outfit" mentality, this herd instinct that terror and propaganda had drummed into him. It was almost a sign of individuality when a soldier, in addition to the mere drive to submerge himself in the mass, could summon up a few vague notions about comradeship or defending the fatherland, or if he was just naturally pugnacious. The average German soldier in the last war was neither drunk nor lost in a dream; he was spell-bound; under the influence of the evil eye, a man loses sight of the hypnotist's eyeballs. His consciousness is disconnected, he responds to nothing but the spell.

They ought to admit it—it's no disgrace—and drop their latest subterfuge: the self-justification that they were bound by their oath.

I agree that for many officers the oath was a problem. But never in any of the outfits I served in during the war did I hear an enlisted man waste words on the soldier's oath. And if they never mentioned the oath, it was certainly not because they thought it too sacred to be spoken of.

I myself took the oath on a bright sunny morning in March 1940, in the courtyard of an army post near Rastatt. Standing in the second rank of my training company, I made a right angle of my elbow, raised my swearing hand, and, pausing after each phrase, recited the words in unison with the others:

"I swear by God this sacred oath: I will give unconditional obedience to Adolf Hitler, Führer of the German Reich and People and Supreme Commander of the Wehrmacht and, as befits a brave soldier, will be prepared at all times to give my life in fulfillment of this oath."

While speaking these words without batting an eyelash, I couldn't help smiling inwardly at the sewer rat's clumsy attempt to bind me to him. It takes very little thought to unmask the absurdity of such an oath.

Under the sewer rat's regime anyone who resisted the draft was executed or at the very least sent to a concentration camp for years. Anyone who, responding to the herd instinct, had become a soldier but had refused at the last minute to take the oath would have met with the same fate.

In other words, the oath was taken under compulsion. The penalty for refusal was death. Hence it was null and void.

An oath pronounced by an unbeliever doesn't commit him in any way.

A believer knows that an oath binds him to God. An oath or sworn testimony is always given voluntarily. (One can be released from it only if the oath itself is shown to be wittingly or unwittingly at variance with God's truth.)

Nowhere is the dialectical relationship between constraint and freedom more evident than in the matter of an oath. An oath presupposes the freedom of the man who takes it.

An oath is a religious act; otherwise it is meaningless.

But most German soldiers didn't believe in God; or else they were indifferent to religion and never, except in moments of extreme loneliness or at the approach of death, asked themselves whether they believed in God or not.

Accordingly, most German soldiers were not even qualified to take an oath.

Nor was their Führer qualified to receive one, for he denied the existence of God and persecuted all religious movements because they tended to reduce his person to its natural proportions in the minds of the people. He replaced the godhead, which arches over all men including himself, with a concept which, though empty, bears the mark of terror: providence.

Only a believer deciding in full awareness to take this oath would have been qualified to do so. Were there any such believers? Is so, they were stricken with blindness. They took a grave sin on themselves.

Because, if they had had a spark of reason, they would have told themselves that God could not possibly have been interested in their obeying the sewer rat—and unconditionally to boot. And if they were unable to grasp this with their reason, their feeling must have made it clear to them that in demanding that an oath be sworn to him the Luciferian rat who stormed and raged against God was desecrating the sanctity of the oath.

But believers and nonbelievers alike, they were all bewildered.

Their fathers and grandfathers, the men of all previous generations had taken soldier's oaths. As they swore, a potent primordial taboo had descended on them; they were incapable of seeing the absolute emptiness behind the glass bell of a godhead invoked in words. For at a certain point in history the space behind the glass bell of the oath became empty.

That point is the French Revolution. The conservatives of all countries take a cynical pleasure in pointing out that they derived the principle of universal conscription from one of the most revolutionary events in history. That is true, but it is equally true that they took nothing else from the Great Revolution, that they did not take the principles of liberty, equality, fraternity, and the rights of man.

Be that as it may, the modern European states began in the early nineteenth century to introduce universal conscription in their territories. There had been a certain amount of coercion even earlier. But in principle military service had been voluntary, though the soldier had slowly changed in character: from the lansquenet to Frederick the Great's guardsman. The lansquenet took his oath of his own free will; those who were pressed into service could not be counted on.

But universal conscription left a man no choice. He was compelled to serve. And though compelled, he was made to take the old oath of the volunteer lansquenets and guardsmen.

The oath still had a semblance of meaning as long as the majority believed in God and as long as the head of state, the prince, felt himself to be a prince by the grace of God. As long as the idea of the fatherland was still a universal idea, and the law, at least in its foundations, was still autonomous.

But these universal ideas dwindled, the majority ceased to believe in God, and a large minority even began to question the idea of the fatherland. What remained was sheer power, which to be sure took on a mythical radiance for some men, while to others the imperialistic character of the epoch became evident.

In the course of this process universal conscription became a manifestation of power and lost the meaning it had held for one brief moment in history. Born from a surge of idealism, it unmasked idealism as an illusion a century later.

And the religious act of an oath freely taken, the oath of free warriors once sworn on the Rütli, became an act of shamanistic magic, celebrated by conscripts, recited in the void of drill fields without even the walls of a dead faith to echo it.

That was why I never heard an enlisted man in any of the outfits I served in during the war waste words on the oath. Amid the absurdity of the sewer rat's war each man dimly sensed the absurdity of universal conscription and of the soldier's oath. In the imperialistic and ideological war, to which Hitler gave its purest modern form, military service and the oath came to be regarded not as a bond, but as absolute coercion. An epoch had come to an end.

It became obvious that compulsory military service and the compulsory oath were an offense against human rights—even in those modern states, or power complexes, that are humane enough to grant a few of their citizens the conscience to become conscientious objectors.

Only a free man can decide to go to war.

An oath can be sworn only by believers to a believer. The army of the future can only be a volunteer army. To judge by the situation of faith today, an oath in such an army is inconceivable.

A volunteer army of this kind will be enormous if it engages in a just defense against an unjust aggressor. At the outbreak of the war, many more volunteers will flock to it and the army will be helped by the countless bands of partisans that are the immediate consequence of the crimes of an enemy who has succumbed to the lure of power.

The society that engenders such an army, even if it loses many battles, even if it is not victorious, will nevertheless lay the foundations of the future. Even in defeat its spirit will win out; on the historical plane, the victor will be the loser.

In dealing with an old-style conscript army, a man can invoke his fundamental rights if he really wants to.

In response to the extreme coercion of universal conscription and a compulsory oath he can choose the extreme form of self-defense: desertion.

I wish I had known all this when I stood beside my upside-down bicycle on a road in Central Italy, peering in all directions like a hunted beast. But perhaps in the moment of action it wouldn't have been good to know too much, to have all these arguments and counterarguments in my head; at such times too much knowledge can be a handicap. As it was, I merely looked around, took note of the terrain, and thought—with an enormous sense of triumph—of the freedom I had created for myself.

The road twined around a long hill. I took my bicycle and dragged it up the slope, perhaps a hundred yards, until I came to a dense acacia copse. At a point where I could no longer be seen from the road, on which from time to time a dispatch rider or a truck or a few stragglers trying to catch up with the great retreat passed by, I stopped. I made myself comfortable and soon fell asleep. Now and then I woke up and blinked through the tree cover at the low-flying planes that were flitting about, releasing occasional bursts of machine-gun fire at some target or other on the road.

At five in the afternoon I decided to shove off. I ate a few crackers—I had provided myself with crackers and chocolate for my venture—and made my preparations. I wrecked my rear tire so thoroughly that any inquisitive eye would recognize it to be beyond repair. Then I went back down the road and, pushing my bicycle, started on my way. Most of the planes had vanished, and I only once had to take cover from a plane that was investigating the road. The road was perfectly still, as though the war had taken time off for Sunday. Now and then I passed a few retreating soldiers, but no words were exchanged, except with a sergeant who pointed vaguely southward and informed me unasked that his radio car lay blown to pieces somewhere "back there." "The Americans are back there," he added. "Thousands of them."

But there must be plenty of German troops too, I said, eager for what information I could get. Had he seen my unit?

"A bicycle unit?" the sergeant asked with a critical look at my bike. Yes, he'd seen a few poor lunatics back there—and again he pointed. According to him, they were just about the only Germans between us and the enemy.

"Hurry up, man," he said with a grin. "Maybe you'll make it before your outfit is captured."

"It can't be as bad as all that," I said.

With a broad, expressionless laugh, the sergeant left me.

For a while the road passed through fields, then it began to twine uphill and down as the landscape grew wilder. Now the hillsides were studded with cliffs, and in the light-colored porous stone I could see the entrances of caves. Outside one of them a Ukrainian was on guard; he told me in broken German that there were big ammunition dumps in these caves.

In the dusk, the landscape became more and more romantic. For the first time that day, clouds filled the sky, and thanks to the overcast, I made good progress. Now and then I felt a gust of warm wind. As I rounded a bend, the small town of Vejano appeared in the valley below. I stopped and looked down, hoping that no one from our squadron would be there.

Vejano looked totally deserted in the waning light. Smoke rose from none of the chimneys surmounting the flat, gray, shingled roofs. I saw that a few of the houses had been hit by bombs. Finally I summoned up courage and entered the town.

The houses were tall, gray, and deserted; like the houses of all small Italian towns they were built of stone blocks, hewn every which way. In the narrow streets I heard nothing but my resounding footsteps and the clatter of my bicycle. I stopped and thought: houses; I could stay here and wait till the Americans came. Houses; maybe with beds, with rooms, with corners to hide in and wait. Hesitantly I passed through a gate. Inside it was dark and musty, smelling of straw and cold stones and excrement. There was a winding stone stairway, cold, gray and lonely. There was a shovel leaning against the wall. I turned around and went out again. In the dark, glassless window frames the strings, to which washing or ears of corn were ordinarily fastened, hung motionless.

Amid the dark houses of Vejano, inhabited only by rats and marauders and offering no safety, I thought of God and nothingness.

There is no longer any safety in houses, because freedom, except for the freedom of rats and marauders, no longer lives in them. Only when reduced to ruins do houses return to freedom.

Freedom lives in the wilderness.

I like to escape into wildernesses. I mean the shore of the cottony sea near Kampen, in the dunes, listening to the thunder of the October surf; I mean the cliffs of Cap Finistère, the upper Tet valley in the eastern Pyrenees, the ponds of the Camargue, the maple trees at the foot of the Lalider cliffs, the flocks of sheep on the Montagne de Lure, the shell-blasted woods on the crest of the

Schnee-Eifel, a brackish Mississippi cove ringed about by motionless pelicans, the great forests of New Hampshire and Maine. I also mean those big-city neighborhoods where the buildings are becoming a wilderness, as in Rome, in the areas on either side of the Corso (where baroque churches and fountains bloom like orchids), on the Hamburg waterfront, in Paris on the left bank and in Montmartre. One December morning the Place du Tertre appeared to me as a gray, enchanted clearing in the woods. It dreamed—a dream in primeval violet.

I like to leave houses behind me as I did that afternoon in Vejano and go out into the wilderness, because it's only in the wilderness that I can be alone with God or nothingness.

Freedom is being alone with God or nothingness.

I don't really know whether God exists. But it strikes me as absurd to assume that He doesn't.

If God didn't exist, there'd be nothingness instead. Think of it: nothingness. It would be every bit as holy as God. As immense and immensely binding as God. God would enter into nothingness and make it divine. Nothingness would be God.

Already God and nothingness have become identical in the minds of those who see the world as nothingness. All nothingness-thinkers are religious thinkers.

At that time, as I've said, I didn't waste a thought on the soldier's oath. But I was dimly aware that no oath could come between God and me.

(I admit that a man can also speak to God from within a community of believers. But such a community no longer existed. The church was an empty house; God could no longer be encountered in houses, but only in the wilderness. I don't mean that God has to be worshiped in the woods, of course not. I'm not a nature fetishist. I'm speaking of solitary excursions into God's wilderness. These are indispensable to every believer, even if he belongs to a living church.)

I was in immediate contact with God. Like all human beings I had the eternal human right to protest against everything that tried to intervene between God and myself. The spirit of the old Protestant revolutionaries who were my ancestors has always been alive in me.

I'm not even sure God exists. But I've always prayed to Him.

In the streets of Vejano I prayed: Let me come unto Thee in the wilderness! Help me. Let me be alone with Thee.

On the way out of the city, where the road descends into the gully, there was a large, half-ruined arch, once a gate to the city. Massive, dark, and menacing, it stood in my path. I passed through its dark vault.

In the gully the cliffs rose white and phosphorescent from the dark-green meadows on either side of the softly gurgling river. I crossed a bridge, then the road wound slowly upwards, bordered by cliffs and by slopes covered with pistachio trees; yellow blossoms shimmered faintly in the dusk.

Arrived on top, I stood on a knoll amid ripening wheat fields. There was still enough light for me to see that there were little thatched huts in the fields, *capannas*, as the Italians called them; they looked like tents.

After studying my map in the waning light, I said to myself: The squadron has gone on to Oriolo, which it will certainly have to evacuate in the morning. I'll head southwest across country. I can't stay on the road, because if the squadron decides to fall back during the night it will come this way. I'd run right into them.

I had no way of knowing that the squadron had been captured long ago.

On my right a slope descended into the valley. I couldn't see the bottom. I went down a short way until I found a *capanna* that couldn't be seen from the road. After hiding my bicycle in a wheat field, I sat down outside the *capanna*. By then it was almost dark. I ate some biscuits and chocolate and drank water from my canteen. The scene was lonely and majestic, a wild mountain country under an enormous cloudy-dark sky. The hills and valleys extended for miles; on the western horizon the evenglow lingered on and on. Now and then there was a flash of summer lightning.

The hut was nothing but a straw roof set directly on the ground. I hung a shelter-half over the entrance and lay close under the slanting walls, as in a tent. Strange to say, I actually slept for a few hours.

It was fairly light when I was awakened by the swishing sound of a horse walking through tall grass. Looking out, I saw a civilian coming down the slope, a young Italian peasant leading a scrawny horse by the halter. He was wearing black trousers, a dirty shirt, and a battered old hat with a broad brim. At first sight of me he was frightened, but then the eyes in his dark face grew curious and cold. I went up to him and asked him if he knew where the front was. He didn't know exactly; it was a stupid question anyway, because at that time there wasn't any front. As a matter of fact, experienced soldiers have assured me that in the Second World War there was never anything that could reasonably be called a "front," not even in Russia.

We stood looking southward and I got the Italian to tell me what was what. He pointed out a group of buildings on a hill far in the distance. The monastery of St. Elmo, he told me. A monastery, I thought, not bad. Monasteries are havens of refuge, if the monks in them are Christians. Maybe, if the Americans don't get here soon enough, they'll take me in for a few days and hide me. But I wasn't so sure; maybe the Catholic Church was just another big bureaucracy and the monks went by precise regulations that didn't provide for harboring a deserter. Because that would have meant taking sides in the war. Still, it seemed possible that they would side with a fugitive knocking about between the two warring powers. Be that as it may, the monastery was well situated, to the southwest, west of the road that I had to avoid because in this war of movement the military would be using it. My tactical problem was to approach the Americans not frontally but from the flank. I decided to take the monastery as a landmark all that day.

I showed the Italian my bicycle and made him a present of it. He looked at it avidly and pushed it deeper into the wheat. At that moment the bomb fell. It hit the road some fifty yards away. It fell from a clear sky, we hadn't heard it coming and we hadn't heard the plane. We didn't even have time to throw ourselves on the ground before the rubble rained down on us; we stood there speechless, while the horse galloped wildly about. Then it was perfectly still, not a plane to be heard; all about us lay the transparent, dew-glittering silence of dawn. We parted with a mumbled "*Addio*" and "*Buon viaggio.*" I went down into the valley, leaving the war road for good, while he took a path leading northward along the hillside to Vejano, whence I had come.

In the valley I again saw light-colored, creviced cliffs. The region was very wild, I saw few tilled fields, the whole countryside was covered with bushes and rank grass, interspersed with solitary trees spreading their umbrellalike crowns over the hills.

That morning, the morning of June 6, 1944, the air trembled with restrained excitement. If I'd known then what I know now, the silence wouldn't have seemed so inexplicable; I'd have known the reason for the magic spell that had been cast on the war between the Tyrrhenian and Ligurian seas. That day the Italian war put its ear to the ground to listen to the war in Normandy. Listening in silence, it heard the sound of ships plowing through the night sea and the heartbeats of three hundred and fifty thousand men going ashore; it heard the thunder of twenty-five thousand air missions between an island and a continent and the deadly crash of ten thousand tons of explosive dropped by the planes. It also heard the heartbeats of those who took to their heels and the fine Atlantic night rain through which they fled. There was no moon to comb their hair by, only night and wetness and death-dealing lightning flashes, not even a dust-cloud triumph was left to them, even a moon-pale dying dust-cloud triumph was denied the defeated western army.

While I was sleeping in the *capanna*, the outcome of the war was determined. While I for the space of one day was disengaged from the fate of the masses, that fate was being decided.

But no one can free himself from the fate of the masses for more than a day. I was with them again a few days later—to get ahead of my story—when after standing in a long line of prisoners I climbed into one of the trucks that were waiting for us outside the camp. The drivers were Negroes. They let down the tail gate and shouted: "Get in!" Two Negro guards climbed in after us and sat down on the now closed tail gate, with their carbines in their laps. Then the trucks drove off.

The roads they drove on were bumpy and the country was devastated. At the entrance to the cemetery a detachment of Negro soldiers was waiting for us. Under the supervision of a white officer, spades, picks, and shovels were handed out. We were organized into work teams. The air was filled with the cloying smell of corpses. We began to dig graves. The calcareous soil was dry and hard. It slid off the gleaming bright spades in great clods. In the searing heat canisters of water were passed around, but the water stank of chlorination and of the chloride they sprinkled on the corpses, and after a few swallows we put our cups down in disgust. Whenever we looked up from our work, we saw wooden crosses all around us, in enormous rectangular fields. After we'd dug a number of ditches, we were led away to fill the sacks.

We were given rubber gloves and high rubber boots as a precaution against infection. We took long white linen sacks from a pile and threw them over our shoulders. The corpses lay in long rows in the middle of the cemetery. From a distance they looked like shapeless clods strewn with white powder. The dead found on the battlefield of Nettuno had been brought to this obscure cemetery. Many of them had been lying on the battlefield for weeks. They were black, and fermentation had set in. The stench was frightful.

The skin on the faces and under the tattered clothing of some who had not been dead for so long was of a lighter color. Some were armless, legless, or even headless; they had been under the fire of land and naval artillery. The flies clung to them in black clusters. Under the rising sun the bodies lost their rigidity and became soft and gelatinous. We stuffed the spongy masses into our sacks. Then we carried the sacks in wheelbarrows to the ditches and threw them in. They fell to the bottom with a squushy sound.

That was the fate the war held out to the masses. A line of development that could be plotted with precision led from Nettuno, Omaha Beach, and Stalingrad to these mounds of corpses. That line, which could have been read in the palm of history, had begun on the morning when Hans Bertsch, covered with blood, staggered to the bar in the Volkartshof, when his eyes looked through us at the windows, behind which night was falling on the streets of the years.

That was the beginning. The symphony of inhumanity had struck its opening chords. There is no point in setting an earlier date; everything that had happened before had been an end. An epoch had drawn to a close when my father collapsed on the road of history, when on his deathbed he sang the Lutheran hymn. Those who came after the old German conservatives began something totally new: the face of God was no longer present to them when they crowned the heads of men with blood and wounds. I too would have been buried in that cemetery near Nettuno if I'd been standing a few yards nearer the road that morning when the bomb fell. But chance has little latitude; it can decide whether to send a man into captivity or death—but it can't exempt him from the fate of the masses. Nor can it alter the fact that men will try time and again to escape that fate, especially when it seems to leave them no other choice than that between death and captivity. But in fighting fate we are not free. We are never free, except in the moments when we drop out of fate. Such moments often take us by surprise. When the bomb struck and the Italian and I just stood there instead of throwing ourselves on the ground, freedom came to us in the expectation of the shell fragments that would pierce our skulls. Afterward we'd be dead, our faces buried in a patch of field. But before the fragments, the moment of surrender to God and nothingness would have entered into us.

From the moment of freedom—I repeat: never in our lives can freedom last longer than a few breaths, but it is for those few breaths that we live—from it alone we derive the tempered consciousness that opposes fate and creates a new fate. For many centuries European art was a battle of the will against historical fate. When it had traveled that path to the end, Picasso and Apollinaire let themselves fall into freedom. Still smoky and smoldering, they emerged with gleaming metallic tablets in hand: they had saved art and changed the course of fate.

Art and man's struggle against fate are accomplished in acts of absolute, irresponsible freedom, of surrender to God and nothingness. I found confirmation of this belief years later when I saw the greatest work of art I have encountered since the end of the war, the film *The Bicycle Thief*, directed by Vittorio de Sica. Everyone knows the plot: a poor Italian worker's bicycle is stolen: he tracks the thief, trying desperately to get it back, and the story ends with his pathetic and unsuccessful attempt to solve his social problem by himself stealing a bicycle. At moments, between the phases of action, the miracle of freedom appears in the face of the man whom De Sica picked off the street to play the part, and into that freedom he plunges at the end when, having failed, he vanishes in the stream of mass fate. The miracle is most evident in the moments when, forgetting his harassment, he turns to his grave young son, who accompanies and guides him. This dream-and-play miracle lives in the concise sharpness of an Italian cityscape, in a photograph that reminds me of Signorelli's frescoes in Orvieto, of Louis Armstrong's trumpet, of Ernest Hemingway's language when he describes a bullfight or a market in Venice, or of the ruins of Grosseto, covered with pink dust after an air raid.

And so the young Italian, who—I remember now—looked like De Sica's hero in that film, wished me *"Buon viaggio,"* and I started on my march through the wilderness. Down into the valley. Jagged rocks. Solitary trees on hilltops. On my map the region was marked *campagna diserta.* "Diserta," I thought, the same root as "desert." The right place for deserters. Deserters are people who go out into the desert.

My desert was very beautiful. At my feet lay carpets of yellow and violet flowers. Carried over the hills by the wind along with gaudy red-gold butterflies, the scent of thyme and lavender mingled with light-blue rosemary blossoms and the big yellow flowers of the pistachio trees. Under the great golden sun, a pine cast its light shadow on the windblown heath. Again valleys opened up, chalk-white river beds bordered by jagged cliffs and silent silver-green thicket. I went down into the valleys and had a hard time making my way through this jungle, inhabited by green, silver, and clay-brown snakes and lizards. But then came another rise and on top, on the heights of the Tuscan Campagna, I found the cool wind again. I lay down on the flowers and ate when I was hungry. I looked at my map and compass and searched the southern horizon, sometimes catching sight of the monastery, which was nearer now.

But far in the east rose the Apennines, tall and noble in desert brightness, and closer to me, surrounded by an army of hills, steeped in sunlight and waving in the wind like a flag, stood the solitary Soracte, chivalric and volcanic and dead, majestically dead amid the melancholy of that wild, dead countryside, which like all wildernesses lay at the end of the world, at the end of life, where our star hovers dead beneath the gigantic empty sky of nothingness.

Late in the afternoon I came to the edge of an enormous wheat field that flowed gently down into a valley. Behind the trees on either side of the valley I saw houses. I heard the sound of moving tanks, a higher, steadier sound than that of the German tanks I was familiar with. I heard the clanking of caterpillar treads. The sounds seemed far away in the red glow of the waning western light. And then I did something colossally dramatic—but I did it: I took my carbine and threw it over the surging waves of wheat. I removed my cartridge pouches and bayonet from my belt, grabbed my steel helmet, and threw the lot after my carbine. Then I went on through the field. Down below I found myself in the jungle again. I struggled through, the dense thorn bushes scratched my face; it was hard work. Then, panting, I climbed again.

In a hollow on the far slope I found a wild cherry tree; the ripe cherries were a bright, glassy red. The grass around the tree was soft and dark green in the evening light. I took hold of a branch and started picking. The hollow was like a room; inside it, the sound of the tanks was muffled. Let them wait, I thought. I have plenty of time. The time is mine as long as I'm eating these cherries. I gave my cherries a name: *ciliege diserte,* forsaken cherries, deserter's cherries, the wild desert cherries of my freedom. They tasted fresh and tart.